NEVERTHELESS
SHE PERSISTED

www.davidficklingbooks.com

Also by Jon Walter

Close to the Wind
My Name's Not Friday

JON WALTER

NEVERTHELESS SHE PERSISTED

David Fickling Books

31 Beaumont Street
Oxford OX1 2NP, UK

Nevertheless She Persisted
is a
DAVID FICKLING BOOK

First published in Great Britain by
David Fickling Books,
31 Beaumont Street,
Oxford, OX1 2NP

www.davidficklingbooks.com

Hardback edition published 2018
This edition published 2021

Text © Jon Walter, 2018

978-1-78845-026-3

1 3 5 7 9 10 8 6 4 2

Papers used by David Fickling Books are from well-managed
forests and other responsible sources.

MIX
Paper from
responsible sources
FSC® C018072

DAVID FICKLING BOOKS Reg. No. 8340307

A CIP catalogue record for this book is available from the British Library.

Typeset in Sabon by Falcon Oast Graphic Art Ltd, www.falcon.uk.com
Printed and bound in Great Britain by Clays Ltd., Elcograf S.p.A.

'*Votes for women, chastity for men.*'

Christabel Pankhurst

Foreword

Victorian England saw the role of women change as they entered the workplace. The movement for women's suffrage had been in existence since 1870 but was given a new momentum by the formation of the Women's Social and Political Union in 1903. Unlike the other suffrage societies, their policy of direct action caught the headlines with the *Daily Mail* coining the term *suffragette* to distinguish them from their more traditional suffragist counterparts.

By 1910, thwarted by consistent broken promises, their militancy was increasing and this included hunger strikes which led to force-feeding in many of Britain's jails. In 1913, fearing the death of a suffragette in jail, the Government introduced an Act of Parliament which became known as the Cat and Mouse Act. This allowed for a hunger striker who was at death's door to be released from prison on licence and then re-arrested once their health was restored.

No hunger striker died directly from their actions, either inside or out of jail, but the Act was unpopular with the public who considered it unfair. It also proved difficult to implement due to the success of the suffragettes in evading the police who tried to re-arrest them.

1

Clara comes as soon as she is able, hurrying along the Seven Sisters Road and arriving at the door of the small terraced house. She lets herself in, her father standing at the sound of the latch then sitting back in his chair when he sees that it's her. She takes off her coat, finds a hook from which to hang it. 'Is she upstairs?' She already has a foot on the first step and he lets her go without a word, though she feels his eyes upon her till she makes the landing.

The bedroom she enters is dim, lit by an oil lamp that stands on top of a small chest of drawers. Clara turns it up and sees her sister twist in the bed, escaping the light like an insect unearthed.

'Don't!' Nancy puts a hand over her face. She pulls the sheet up high across her shoulders.

Clara tuts. 'I need to see you, don't I?'

'There's nothing to see,' says their mother, sitting grim-faced on a chair in the corner of the room.

Nancy pants like a dog. 'Make it stop,' she whines. 'Oh, make it stop!'

Clara goes to the bed and kneels. She puts a hand to Nancy's head because it seems the right thing to do.

'She won't let it come,' says their mother bluntly.

Clara takes hold of her sister's wrist and lifts her arm away from her face.

Nancy shuts her eyes. Her nose and mouth are tight and small, her legs curled up into a ball beneath her. 'It hurts Clara. It hurts me terribly and I can't make it stop.'

Clara looks to her mother. 'How long's it been now?'

'Since lunch time. I came to get you straight off.'

'I couldn't get away.'

'I left a message at the door.'

'I had to finish up before they'd let me go.'

Her mother shifts in her chair so that she won't have to look at either of her daughters. She crosses her legs and sets her chin.

'Did you send for the midwife?' asks Clara.

'He wouldn't let me.'

'Well he's daft.'

'Said I should know my way around by now, what with having had the two of you. He says we'll have to manage it between us.'

Clara stands and walks across to the bowl on the dresser. The water is cool to the touch. She takes a flannel, dips it, then wrings it out and brings it back to the bedside. Nancy's hair is sweaty and stuck to her forehead so Clara pushes

4

it back behind her ears and holds the cloth to her brow. She turns the bedclothes back so they are down by Nancy's knees and when Nancy makes a grab for them she stops her hand. 'You're too hot, Nancy. You need to be cooler.'

'She's ill,' says their mother. 'She ought to stay in bed.'

'She's not ill.'

'I want to go to sleep,' Nancy complains. 'All I want is to go to sleep.' She screws her eyes tight shut as another contraction comes to meet her like a wave rolling in towards a shore. 'Oh make it stop; someone *pleeease* make it stop!'

Their mother arrives at the bedside. 'Should of thought of that, shouldn't you!'

Clara glares at her till she returns to her seat. 'I'm going for the woman.' She straightens her skirt. 'I shouldn't be long. Don't let her get too hot.'

When she opens the bedroom door, her father steps back. Clara walks past him. At the top of the stairs she says, 'I'm going for the woman.'

'No need,' he barks then follows her down the stairs.

She half expects his hand on her shoulder – if he means it then he won't let her go – but he stays at the foot of the stairs as she crosses the parlour and fetches her coat. She puts her arms into the sleeves and lifts her hair free of the collar.

'Didn't you hear me?' He raises his voice but she knows now he's only doing it to save face, like a dog snarling at a passer-by. 'I said there's no need!'

'There's ways to do it right, same as anything,' she tells him calmly. 'Something might go wrong.'

'Wouldn't be terrible, would it?' He walks over to his chair and sits himself down. 'Might be the best way. Might be better for all of us.'

Clara slips out into the street and walks quickly, thankful to be away from him. The woman she brings back to the house is terse with common sense and hardly looks at their father, save to nod in his direction as she takes to the stairs. That annoys him and he makes a grab at Clara's arm as she passes.

'I won't pay her,' he hisses. 'You know that, don't you?' But he lets her go. 'Like living with a houseful of cats,' he mutters as she reaches the landing.

Her mother stands with the midwife at the dresser. 'This water's cold,' the midwife tells her.

'We've been keeping her cool,' says her mother, glancing at the covers that are up around Nancy's neck again.

The woman walks to the bed. She pulls the covers back so Nancy is exposed, all curled up and whimpering. 'C'mon, pet.' The midwife takes a hold of her shoulders and eases her round till she can see her face. She plumps up one of the two pillows. 'Try to sit up a bit.' But Nancy wails, all frightened and lost. The woman nods to Clara. 'Bring me my bag.' She orders their mother downstairs for hot water.

Clara watches as the midwife lifts Nancy's nightdress up around her hips. The sudden nakedness shocks her and she turns her back. But she knows she's of no help to anyone like that. The loss of control makes her feel faint. She gives herself a talking to. This is happening. This is actually happening and nothing she can do will change it now, so she'd better get used to it, the same as Nancy has to. She takes a deep breath to clear her head then turns back to the bed.

The midwife has her hands on Nancy's belly. She presses gently on the sides as she moves up towards her navel then takes a small wooden trumpet from her bag, puts one end of it over Nancy's belly button and the other to her ear. 'Has he been kicking much?'

'I don't know,' says Nancy, all surly and tired.

'What? You haven't felt him? You must have a belly of stone then cos he's got a good heart.

'Has he?'

'Nothing wrong with him there.'

Nancy clenches at her pillow, bringing it up to her face as another contraction arrives. 'Why won't he come then?'

'Not ready yet.'

Nancy bursts into tears. She howls and screws up her face and shuts her eyes.

The midwife quickly takes her hand and puts it firmly at the top of her belly. 'Feel him kicking? There! Can you feel that?'

Nancy's face opens up, all wide eyed in wonder. 'Is *that* what it is?'

'Didn't you know?'

Clara steps closer. She wants to touch her sister's belly too, to feel what it's like to have something alive and kicking at your insides.

Something happens that makes Nancy break into

laughter. 'Oh, oh the little bugger.' She moves her fingers to the bottom of her belly. 'He's trying though, isn't he?' she asks the midwife. 'He's trying to push himself out.'

The three of them watch in silence, the way you wait for nature, but then quite suddenly the shape of a foot curves across Nancy's belly, like a fish turning in water, and the sisters look for each other, needing to know the other saw it, both of them holding their breath with the wonder and the horror of it.

'Come and help your sister up.' The midwife moves to let Clara in and together they take hold of Nancy under each arm and bring her to her feet.

'Where's she going?'

'She's not going anywhere. Just walk her round. It's good for the both of them. Helps get things going. Gets some air in the lungs.'

Clara's almost too scared to touch but she puts an arm around Nancy's waist and it's not as strange as she might have imagined. The two of them lean into each other. They walk together round the bedroom, holding each other's hands, taking five steps to the window and then back again. They'd shared a bed until a year ago, and Clara knows her sister's body, the shape and line of her beneath a nightdress, though never like this, never bursting and brazen and careless. Nancy's not a girl to have heavy breasts and a large round belly. She's a quiet girl. Never says boo to a goose.

Their mother returns with warm water and startles at the sight of them. 'What are you doing out of bed? You should be resting.' She looks for the midwife's approval but gets none. 'I'll get a pan,' she says and makes for the door again. 'Your father says you've driven him down the pub.'

The midwife takes their mother's chair. She produces knitting from her bag, keeping herself to herself as the sisters pace the room.

Clara hadn't thought it would be like this. She'd come home to look after her younger sister, to tell her what to do like she always had. Only Nancy is going through something that is new to the both of them, probably the first time she has ever done something before Clara. Still, Clara thought to bring the woman. That was something useful at least. 'Does it feel better when you walk?' she asks Nancy.

'A bit.' After another turn of the room Nancy says, 'We haven't done this for a long while.'

'We've never done this at all!'

'In the park we did,' Nancy reminds her. 'We used to walk together in the park.'

'Not for a long time,' says Clara. 'Not since we started working.'

'No,' says Nancy. 'Not since then.'

Each time the contractions come, the pair of them stop by the window and Nancy holds onto the edge of the dresser, bends herself forward and breathes deeply. Clara keeps a hand in the small of her back. When she can walk again, Nancy pushes her head into Clara's shoulder and the pair of them shuffle round the room till they have lost track of the time and who is there and who is not.

Their father comes back from the pub. They hear him slam the door shut behind him. 'Is it done yet?' he shouts up from the front room. They hear his boots on the first few stairs but then their mother's voice, telling him to come away and leave them be.

'No better than witches.' He cusses and descends again.

The midwife makes Nancy eat a biscuit and take a mouthful of water and then they go back to knitting and walking, knitting and walking. A little while later Nancy's arm stiffens around her sister's neck. 'Oh . . .' she says and pinches at the waistline of her dress. 'Oh . . . oh . . . I think something's happened.'

Both of them step back from each other. Nancy's nightgown is wet at the front and there's a puddle on the floorboards.

'That's good,' the midwife tells them. 'That's just right.'

Nancy tugs at the neck of her nightgown. 'I want this off, Clara. Help me get it off.'

Clara gathers the hem and lifts the cotton gown up over Nancy's head.

Once Nancy stands naked, she reaches for Clara's neck again. 'Oh!' she groans.

Clara holds her tightly by the elbows as Nancy bends her knees and rolls her hips. She's moaning now, finding something deep inside, something that is animal and giving it a voice, so that Clara thinks she seems almost possessed, as though her sister is being used by a force that cares nothing for any of them. Nancy gets heavier to hold, sinking down

10

toward the floor and Clara has no choice but to follow, till they are both on their knees, looking like cattle calving on a barn floor and lowing in the half light.

The midwife comes and kneels beside them. She doesn't appear to be shocked at all. 'Better to breathe him out, girl. Don't rush it. Let him come in his own time.'

Nancy raises herself, squats upright on her knees and Clara tucks in behind her, letting Nancy lean back into her chest, though it takes all the strength in her back to stay there. She can feel Nancy tense and stretch, can feel the tremor of her bones and muscle. For the love of God, she thinks, why'd you let him do this to you? And then everything changes again. Nancy stops moaning. She is staring at the door handle as though it's the most important thing in the world.

The midwife appears in front of them holding a warm flannel that she presses up between Nancy's legs. 'You can feel the baby's head,' she says and takes hold of Nancy's fingers. 'Go on. You won't hurt him.'

Nancy eases herself off Clara's thigh and lowers a shaking hand to touch for herself. 'He's there, Clara!' She throws her head back, laughing, her face glowing like a rising sun. 'He's really there!'

'Next one'll bring his head out full,' the midwife tells her and it comes immediately, Nancy rising up in Clara's arms and then bearing down again, the force of her pulling both sisters forward to the floor so the midwife has to push them back against the side of the bed with a hand on

11

Nancy's sternum. 'We've got the head,' she tells them. 'He's a stargazer, this one, got his eyes fixed on higher things. Now save your strength, girl. Don't push till you have to.'

Nancy breathes deeply. She drapes herself from Clara like a puppet. Suddenly she heaves herself forward again with such force that Clara has to let her go then bring her back again, the way you coax a kite into the air. And then something gives. Nancy falls forward again and suddenly Clara sees the baby, the head and shoulder of him, all blue and grey and slipping out into the world, a startled hand grasping at thin air and Clara reaches out, catching him by the shoulders just before he comes again, a second later, being fully born into her hands.

For a brief moment there is nothing in the world but the two of them staring at one another and then the midwife is beside her, holding a piece of cloth that she wraps around the little creature, leaving the pulsing grey cord to hang as she passes the baby back for Nancy to hold.

Clara slumps like a bag of bones on the bedroom floor. She watches Nancy sit back against the bed, looking at her baby in disbelief. 'What'll I do with it?' she asks the midwife.

'Go on and see if it'll feed.'

Nancy eases the baby to her nipple with a hand behind its head. 'I can do it,' she says, all disbelieving and proud. 'Clara, look. He wants me. See?'

'It's not a he,' laughs the midwife. 'Have a look for yourself. It's a baby girl.'

'Oh,' says Nancy, as though that changes everything. She looks at the baby closely. 'Isn't she lovely though?'

Clara goes to wash her hands in the bowl. The midwife comes and does the same.

'Should she be holding it?' Clara whispers, but the midwife ignores her and she feels ashamed for having asked. Her father's footsteps pass the door as he goes to his own room. 'I better wash this floor,' she tells the midwife.

Her mother is sitting alone in the kitchen. 'Is she done?'

'A baby girl.'

'Well, that's that then.' She opens a cupboard door and closes it without bringing anything out. 'You'll be going back, I suppose.'

'I've got a shift first thing.'

Clara fills a pan full of water and puts it on the heat. When it's halfway to boiling she pours it into the bucket and finds the scrubbing brush. She meets the midwife coming down the stairs and pays her from her own purse before she lets her leave. She takes the bucket up to the room. She turns the wick a little higher on the lamp. Nancy is almost asleep, propped upright in bed with the baby on her chest.

Clara gets down on her knees and begins to scrub at the floor, beginning in the middle of the room where Nancy's waters broke and moving back toward the bed. God she is tired. She hasn't stopped to rest since breakfast and her back aches terribly. She gets a glimpse of Nancy closing her eyes. 'Nancy? Nancy! Don't go to sleep now.' And then more softly, 'I've got to take her. Remember?'

Nancy startles awake. 'Not now, Clara. Please. Not till the morning.'

'It won't get any easier, will it? Better to do it straight off.' She stands, putting the brush into the bucket. The only way to do this is to be practical. To keep busy. She thinks of her mother as she folds away the unused linen and stands over the bed.

Nancy looks like a little girl holding onto a doll. 'Just a bit longer?' she asks. 'Only a moment more.'

Clara frowns, but she goes back downstairs with the bucket and brush. She pours the water down a drain in the yard then goes to the pantry for the wicker basket that her mother takes with her for the shopping. She lines the bottom with a blanket that is warm and soft enough to weaken her resolve. Perhaps it is better to wait till morning? It might not do to go knocking on doors in the middle of the night, waking half the neighbourhood. That's the sort of thing to start people gossiping. She tells herself to stop it. It's better done as soon as possible and anyway, the woman has been forewarned. She knows what to expect.

She returns to the bedroom, steps inside the door and puts the basket on the floor by the side of the bed. Nancy begins to cry.

'Come on, now,' Clara says gently. She leans across and puts her little finger to the side of the baby's mouth. 'See? That's how you do it without waking her up.'

The baby stirs then calms herself back to sleep as Clara lifts her up. For a moment she lies naked and warm on the palm of Clara's hand but she daren't hold onto her. She lays the baby in the basket and covers her up and Nancy rolls away till her back's turned and Clara thinks, that's it then. Better done without the fuss. She closes the bedroom door quietly.

The house she goes to is close enough and the woman answers her door without Clara having to knock a second time.

She takes the basket with only a quick glance inside. 'Does it have a name?'

Clara hadn't thought about that. 'No,' she says. 'Does she need one?'

The woman shrugs before she shuts her door.

2

There's a moment when she wakes. A moment when the world feels warm. Before Nancy feels the loss of her, the dread of knowing she's gone, slouched deep in her belly where the baby used to curl asleep.

The need to urinate grips her and she's up and out of bed, kicking about for the pail till she stubs it in the half gloom of the curtained room. She hitches up her nightdress. Crouches. Rattles the handle on the edge of the bucket, what with all the worry in her thighs, and it stings when she lets go. Hurts all over again. In her elbows and knees. In the small of her back and that space between her shoulder blades. All the pain and the aches of her.

The baby could still be here. She lets herself believe that she might be. Perhaps still in her bed, breathing quietly under the sheets or tucked up tightly in a basket somewhere out of sight. Maybe Clara couldn't do it. Perhaps the baby is there on the floor? Just the other side of her bed? If only she could stop weeing she might hear her, but it takes a lifetime of squatting till she falls forward onto her knees and crawls across the floor, her hope the size of a candle.

She holds her breath, peering past the end of the bed into the gloom of an empty floor. She puts a hand beneath the bedclothes, makes a single sweep of the sheet, just in case the baby might have somehow flattened out in the night, in case she's thinner than Nancy remembers. She was such a little thing. She might still be in there, tucked up sound asleep and Nancy not noticed. Be just like her to get it all wrong. The baby could be anywhere. Anywhere but here.

Clara took her like she said she would. Like they all agreed. She's never been one to change her mind, not when she's decided that something is right. The disappointment rattles down into her chest like a coin into a piggy bank. Something to save for a rainy day. She tells herself she's stupid. Missing her. It was only last night that she even gave her a thought. Only when she touched the baby's head. Till then she didn't want to think about it.

They've got a newborn in the house next door. She can hear it through the walls when it gets a wail on. And it's not their first. They've got the two, with only a year between, though the woman says she doesn't have to work any more, says she gave up her job once they were married because he earns a good enough wage without her having to take in too much needlework. Nancy couldn't say for sure what he does, but by the look of him, it's an office job and it feels strange to have a woman, only a few feet the other side of a wall, leading a life so very different to her own.

Father is sweet to her once she comes downstairs. His morning mood. He tells Nancy she should stay in bed for a day or two and when Mother asks who'll do the washing and the floors, he tells her to hush her mouth and get used to it, says she'll have to anyway, once the girl's gone. They don't mention the baby. Nancy takes a slice of bread back to her room, thankful for the peace and quiet of it and wondering why she feels so strange. She's not herself today. She has to remind herself to chew. She looks at her feet. Both of them are swollen and pink, with fat little toes that have lost any grace they ever had. She runs a hand across her belly, finds it saggy and flat, something like old Mrs Oliver's bloomers, pegged out to dry on her clothes line after washday.

She's only been back in bed a moment when her father knocks, just the once, and slides around the bedroom door. He closes it softly then stands with his back to it, his eyes on the floor, wringing his hands as though he's shaping the words he wants to use. Nancy sits up straight. Puts her spine to the bedstead. Brings her knees up into her chest.

'I wanted to know . . .' He stops sharp. 'Wanted to ask . . .' He falters again, then finds his fuse, stabbing a finger at her. 'You have to tell me what you intend to do!' He takes a few quick steps but then retreats and Nancy enjoys his uncertainty. These moments don't come often. He tries to begin again using a softer tone. 'You could still stay here. Nothing needs to change. Not now it's all done.' He turns to face the window, pretending to be interested in something – a cart or maybe a woman walking past on the pavement beneath. 'You belong here. This is where you were born.' He coughs, perhaps regretting the mention of a baby. 'Your mam and I . . . we need you.'

He waits for her to speak and when she gives him nothing he begins again. More formal now. 'So I thought you ought to know that when you find another job, well, you can keep half your wages. Whatever you earn. Half your wages.'

She knows it's a dangerous game to stay silent – he might explode at any moment – but there's not a word in her head, not a thing she can say that might help her or that wouldn't be a lie.

His eyebrow twitches. She thinks this'll be the start of it but he shakes his head, gets rid of any notion he might have had to hit her, though his mouth still looks mean enough to spit the width of the room. He plunges both hands into his trouser pockets. 'Your sister thinks she knows what's best but she doesn't always.'

'She shouldn't have taken the baby,' Nancy says, then regrets it immediately, tries to soften it. 'Not like she did, I mean, in the middle of the night, without me getting to say a proper goodbye.'

'That's typical though. Isn't it? Getting us all to do as she wants. She's always been the same.' He sneaks a longer look at her. 'So I'll tell her. Shall I? Tell her you're staying put and finding your own way?' He walks to the bed, sits on the edge of it, his body now free of the tension that made him stiff legged only a moment ago. He puts a hand on her knee and the touch of him makes her lose herself, makes her go to that place where she's nothing at all. Not a thought or a voice. Nobody.

'She wants to see us Thursday,' he says softly. 'Shall I tell her then?'

A baby starts to cry, begins to wail through the wall at the back of her head and she feels the rush come on, the milk that drops down into her breasts and drips, filling her with horror. She nods quickly, pulling the sheet up to her neck, knowing a yes will make him leave her be.

By the Thursday, her feet have lost the swelling and she is able to wear shoes. She wraps the strapping round her breasts like a bandage. It's the first time she's been out for nearly a week. First time she's needed a coat.

They arrive at the coffee shop before Clara. Nancy sits away from her mother at the table. They order a pot of coffee. Three cups. Her mother says they won't have cake – after all, it's a coffee shop – and Nancy says she doesn't mind. She thinks the less she opens her mouth the better.

By the time Clara arrives, the three of them have fallen to silence. Father has taken up a paper to look respectable but Nancy knows he won't be reading it. He lays it down as Clara sits and Nancy finds herself between the two of them. She pushes her chair further out from the table.

'You've already ordered,' Clara says.

'We didn't know how long you'd be,' says her father.

'Well I'm here now. Perhaps we'd like some cake?' She motions for a waitress and Nancy thinks that's just like her, never making do with what there is, always wanting something more. She half resents it but admires it too.

Clara takes hold of her hand and squeezes her fingers. 'Nancy? You must be in need of some cake. How have you been?'

'She's been ill,' says their mother.

Clara keeps hold of her fingers but Nancy feels no comfort in them. 'Is this the first time you've been out?'

'What can I get you?' asks the waitress, suddenly at the table.

Clara gets into a fluster, letting go of Nancy's hand and snatching at a menu that she doesn't bother to read. 'Muffins, please. Two muffins with butter and a cup of coffee for me.'

'We won't be stopping,' says their mother. She makes a point of finishing her coffee and setting the cup down in its saucer.

Her father folds his paper in half. 'We're here to tell you that Nancy won't be taking up your offer of a job.' He sits up straighter in his chair. 'She'll be staying with us for the foreseeable future.' He lays his hands flat on the table as though that's an end of it.

'To do what?' Clara raises her voice. 'They won't have her back in the shop. They'll have given her job to someone else by now.'

Nancy blushes. She knew it would be this way, like birds pecking and pulling the meat from a carcass.

Now Clara turns on her. 'Is this what you want, Nancy? The interview is arranged for tomorrow, and if you get it, you can begin within the week.'

'She won't be going for the interview,' says their father.

Nancy pulls her hands from the table top and puts them in her lap.

'She has to,' Clara says. 'It's all arranged.' She straightens her neck, lifting her chin and eyeing him like a ruffled swan. 'I've put myself out for this and she'll be letting me down if she doesn't show.'

'She won't be coming.'

'Then I want to hear it from Nancy.'

But Nancy hasn't got the will to speak and even if she had they wouldn't listen.

'You know what she's like,' says their mother.

Her father sets his cup down with a rattle. 'I said it before. There's nothing to be talked about.'

'No,' Clara agrees with him. 'There never is. Just like the father of her baby. There was no more to be said of that either.'

The waitress arrives with the muffins and sets the plate down with a roughness that says she's heard enough of their business to make up her mind about them.

'Please, not that again!' their mother says as soon as the waitress has left the table. She stands up and reaches behind for her coat. 'It was that boy from two streets down.

Richard whatshisname, the fella with the bright blond curls.'

'Richard Carter?' Clara exclaims far too loudly. She lowers her voice. 'It was not! I can tell you that much.'

Her mother dismisses them all with a flick of her hand and makes for the door. 'Tom? Come on, now.'

Nancy is relieved to be leaving before any more gets said.

Her father half stands. 'Come on, Nancy,' he says softly and takes hold of her arm, lifting it at the elbow. 'Come along with us now.'

Nancy is rising from her chair when Clara grabs her other arm, pulling her back down. 'I'll tell if I have to,' she hisses at him over Nancy's head.

He lets go of her. 'Do as you please,' he says and then, 'Good riddance to the both of you.'

Clara keeps a hold of Nancy till the door to the coffee shop has closed behind them. 'This job is important, Nancy. You'll be living in. It's a good enough wage. And it'll keep you safe.'

'Yes,' Nancy says. 'You told me.'

3

Clara gives Nancy a story that has to be rehearsed – of why she left her old job, why she wants a new job and the date of a birthday that makes her five years older than she actually is. Nancy feels a thrill to be older than her sister, until she realizes that Clara must have lied about her age too.

She told her, 'Brand new stockings, a starched handkerchief, a pair of flat shoes with buckles cleaned to a shine and your dark blue dress, washed thoroughly and pressed.' There was more. 'Pin your hair up, Nancy. And clasp it tight. You can use the one I gave you last year, the plain brass one. That would be very suitable.'

When she arrives, Nancy thinks the prison looks like a castle. It has towers and high walls. It has a tall black gate, the sort you find in ghost stories and far too frightening for Nancy to knock on, so she is glad Clara has told her about the small entrance, just a normal sized door, built into the brickwork at the side.

The woman at the desk doesn't turn her away like she half expects. She says Nancy is on a list and someone will be along shortly.

A warden arrives. 'Miss Cooper? Please follow me.' The woman goes ahead of her without any inclination for conversation, walking quickly enough that Nancy is always a step or two behind. She wears a long-sleeved dress of dark blue cloth that reaches to the floor. On her head, a matching bonnet ties tightly under the chin. She leads Nancy out of the building and across a small courtyard, hemmed in on every side by tall dark walls. They go through another door and into another corridor. They pass other wardens, all dressed identically and walking with their hands clasped in front of them. Like nuns, Nancy thinks. Or dark angels. All austerity and sharp edges. Every one of them untouchable.

The woman stops at an oak door, which she swings open. 'Please remain here.' She invites Nancy into the room with an open hand but does not enter herself. She closes the door once Nancy steps inside.

The room has a desk with a chair and a shelf with three books but there's no window and Nancy waits a long time with nothing to do but listen to the conversations of women that pass in the corridor.

Eventually the same warden returns with an examination paper. It has questions on comprehension and basic maths. She gives Nancy a pencil and ruler. 'I will return in twenty minutes to collect it.' She takes in the clock on the wall to their left and then leaves, closing the door behind her.

Nancy takes a deep breath, scratches her name on the top of the sheet and begins.

The Matron of the prison is called Miss Hardgrave, and by the time Nancy gets to meet her, she already has the marked examination paper available on the table in front of her. She is dressed in a simple day suit of grey cloth, which should make her more approachable than the wardens, although she doesn't smile or shake Nancy's hand. Neither does she ask her to sit, leaving Nancy to hover behind the empty chair opposite her own.

'What is your name?'

Nancy knows that it is written on the top of her paper and that this is a game, a way of emphasizing who is in charge here. 'Nancy Cooper, miss.'

'No second Christian name?'

'No, miss.'

'And your age is twenty-four? Am I correct?'

'Yes, miss. On the fifth of May just gone.'

The Matron consults her notes. 'Please, take a seat,' she says with a voice that implies that Nancy could have sat down as soon as she entered the room if only she had been bold enough. 'For the last three years you have been working as a shop assistant at a department store called Freeman's, but you left six months ago.' She lifts her head just enough to see over the metal rim of her glasses. 'Were you happy there?'

'Yes, miss. Happy enough. It was hard work, but enjoyable. I liked meeting people.'

'And yet you gave it up without another job to go to. Why was that?'

'My father was taken ill, miss. He needed looking after and we decided I should be the one to do it rather than Clara.'

'Yes, of course – your sister.' The Matron smiles briefly at the mention of Clara's name. 'And how is your father now?'

'He passed away last month, miss.' Nancy's mouth saves her, working quicker than her brain, though the dread of lying takes the blood from her cheeks.

'I am sorry for your loss,' the Matron says kindly and then, for a moment, she seems bewildered, as though she has lost her place while reading from a book. She consults her notes again, tapping at the examination paper with a crooked finger. 'This is . . . unremarkable . . . though I have read a lot worse.' She shuffles the offending paper to the back, replacing it with a new one at the top. 'I see that Freeman's have supplied you with references.' She flicks an eyebrow upwards. 'Stand up, please, Miss Cooper.' She points to where she wants Nancy to go. 'Over there, so that I can see you.'

Nancy steps into the middle of the room as Miss Hardgrave looks her up and down – sees right through her, she's certain of it. 'Lift your dress, please, Miss Cooper.'

Nancy doesn't hesitate, bunching the material in both fists and raising the hem, knowing that anything more than an inch above the knee would be indecent. She has already been warned by Clara.

27

The Matron begins with her feet. 'That's good. Sensible shoes. Stockings without holes. Turn around now.'

Nancy does as she asks, keeping her gaze to the wall as she pivots on the ball of her foot, trying not to think how she might look to someone else's eyes but meeting the gaze of the Prime Minister and the new King George, whose portraits hang above the fireplace.

The Matron nods with satisfaction. 'Thank you. You may lower your dress and sit back down.' Nancy returns to her seat. 'It's the details which can't be seen that reveal the most about us, Miss Cooper.'

Nancy is relieved, thinking that'll be the worst of it. Everything has gone exactly as Clara said it would.

'You seem a little quiet for us,' Miss Hardgrave tells her in a tone that is sharp enough to cut through any optimism. 'If you are to be successful in this work you cannot afford to be meek.'

'No, ma'am.'

The Matron pauses, intending to give the maximum effect to what she will say next. 'Would you like to know how many murderers we have here?'

Nancy can't stop her eyes from widening and she drops her head, wondering how she should respond. The Matron must be teasing her and she decides it's better to stay silent than risk a wrong answer.

'We have five, Miss Cooper. All of them murdered either their husbands or their children but I doubt you could tell them apart from our other inmates. Women do not make master criminals, Miss Cooper. Neither are they disposed to cruelty or violence. Thankfully, unlike men, it is not in our natures. Most of the women entrusted to us are prostitutes or alcoholics, guilty of little more than feeble-mindedness. The women here might elicit your sympathy, but they do not need it and it would do them no good. What they need is for you to set them an example. They need you to be a woman of exemplary character. Can you tell me what that involves?'

Clara told her nothing of this and Nancy panics. 'Should I be honest?'

'That would be the very least requirement,' Miss Hardgrave answers her grimly.

Nancy remembers what Clara has told her about the work the prisoners do here and how it is supposed to reform them. She reels it off as a list. 'I should be hard working and clean at all times. I mean hygienic – knowing how to do the laundry and scrub a floor – that sort of clean. And sewing. I should know how to sew and I do, miss. I know how to sew very well.'

The Matron nods in agreement. 'Knowing how to keep a household is an essential skill, Miss Cooper, but above all you should be seen to be virtuous.'

'Yes, miss. Of course, miss.'

'Once a woman loses her virtue and her dignity she has nothing.'

'No, miss.'

'And the women here *do* have nothing. You will need to set them an example, Miss Cooper, and you must never let it slip. It's the only hope for all of us.' The Matron pauses. She takes another long look at Nancy, her finger tapping at the table top.

Nancy thinks of the bandage that still binds her breasts. Perhaps the Matron has guessed for herself.

'Your sister has been with us for just over a year and is doing very well. In the circumstances it seems foolish not to give you the opportunity as well, so I will agree to you working with us as a prison hand for a probationary period of three months. You will accompany the staff in their work to gain your practical experience with an expectation that you become a warden and enroll in the training programme. Do you have any questions?'

'No, miss.' Nancy smiles with relief. And she remembers to say, 'Thank you, miss,' before she leaves.

4

Miss Jackson, the prison supervisor, has a smudge of a face, with features that are only half formed, like a moon or a child. Clara thinks it is the sort of face a man might find either pretty or plain but she has no way of knowing which and mistrusts her because of it. Miss Jackson tells Clara she should meet her sister at the gate in ten minutes' time. 'I thought you might like to settle her in. It will reassure her to have a friendly face.'

Clara resents this, though she can hardly refuse. She doesn't want Nancy to assume that she will be here at her beck and call. It would be better for them both to be independent while they work together and anyway, she still isn't sure if Nancy will come at all. The possibility of returning to Miss Jackson with the news that her sister cannot be relied upon irritates her further and she takes herself off down the corridors at a brisk pace, her hands

31

clasped in front of her more tightly than usual.

The notice board contains the staff rota and a list with the location of each warden's room. She runs her finger down the line of names. Nancy Cooper has the number 501, which, Clara notes with some satisfaction, is in a different part of the building to her own room. She knocks on the office door, then enters. Miss Penny, the secretary, sits behind her desk as usual. She is given to wearing blouses with floral patterns, which emphasize that her role is purely administrative and really could be in an office anywhere. It just so happens it is here.

She has the key to Nancy's room waiting on her desk. 'I thought it might be you.' She picks the key up quickly and holds it at arm's-length. 'How exciting to have two sisters on the staff. I shall have to take special care not to confuse you on the payroll.'

Clara forces a smile and clips the key to her leather belt so it nestles in among the others.

She is relieved to find Nancy already waiting at the front gate, though she looks nothing short of terrified, sitting with her hands folded in her lap like that, and Clara remembers how her sister used to be at school, always afraid of doing the wrong thing. Her resentment disappears immediately. 'I said you could do it!' She hugs Nancy hard enough that she drops her holdall to the floor.

'I didn't think I would,' Nancy tells her. 'I forgot half the things you told me.'

'Like what?'

'I don't know . . . I didn't blow my nose so she could see that my hankie was clean.'

'Well you can't have done too badly or you wouldn't be here.' She leads Nancy along the corridor that takes them into the prison. 'I bet the old dragon looked at your shoes. How far up your leg did she make you lift your dress?'

'Just above the knee.'

'Then she must have liked you.'

'I don't think so.'

She puts her mouth close to Nancy's ear and whispers a perfect imitation of the Matron. 'It's the details which can't be seen that reveal the most about us, Miss Cooper.' They giggle like little children.

'I'm on three months' probation,' Nancy reminds her. 'So it's not like a proper job.'

'Then we need to make sure it becomes one.'

They pause at a tall dark door. 'This is the first locked door. From here on we're in the prison proper, so we must behave properly, the way we would if we didn't know each other.' She takes a key from the ring at her waist, unlocks the door then locks it behind them. Seeing the look in Nancy's eyes, she touches her shoulder lightly. 'You'll get used to it.'

They follow the corridor before turning to the right and then again to the left. They go through more locked doors taking them deeper inside the prison. When they pass a window, Nancy stops to see the sky.

'That looks out onto the exercise yard,' Clara tells her. 'So now we're in the centre of the prison.'

'How do I get out again?'

Clara points away to the right. 'The main entrance is that way. Keep the yard in mind and you'll start to see the logic of it but it does take a little getting used to.'

A metal grille forms a long wall that divides the entrance to the prisoners' wings from the other parts of the building. Behind it is a hall with three lines of trestle tables, each of them filled with women who are sitting on the benches in silence, all of them at needlework, sewing patches onto dresses or darning the holes in countless pairs of woollen stockings. Nancy stares at them. She lifts her eyes to the first metal gantry. Four floors rise above her, each with a circle of black cell doors that stand out against the white walls like keys on a piano. Clara unlocks a section of the grille which opens as a door and Nancy creeps inside, keeping her eyes to the floor and holding her bag up around her chest. Two wardens walk between the tables towards them, their hands clasped behind their backs.

Clara leans in closer. 'It's all right, silly. They're not interested in you.'

She takes a metal staircase up onto the next floor with Nancy close behind, then she takes the next flight and then another. On the top floor, Nancy pauses, looking out over the railing to the hall below. Clara did the same thing herself when she first arrived. Below them, the women are being told to form two lines and they shuffle into place without a word being spoken.

Clara takes Nancy's key from her belt and unlocks the

first cell door they come to. 'It's not much,' she tells Nancy. 'But you can do what you want with it.'

Nancy looks confused. She steps inside to see what it is she is being shown. The cell has a bed, a chair and a small table with a basin. The window halfway up the opposite wall has bars across it. 'Do I have to live in a cell?'

'It's your own room,' Clara tells her quickly. She feels guilty that she hasn't already warned her but she hadn't wanted to scare her off. 'And you have a key.' She holds it up in front of her sister's face. Nancy looks about to cry. Clara closes the door to give them some privacy in case there is a scene. 'You'll enjoy having a room to yourself,' she says briskly.

'I've had a room to myself since you moved out,' Nancy reminds her.

Clara becomes officious, pulling at the front of her uniform to straighten it out. 'Well you needn't worry. You'll be working too hard to spend much time here.' She brings Nancy's bag from the floor to the bed then walks to the table, fills a tin mug with water from a small enamelled jug and holds it out. 'Honestly, Nancy, it's not as bad as it seems.'

Nancy takes a sip then puts the cup down. 'I don't have any keys for the other doors.'

On the back of the cell door hangs a dark-blue uniform, the same as Clara's, and she goes to it, puts a hand into the large square pocket and brings out a ring of keys. She clips Nancy's cell key with the others then dangles the ring in front of Nancy's nose. 'You're not a prisoner here. Sometimes it *is* difficult to remember, but you can come and go as you like.'

'Where's your room?'

'It's off the infirmary. I can show you another time.'

Nancy looks back toward the cell door. 'And who else is up here? What about next door? Is there anyone in there?'

'I'm not sure. It might be empty. We can take a look.'

'Oh no, I couldn't. What if someone sees?'

'Come with me.' Clara takes Nancy by the hand and leads her back out to the gantry and along to the door of the next cell. She points to a small round piece of glass in each of the doors. 'It's called a bull's eye. You can view the whole cell without being seen yourself.' She puts her own eye to the spy hole. An elderly woman sits beneath her window, very deliberately counting something out on her fingers as if using them for worry beads. Clara beckons Nancy to take a look and when her face is up against the door, she whispers, 'This woman is as good as gold. She won't give you any trouble.'

Nancy watches the woman for a minute or more. 'What did she do?' she asks as they return to her room.

'I don't know. Sometimes they tell you themselves but you don't tend to ask. Given her age, it'll probably be forgery. Something financial. You can always check her records in the office if you're curious.'

Nancy points to the glass eye in her own cell door. 'But they can look at me too!'

'Not if you keep your uniform hanging on the back of your door. Or better still, pin a spare handkerchief over it.' She takes hold of the dress as they go back inside. 'You should try this on before I go. I need to know if I chose the right size.'

That was tactless. Until recently, the two of them have shared the same clothes. Clara pushes the dress into Nancy's chest and then walks to the foot of the bed, keeping her back turned to give her sister some privacy. Above the bed is a shelf with books. All of them are standard issue for a prison cell – a Bible, a prayer book, a tract called *The Narrow Way* and a thin volume entitled *A Perfect Home and How to Keep It*. She picks up a thick pamphlet of the prison rules and pretends to find it interesting. 'You'll have to learn these,' she says, absent-mindedly flicking through the pages.

'What? All of them? Off by heart?'

'It's not as difficult as it looks.' She replaces the pamphlet on the shelf. 'Most of them are common sense.' She turns to find Nancy doing up the last of the buttons on her uniform. 'There you are! Now you look just like me.'

Nancy stands awkwardly, all arms and legs, as though it's her body and not the dress that doesn't fit. She runs a finger round the inside of the stiff short collar. 'I can't breathe properly.'

Clara goes to her and feels for herself. 'There's plenty of give in it. You're probably just nervous.'

'I don't think I can do this.'

'Yes you can, Nancy. I felt the same way when I first got here.'

'I don't even know why I'm here.'

'Yes you do.'

'Does anyone know about the baby?'

'No one.'

Nancy pulls at the dress from below the belt, flattening out her stomach. 'You look like angels. All of you do. I don't think I can carry it off.'

'Everyone has secrets, Nancy.'

'You don't.'

Clara thinks of Ted. She'll be late for him if she doesn't hurry. She reaches up, puts the bonnet on Nancy's head then ties the strings tightly under her chin. 'There now. You look as proper as the rest of us.'

'Is there a mirror?'

'Didn't you think to bring one? Well, never mind. You'll just have to use my eyes.' She takes a couple of steps back to get a good look at her sister. 'You look perfect. Now come with me so I can show you where the recreation room is. There's a fire in there, the seats are comfortable and there's nearly always someone about so it's a good place to go if you want some company.' She feels better at the thought of leaving Nancy there rather than mulling in a room on her own.

On their way, she takes her to the office and shows her the rota. 'You begin tomorrow at 5 a.m. Breakfast is in the canteen at 4.30.' She shows her where to go, pointing out the easiest way to get there from her room and reminding her of the left turn when she comes to the wooden crucifix hanging on the wall. At the door of the recreation room she tells Nancy she must go in on her own. 'You'll feel better for doing it yourself.'

'Don't make me. Stay a few minutes at the very least.'

But Clara won't be moved. 'I have an evening off and I'm going out. I don't want to be late.'

'Where are you going?'

'Just out. I'm meeting with a friend. I make a point of going out on my evenings off and you should too or you'll never get to see the light of day.' She puts her palm into the small of Nancy's back and urges her gently towards the door. 'Go on. No need to knock. Just go straight in.'

Nancy takes a deep breath then walks inside. Clara hurries back to her room and changes out of her uniform. She has already chosen what she will wear. The skirt and blouse are laid out on the bed and it's just as well because she doesn't want to be late again. Ted will be waiting for her, standing cap in hand and ready at the prison gates. He's as good as his word that one. She had let him down only the other week when she met Nancy at the coffee house. The week before that had been the birth and he'd had to stand around in the rain because she didn't even have a moment to get a message to him. He'd been hurt then – more than she expected – though he had the good manners not to ask her what the family problem was about. Ted is considerate like that. That's part of the reason she likes him. Still, she knows it doesn't do to lead a man on.

'Clara!' he calls out to her as soon as she steps outside.

'Hello, Ted.'

He leans across and pecks at her cheek. 'You got off on time then.'

'Regular as clockwork that place,' she tells him, all the formality of the prison disappearing from her mouth.

Ted makes a joke of pulling up his sleeve. 'I ought to set me watch. I've been using Big Ben till now but I heard it's not reliable.'

'Come on.' She urges him away from the front gates and the threat of gossip from the woman at the desk. Once they are well away she gives him a proper smile. She's been looking forward to seeing him. 'So where are we off to?'

'It's a surprise,' he tells her and sets a quick pace along the crowded main road.

'What if I don't like surprises?'

'You'll like this one.'

'I may not.'

'Well if you don't then I'll have to do better next time. But we shouldn't hang about. We've got to catch the omnibus.'

They pass a woman selling sprats from a barrel on the street corner, three for a farthing with the smell of them coming out to meet you before you've even set your eyes on her. At the corner, past the new fashion shoe shop and the Marks and Spencer, Ted sees the bus he wants to catch, the number 14 to Brixton, and they run across the street holding hands, dodging past the back legs of horses and other people crossing the busy road. There's room up top and it's warm enough to stay there.

'It said Brixton on the front,' she tells him. 'Are we going all the way?'

'Oh yes!' he says, sounding ever so pleased with himself. 'We're going all the way!' When she blushes he doesn't laugh at her but blushes too, at least she thinks so. 'Sorry. I didn't mean that the way it came out. We're going to the Brixton cinema. Electric Pavilion. Have you been before?'

'Once or twice,' she tells him but she's glad to be going again and when they get there Ted makes a point of paying for the decent padded seats, the ones near the back, away from the pianist and the kids that like to chatter through the newsreels. He shares a bag of boiled sweets while they watch a travel piece about the pyramids of Egypt and Clara laughs so much at the camels that Ted pretends he's embarrassed by her.

She hasn't felt as happy as this for a long while, not since all this business with Nancy, but now that it's over she can begin to relax, and she likes being here with Ted, sitting in the darkness and the thick smoke of cigarettes, cheering and booing at the screen along with everyone else. They watch a film from America called *The Girl and her Trust*. It's about a telegraph operator, a woman, working with all the men at a remote railway station and all of them are making eyes at her, thinking that's all she's good for until she saves the day when some thieves steal all the money. Clara claps loudly when it finishes and Ted puts his fingers in his mouth to whistle. The evening finishes with a news piece about the funeral of Emily Davison, the suffragette who was killed by the King's horse at Epsom.

'That's a shame what happened to her,' says Ted, once they're stood outside on the street. 'But she brought it on herself.'

'Did she?'

'You can't go running in front of a galloping horse and expect to come out all right at the end of it.'

'No,' says Clara. 'No. I suppose not.' They walk to the edge of the street, away from the couples that are still coming out of the cinema and chattering about the bits they liked the best. 'I don't suppose you've got the vote?' she asks him.

'Course not.'

'You could get it though, once you do well for yourself.'

'What? You mean once I'm in charge of the bank? I don't think I've got it in me.'

'You could though. Who would you vote for?'

'I don't know. I'm not sure if I'd bother. None of them seem to make much difference.' He looks along the busy street where the gas lamps are being lit and Clara thinks he looks uneasy about something or other.

'Are you all right, Ted?'

'I'm sorry, Clara,' he says, 'but I don't have the money for a meal out. I brought along a picnic instead. I hope you don't mind. It's nothing much but it'll keep the wolf from the door till you get home.' He points across the road to a small fenced-off piece of park. 'We could sit down there, if you like.'

Clara doesn't mind at all. Most men would have borrowed

the money rather than admit they were short. Or they might have lied to her, making up some excuse, though she doesn't need one. She admires his prudence. They find a bench that is sheltered by a cedar tree, just inside the main gate, and they sit close together, the sky turning from blue to black above them.

'How did you get on with your family business the other week?' Ted asks her. 'Is it all sorted out?'

'Yes, thank you, Ted. I think it's all over and done with.'

'That's all right then. For a moment I thought I might have to offer my help. I could have met your father.' He winks at her, knowing he's being cheeky. 'I'd have made a good impression.'

'I know you would.'

'I could've let him know I'm in regular work. A decent job. What's your father do again?'

'He works for the post office, Ted. I thought I told you.'

'That's right, you did. Well, we're well matched.' He takes her hand and lowers his voice. 'I'd let him know my intentions towards his daughter are honourable.'

'Then you'd be wasting your time because he couldn't care tuppence.' She laughs when she thinks about it. 'Anyway, Ted. We hardly know each other. You don't want to meet my father till you have to. Maybe after a little while you won't want to any more.'

'That won't happen.' He produces a pack of sandwiches from his bag, unwraps the brown paper and offers them. 'There's ham and cheese or boiled egg. We've got one of each.'

She takes a ham and cheese. 'Who made these for you?'

43

'I made them myself.'

'Did you?'

'Yes, I did actually. Nothing wrong with that, is there?'

She shakes her head. 'No, Ted. There's nothing wrong with that at all.'

He's got a bottle of stout and he pops the top with an opener from his key ring then gives her the first swig. 'You must have lots of them at work.'

'Lots of what?'

'Suffragettes.'

Clara knows it doesn't do to gossip. 'Well, yes, we've got a few.'

'I bet they're a handful.'

She could tell him a thing or two but it wouldn't be worth the risk and anyway, she doesn't want him to know some of the things she has to do. 'They're hard work,' she admits, though the hardest part is deciding whether she agrees with them. 'They don't make my job any easier.'

Ted shakes his head. 'No. I don't suppose they would.' He takes a bite from his sandwich. 'I couldn't ever do your job, Clara. I'm sure I couldn't.'

'You'd be too soft hearted.'

'I think I would.'

'But you'd do it if you had to. You'd be like everyone else if you didn't have a choice about it.'

'I suppose so. But it'd be nice not to have to, wouldn't it? I mean, a girl your age. You must be thinking what you'll do when you get married.'

She feels a sudden sharpness in her mouth, like tasting salt when you're expecting sugar. 'Did you know that some of the suffragettes think marriage is a form of legalized prostitution?'

Ted nearly chokes on his sandwich. 'Blimey. That seems a bit harsh.'

She stands up from the bench, brushing the crumbs from her long skirt. 'I ought to be getting back, Ted. If I'm late they won't let me back in.'

'Yes, of course.' Ted jumps up quickly. He puts the remaining sandwich away in his bag then offers her the last of the beer. 'Clara . . .' He puts a hand on her arm. 'I hope I haven't offended you.'

'Not at all.'

'I have,' he says. 'I can see it. But I don't want to talk about nothing. I know I like a joke or two but I want to know what you think about things. I really do. I want to hear what you've got to say but I'm sorry if I was clumsy.'

She thinks that pretty decent of him. If this is worth it at all, it's because she can talk with him. And there's no one else. Not like Ted. She takes the bottle and swigs the last of the beer. 'We've still got a lot to find out about each other, haven't we?'

'But we're going steady? I'd like to think we are. I mean, if you want to.'

Tell him you can't, she thinks. Tell him you won't. Tell him anything but yes. Because she knows this whole thing is impossible.

'I think we are,' she says.

Ted can't keep the smile off his face. He holds her hand all the way to the high street, searching for the omnibus that will take them back across the river. Once it arrives, they sit up on the open deck again, pointing out places or people they see from the top of the bus. And he's fun to be with. He's easy. An antidote to all the stiffness in the women at work. And he's not bad looking either, not a real bobby dazzler but pleasing enough, with an open face and a jaw that looks reliable. She could do a lot worse, she tells herself, though she needn't have a bloke at all. Still, she'll be a long time lonely before she's dead. So why not enjoy it while it lasts?

She gets a sudden surge of regret, not from being here with him now but for the future. Because she knows the way it'll go. They'll see each other once a week until she decides enough is enough. Or maybe he'll stop it himself. That's normally the way of things for a girl like her. And if neither of them stop it, then it'll change. It'll start to get serious, and after a while he'll ask her about whether they should get engaged. There's no way round all of that. After all that's the whole point of courting, isn't it? But she wishes everything didn't feel so inevitable. Even now, sitting on the top of the bus, it feels like a game. Well, perhaps not a game but a performance, like they've both been handed parts in a play that's not been written by either of them. And there are so many rules to this. All the things you should and shouldn't do.

The script says he'll try to kiss her. He must be thinking about it, so he's bound to ask if he's got the courage, and if he hasn't then he'll probably lunge at her, maybe here on the bus or a few streets from the prison as he walks her home. She wonders when he'll make his move and whether she'll respond or put the brakes on. Only she can't. Not now she's said they're going steady. And anyway, what about her? What does she want? She can't be independent and have a man in tow as well. The two of them don't mix, at least not to her mind.

The bus takes them over Lambeth Bridge, the lamplights playing on the deep dark water of the Thames below. Behind them, a couple are kissing on the back seat, behaving like they're the only ones here. And suddenly Clara doesn't want to wait to find out what Ted might do, she wants to choose for herself, she wants to make her own decision.

Ted is looking the other way and so she touches his hand. 'Ted?' When he turns, she kisses him, awkwardly but open mouthed, their front teeth scraping against each other when they meet.

'Oh,' says Ted. But then they kiss again, for longer this time and they settle down, pressed together in their seats, not knowing how long to go till the bus reaches Holloway.

5

From her cell that night, Nancy hears everything. A key turning in a lock. Every footstep on the stairs. A set of pipes whispers to her while she lies in bed and a woman, somewhere, shouts through the small hours. Every time Nancy thinks she's stopped, the woman shouts again and she never says a word that's intelligible, so Nancy can't be sure what it's about. She'd rather not know and curls into a ball beneath her covers, closing her eyes and counting to one hundred, knowing it will likely all be over when she gets there. And it is. Till she's about to drop asleep. And then the woman shouts again – or it's someone else – and she thinks she might drive herself mad living in a place like this. She'll start to hear babies in the walls.

In the middle of the night, she gets up and goes to her door. Touches her set of keys. She steps out onto the landing. The lights along the corridor are dim but she can still see down into the hall where the lamp of the duty warden stands upon a table. Everything is quiet. She tells herself there's nothing to be afraid of but then jumps in fright when she sees a movement, something down in the shadows at one of the tables. She looks more closely and catches the quick sharp movement of a pecking beak. She leans further over the rail, watching as the bird skips along the top of the table till something spooks it and it scatters upward, showing her the shape of a starling. Yes! She's sure of it! When it settles on one of the ceiling beams she can see it clearly. There's a bird trapped here with her. A starling, living as best it can on the crumbs that are missed when they clear away the food.

5.30 a.m. A bell. A line of wardens parades from behind the metal grille and take to the stairs. Nancy is among them, trying to look as though she knows what she is doing. At each floor, three remain. When everyone is in their positions, a whistle blows. Each team of three takes to the doors, sliding back the covers of the spy holes and looking inside. They open the locks, rattling the keys on their chains. Behind them, the kitchen staff climb the stairs with large wicker baskets filled with bread. They produce hot water from an urn. Each prisoner receives a small brown loaf, two ounces of butter and a pint of tea. A whistle blows. The prisoners bring out their slops, empty them, sluice out the buckets, take a clean bucket and fill it with water. They return to their cells and scrub their floors. They roll up their bedclothes and store them away in the corner. They wash down the planks that make up their beds and polish their utensils with soap and bath brick. They don't complain. For most of them, the work is easier than being at home. A whistle blows. Fifteen minutes till chapel.

It shocks Nancy to see the men. Since she arrived she has seen only women in the prison. The women do everything here but of course it's not the women who are actually in charge. That isn't how the world works, and she feels stupid to have assumed the prison was different. After all, she knows there must be doctors.

The Prison Governor and the Chaplain are already seated on a raised platform as the wardens lead the prisoners to their pews. On one side of the men sit Miss Hardgrave and Miss Jackson. On the other side are four women, dressed in fine-looking dresses of white or black and wearing wide brimmed hats topped high with feathers or flowers freshly picked that morning. It's a wonder they stay put when they bend their heads to pray. Nancy asks one of the other wardens who they are and is told they are from the Lady Visitors' Association. They visit once a week in the hope of befriending the prisoners and to give some instruction on needlework or how to keep a good home, 'because the likes of us can't be trusted to set such a high example.' The warden tightens her mouth, slighted at the insult. 'All we're good for is locking doors.'

Nancy doesn't comment. The other wardens are not like her, not the way she imagines herself. Mrs Armitage has

50

no-nonsense arms, a neck that strains the top button of her blouse and a mouth that only softens when she talks of her son, ten years in the army and on ten bob a week, though it's not enough to bring him home to her from India when he gets his leave. Miss Barraclough, on the other hand, is a penitent of few words who speaks and then apologizes for what she says. Nancy met them both in the common room the previous night, along with Miss Denton, who can't be more than twenty-five and sat slouched and sulking, only perking up when the topic of conversation turned to the Duchess, a new inmate who apparently is famous, though Nancy has never heard of her.

'Imagine Daisy Divine in here?' she had said, her eyes widening with the very notion of it. 'I might ask for her autograph.'

'I'm glad I don't have to work with them,' Miss Greenwood had told her dismissively. 'I went to Miss Jackson and said I wouldn't do it. Special privileges for arsonists – whatever next.'

Mrs Armitage put a stop to the conversation before Nancy could find out who the woman was. 'If God had meant for us to be equal, he'd have made us all men,' she said and she folded her arms to show that should be an end to it.

Nancy wonders if there's a single woman working here who hasn't been thwarted one way or another. Only Miss Jackson seems to have a purpose, but even she carries out her work with a sense of remove, as though her mind is elsewhere. She takes charge of Nancy once they leave the chapel.

'You should see where it all begins,' she tells her and takes her to a large room beside the main courtyard. 'This is where we receive the new girls.'

Five other wardens are already there, including Clara, which is a relief at first, although Nancy doesn't know whether she should be familiar or not. She decides against it and Clara shows her no special favours, not even a nod of the head, so that must be the right thing to do. Nancy is put to work sorting clothing into piles until the Black Maria pulls to a stop in the yard and she is told to form a line with the others. Outside the door, she can hear the bobbies talking to the women as they release them from the van.

'What happened to your shoes, love? How come there's nothing on your feet? One at a time, ladies. Let's be patient, please. Well don't you worry, dear, they'll sort you out inside.'

Miss Jackson finds a clipboard and hovers at the door, ticking off names as the women come through. Nancy watches them carefully, wondering what sort of a woman ends up in a place like this. The first of them can't be more than nineteen. She's still dressed up from the night before in a frilly lilac dress that would be glamorous if it weren't grubby and torn at the hem. She's pretty too, although a smudge of dirt around one eye makes Nancy think of a bruised apple. The next woman is older, dressed in nothing much better than rags. She looks scared and a little mad, with a tick of the eye that she can't control.

Nancy straightens her back and folds her hands together in front of her, trying to look like all the other wardens, though she wouldn't be surprised if Miss Jackson were to suddenly turn on her and tell her to go stand with the prisoners. She wouldn't be surprised at all. She might even be relieved.

Miss Jackson waits till all eight of the prisoners are present. A bobby waves to her from the door. 'Right, that's your lot!' and she signs for them. One of the women tries to speak and she brings her to attention by clapping her hands and shouting, 'There will be SILENCE! Conversation between prisoners is strictly forbidden.'

Nancy puts her tongue to the back of her mouth.

The prisoners are led to another room where there are holding cells for three at a time. Nancy fills out forms with their names and age, their religion and occupation. She writes *none* in most of the boxes that ask for an address and when Miss Jackson checks the form she tells her the correct term is *No Fixed Abode*. Nancy is told to watch them undress, though she doesn't know what she's meant to be looking for and she feels guilty, remembering what it's like to be shamed. To be back at home. She thinks, this is what it must be like to be him. To have the power to push and push, knowing that I won't fight back.

She searches their clothes, puts her hands into every pocket then stores what she finds in boxes, making sure everything is labelled. A hair comb. A locket. Nothing much of any value. At least it's not difficult work, but she has to be told what to do at every step, just like the prisoners, with a warden to watch over her.

She's given charge of a woman with pretty fair hair, a splash of freckles on her cheeks and a cold sore at the base of her spine. She takes her for a bath and is thankful that the water is hot enough for the steam to allow them a pretence of modesty. When the prisoner closes her eyes and leans back in the bath, Nancy worries about letting her rest and hands her a bar of carbolic, nudging it into the top of her arm. The woman smiles a thank you, thinking she means well, but Nancy hurries her along, holding out a towel then marching her half naked to the next room where they find the floor covered in clothes.

There's a pile of green dresses and another of brown. There's a pile of undergarments and another of aprons, all folded and stacked beside some white linen caps. Every item is marked with big broad arrows in black or white, to show it is prison property. There is a pile of hard wooden clogs, none of them in pairs, and a tangle of red-and-black, hooped stockings.

'If you have been sentenced to the third division you will dress in brown,' announces Miss Jackson. 'If you are to go into the second division, then you must wear green. Now help yourself to clothes.'

The women circle the piles, pulling out anything that looks like it might fit. The younger ones make do with the first items they come across, hoping to cover themselves as quickly as they can but some of the others take their time, knowing that once a dress is chosen it can't be changed.

'Do you have anything smaller than this?' a woman

asks Nancy, holding up one of the green serge dresses.

Nancy bends to see if she can find something smaller, sifting through the pile for only a moment before a hand pulls her upright.

'All the clothes we possess are here,' Clara announces loudly to no one in particular. 'So there's no point in asking for anything else.'

Nancy feels her cheeks warm as Clara says quietly, 'It is not our job to do the prisoners work for them, Miss Cooper.'

'Yes, miss,' Nancy tells her sister. 'Sorry, miss.'

Once all the prisoners are dressed, they are given a blue checked handkerchief and a yellow badge with the number of their cell. They must pin this to the front of their dresses.

'From now on and for the duration of your stay, you will not be called by your name but by the number of your cell,' Miss Jackson tells them.

That would make me 501, thinks Nancy.

6

Clara waits at the Matron's desk. She sits upright. Keeps her hands tidy in her lap. She is entirely alone, but she wouldn't put it past the Matron to be watching her from somewhere – a hidden spy hole in a wall or the door that leads away into her private apartment.

This room is unlike any other in the prison, comfortable but still official – a place that sits between the cell doors and the power that keeps them locked. A dull orange glow comes from the fireplace. On the wall above the mantlepiece there are portraits of King George and Asquith, their heads bent towards one another as if they are commenting on what goes on in the room. To the right of the fireplace is a coatstand with the Matron's things – a modest straw hat with a thin blue ribbon running around its crown and a grey coat that errs on the side of practicality. Beneath the coat, Clara glimpses a pretty blue silk scarf with green leaves embroidered along its edge, something that she can't imagine the Matron ever wearing, but then, it's the hidden details which reveal the most about us, she reminds herself.

Miss Hardgrave arrives from the door at Clara's back. She has a stack of papers under her arm. 'Ah, Miss Cooper.' She sounds surprised to find Clara waiting there.

'You asked to see me, ma'am?' Clara asks, feeling the need to justify herself.

'Yes, I did.' The Matron takes her seat at the desk and smiles briefly, a rare enough occurrence that Clara takes to be a good sign. 'I would like to talk about your work. You have been with us a while now. How are you finding it?' She opens a drawer in her desk and produces a small tin of peppermints which she places on the table beside her papers.

'I am very happy with it, ma'am.'

'What do you find difficult?'

Clara struggles to think of anything at all. She doesn't like having to deal with Miss Jackson but she can't say that. She thinks back to when she first arrived, when everything was new, but even then, she was a quick learner. She tries to be honest without saying much at all. 'Well, it's always challenging, ma'am, but I believe I can cope with it well enough.'

'What challenges you in particular?'

'I suppose at the moment . . . well . . . the suffragettes . . .'

'Of course. The suffragettes. Do you have some sympathy with them?'

'No, ma'am. Why would you say that?'

'I know I do. We are all women, after all.'

Yes, she thinks. We are all women after all, though it seems to her the suffragettes take it upon themselves to behave more like men. 'Sorry, ma'am. What I meant is that they won't do as they're told. And then, of course, there's the feeding. It's unpleasant to administer and can be physically very tiring.'

'Yes, of course. You must resent them.'

'How so, ma'am?'

'Because they force us to be cruel when we are nothing of the sort.'

'Yes, ma'am,' Clara agrees with her. 'That's very true.' She understands the closeness of kindness and cruelty and it seems to her the Matron has summed up her feelings very well.

Miss Hardgrave appears glad that she agrees. 'I often have to remind myself that they have chosen their own paths. As indeed, we must choose our own. No virtue is left intact without a struggle, Miss Cooper, and we should see ourselves as the guardians of that virtue, even when called upon to do unpleasant work.'

The sunlight catches the flecks of grey in Miss Hard-grave's hair. Clara wonders how long she must have worked here and the circumstances of her arrival.

Miss Hardgrave takes the lid off the box of sweets. 'A peppermint?'

'No, thank you, ma'am.'

'Please. I insist.' She pushes the box toward Clara, who takes a mint and puts it in her mouth. Miss Hardgrave retrieves the box then does the same and the two of them sit for a moment, sucking on the sweetness of the informality.

'I have been very pleased with your work here, Miss Cooper. You show a very sensible attitude. I think you are fair but firm in regard to both the prisoners and staff. But now you must be honest with me. Do you think of this work as a long-term career?'

Has Clara been dishonest? She doesn't think so, but it often pays to be guarded. 'I'm beginning to think I might, ma'am.'

'You will already be aware of the sacrifices necessary to pursue a career here. But I hope you are also aware of the rewards?'

'Yes, ma'am. I believe I am.'

'Well then. You should know that Miss Jackson will be leaving us. She is to be married, so it appears she does not see her work as a vocation. This means the role of Supervisor will become vacant and I have it in mind to offer you the job.'

Clara's mouth falls open. She hadn't expected this at all. She wets her lips before she smiles but the Matron brings her back down to earth.

'I assume the same temptation will not befall you, should you accept?'

'No, ma'am,' she replies, an image of Ted flashing before her eyes. 'Thank you, ma'am.'

Miss Hardgrave smiles warmly, 'Then you and I will

need to get to know one another a little better. We shall speak again before Miss Jackson departs.'

'Thank you, ma'am. I shall look forward to it.'

Miss Hardgrave puts the lid on the box of mints and stands up from her chair. She motions toward the door with an open hand then pats the sleeve of Clara's uniform as she passes. 'By the way, I was sorry to hear that you didn't feel able to take time off to attend your father during his illness.'

Clara startles, like a rabbit setting eyes on a fox. 'Thank you, ma'am, but he's made a full recovery.'

'I am impressed by your dedication to work but there are always circumstances, family commitments and such like, that are unavoidable. Should a similar situation arise again, I hope you would feel able to discuss it with me.'

'Thank you, but I don't envisage either myself or my sister needing to take time from our work.'

Miss Hardgrave frowns for just an instant. 'Yes. Quite so.'

Alone in the corridor, Clara can hardly contain her excitement. She wants to run and jump with her hands in the air but confines herself to a stretch, rising up onto the tips of her toes with all the satisfaction of a ballerina in full control of her movement. She thinks she has to tell someone. Strangely, her first thought is how proud her mother and father will be, but no, now she's only being silly. She goes instead to Nancy's room. She should have finished her shift by now.

'You'll never guess what's happened,' she says as soon as she has closed the door behind her.

'What?' Nancy looks alarmed.

'You must promise not to tell a soul. Not a word of it, do you hear?'

Nancy stares at her blankly.

'I've just been offered the Supervisor's job. Miss Jackson's going off to get married and the Matron thinks that I . . .'

Nancy bursts into tears.

'Nancy? What on earth's the matter?' Clara hugs her straight away. 'Now you tell me. Has someone been bothering you?'

'I can't do it, Clara. I don't know what I'm supposed to be doing or when to do it and I feel like a fool for having to ask the whole time.'

'It's a bit of a shock at first, isn't it?' Clara confesses. 'I hid in my room every minute I wasn't working and I didn't eat for a week.'

'I don't believe you.'

'I didn't. Certainly for a few days. It took all the courage I had just to step out of the door.' She takes the handkerchief from the cuff of her uniform and holds it out. 'You'll get used to it. It's the same for everyone in these first few days.'

Nancy blows her nose hard. 'I can't even work out when I'm supposed to let them speak. Sometimes I'm supposed to answer their questions and other times I've got to read them the riot act just for opening their mouths. And the way we have to talk to them! That high and mighty tone, speaking over their heads like they aren't even worth looking at. I can't do it, Clara. It makes me shiver just to think about it.'

'It's only a game, Nancy. Everyone knows that, both the wardens and the prisoners. It's a way of marking us both out. Do you see? It lets them know who they are and who we are too.' She can see that Nancy doesn't understand, so she explains again. 'It's like being a teacher. If they talk when they shouldn't then they're testing you. They're asking, who's in charge here? And you answer them in a way that leaves no doubt. That makes them feel safe. Do you see?'

'But I'm not in charge. It's different for you.'

'Come on,' Clara says calmly, feeling more generous than she would usually. 'I'll show you how it's done. Stand over there.' She moves Nancy to the door. 'Now then, pretend it's scrubbing out time. You've seen them doing it this morning.' She drops to the floor on her hands and knees and starts scrubbing with an imaginary brush. 'See here? I'm not doing it right, am I? I'm just swilling about some water. What do you say to me?'

'Don't, Clara.'

'Come on, Nancy. I wouldn't do this for anyone else and you know what they say? Practice makes perfect. Now, I would say something like this.' She changes the tone of her voice, speaking sharply. '"The use of soap and a bit of elbow grease saves time and effort, Miss Cooper." Go on and say it.'

'The use of soap . . .' Nancy stutters to a stop. Her voice couldn't be much quieter.

'Don't look at me when you speak,' Clara orders her. 'It's much easier if you don't meet a prisoner's eyes.'

Nancy begins again, speaking to the window at the end of the cell. 'The use of soap and elbow grease saves time and effort.'

'That's better. Now do it again but with more certainty! And add a question that shouldn't be answered. Try to think of a judge, sitting up on a great big chair with no one to answer him back. Go on. Try it again.'

This time Nancy really does sound angry, like Clara's the one to blame for being locked up with all these spinsters, telling everyone else how they should behave. 'The use of soap and elbow grease saves time and effort. And hurry up too. Do you think I have the time to stand here watching you?'

'That's much better,' Clara says, getting to her feet. 'Once you've got it and you're sure of yourself they'll be good as gold. You'll see. You'll make your own decisions, Nancy, but you have to be able to hold the line or you won't last five minutes in here. Not if they think you're weak.'

Nancy puts a hand to her stomach as though she feels a sudden pain and Clara thinks immediately of the child. If Nancy wasn't weak she'd still have her baby. But then, if she wasn't weak, she'd never have had the blessed thing in the first place. She puts the thought from her mind.

'Has Father asked you for money?'

Nancy nods.

'How much?'

'Four shillings a week.'

'He's got no right. I've been giving him something because

you were at home but I'll put a stop to it now you're here. I've been saving some too. You should do the same. It's a good way to keep going here, to think of what you could buy with all your hard work. Honestly, it is! When I have a bad day, and I still do occasionally, I get back to my room and look at a catalogue. I've got a few of them tucked away. You can borrow some if you want to.'

'There's nothing I want.'

'That's only because you haven't looked. I'll lend you them so you can see what they've got. They have some lovely things, Nancy. Have a guess what I want the most. It's expensive, mind. Over seven pounds, and I reckon it will take me six months or more till I've got the money but I'm going to have it. I've made a promise to myself.'

'What is it?'

'Have a guess.'

'I don't know.'

'A bicycle.' Clara says it in a whisper, almost reverential, the image coming to her mind of the model she has chosen. The Raleigh 17 has inflated tyres, safety brakes and a leather guard that encloses the chain to keep your skirt from getting caught. The advertisement promises speed, ease and grace for the woman who buys it.

Nancy looks at her wide eyed. 'He'll kill you when he finds out.'

They burst out laughing, thrilled at the daring of it and remembering their father's tirades about hussies in bloomers and how indecent it is for a woman to straddle a saddle.

'I'd rather have a motorcar,' Nancy tells her. 'I've never been in a motorcar.'

'You'll be lucky!'

While there are some with sufficient wealth to dream of owning a motorcar, Clara knows it is the bicycle that will carry an independent woman like her into the future. And she intends to have one, whatever her father thinks of them.

7

'Excuse me?' Nancy asks a passing warden at the foot of the stairs. 'Excuse me? Which way to the kitchens?'

The warden points along the corridor. 'Take the next left. Go through the double doors. Take a right. Through the next set of doors and you'll find them on the left.'

Who'd be a new girl in a place like this? Always having to ask the way and everyone too busy to help. She hurries on her way and after the last pair of doors she can follow her nose, the smell of stewed cabbage bringing her to the right place. She steps inside the swinging door. The room is busy. Steaming hot. A clatter of pots and pans. The tap, tap, tap of knives on chopping boards.

Nancy stands out of the way, waiting to be noticed. 'I'm to fetch a tray of food for the Duchess,' she tells the first person that looks in her direction.

The woman nods toward a tray that's ready and waiting

on the side. It's been laid with a carving knife, a fork and a large silver dome that covers the plate. Nancy picks it up, not expecting it to be so heavy and it tilts in her hands, threatening to end up on the floor, fit for nothing but the dogs that sleep in the surrounding alleyways.

'Careful now,' the cook warns her and snaps a finger. 'Hey you, give her a hand with the doors.'

A girl appears from nowhere, a kitchen runner, and she holds the door open then follows Nancy out into the corridor.

'And don't go lifting the lid!' the cook calls after them as the door swings shut. 'They want her to have the smell of it hot.'

Nancy puts her head down and walks briskly, Miss Jackson's voice still in her head, telling her she should better be quick about it. The girl takes charge of Nancy's keys, skipping ahead and opening the doors so Nancy can pass straight through, then catching her up and going on ahead so she is ready for the next. Nancy thinks the girl can't be more than thirteen – probably helping her mother out for a bit of extra money – and she wonders which of them is in charge, whether it's herself or the girl.

'Is she as beautiful as they say?' the girl suddenly asks her.

'Who?'

'The Duchess. Is she beautiful?'

'I don't know.' She shouldn't be asking about her. It's not for anyone to say what goes on here, but she can tell the girl won't leave her be till she gets an answer, so she gives her the truth of it straight away. 'I've never seen her.'

The girl nods like that'll do. She runs ahead and opens the door that leads to the staff staircase but Nancy shakes her head. 'I go the long way,' she says, nodding towards the other door.

'You scared of the rats?' Nancy brings her heels together and the girl, knowing she guessed right, leans inside the door and claps her hands. 'Shoo!' she shouts and stamps down hard so the noise of her heel echoes up the steps. 'There! That'll get rid of 'em.' When Nancy doesn't move she puts her hands on her hips. 'Well they ain't gonna jump at you.'

'I've got food. They can smell it.'

'Better be quick about it then,' says the girl. 'C'mon.'

Nancy takes a deep breath and follows the girl as she hurries up the stairs. She turns the first corner, knowing there's a window on the next flight up that'll give them some light. They don't see any rats, but still run the whole way up, as fast as they are able. By the time they stand at the door of the third floor landing, both of them are breathless and taking big gulps of air, their faces redder than a robin's breast.

'Open the door then,' Nancy tells her.

The girl doesn't move. She nods instead at the big silver dome. 'Shall we have a look? See what a Duchess gets for her dinner?' She whips the lid away before Nancy can stop her and the two of them stand gawping at the whole roast chicken, the delicious smell of it curling up around their heads, all the heat of it escaping. 'What would you give for a dinner like that?' the girl asks her.

'C'mon, now.' Nancy tries to take charge. 'You've had

your look.' She is relieved when the girl puts the lid back on and then unlocks the door.

They step out onto the metal gantry, a line of black cell doors to the left and right of them. On the landing below, a young doctor is leading a procession of wardens along the walkway. Miss Needler and Clara are out in front and Mrs Armitage comes along behind, fumbling with a funnel and a length of rubber tubing.

'I can manage now.' Nancy tries to dismiss the girl. 'Thank you.'

But the girl skips away again. 'You ain't getting rid of me now,' she calls back, already running past the first of the doors. 'I wanna have a look at her, don't I? Which door is it?' she shouts over her shoulder, her voice filling out the big empty hall.

'Fifty two,' Nancy shouts back, hoping it'll keep her quiet once she knows.

The cell door opens as she catches up with her and Miss Jackson appears with a look that says she wants to know what all the noise is for.

Quick as a flash, the girl dodges past into the cell. 'Sorry to disturb you ma'am,' they hear her say, 'but we got your dinner for you.'

She lets the cell door swing wide, showing Nancy a woman on her bed, staring up at the ceiling. Nancy gets a good look at her face and she feels bad for staring. But it's her all right, the famous actress everyone's been talking about. She's so beautiful, it couldn't be anyone else.

'That will be all. Thank you.' Miss Jackson takes hold of the girl's ear, giving it a sharp tug as she hoists her out of the door, but the girl doesn't mind and she leaves the room looking like the cat that got the cream.

'Don't just stand there,' Miss Jackson scowls at Nancy so she steps inside the door, putting the tray down on a small folding table that must have been brought there for the purpose.

Miss Jackson closes the door. 'We brought you some food, Miss Divine. Silver service. We don't do that for everyone, you know. We're treating you like royalty.'

She lifts the lid, revealing the roast chicken. It's got all the trimmings – sprouts and roast potatoes, turnip and gravy, all arranged around the sides – enough to feed a family. The smell of it fills the room like a fog lifting off the Thames and seeping out into the streets.

Miss Jackson hands Nancy the lid. She picks up the carving knife and the skin crackles with her first cut, the juices seeping out around the fork and running in a river down the breast of the bird. She lifts a thick slice of white meat and holds it up so the Duchess can see for herself. 'Bring me Miss Divine's plate please, Miss Cooper.'

Nancy goes to the rough wooden shelf by the bed and picks up the tin plate and spoon, then stands waiting like a proper waitress as Miss Jackson slides the meat from the fork to the plate before cutting a second slice. She puts a roast potato or two beside it.

'There now.' Miss Jackson stands aside to show the

Duchess her food. 'A proper roast dinner, Daisy. You can have as much as you want.' She waits impatiently for the Duchess to answer. 'Miss Divine? Please have the decency to look at me when I talk to you.'

The Duchess stirs. She seems to focus for the first time and fixes her gaze on the chicken. Part of the breast is already laid bare but the whole roast chicken still makes a handsome sight. The Duchess lifts herself up from the bed. She has long dark hair tied loosely at her shoulders. She puts her feet to the floor and although she moves slowly, she doesn't appear to be in any discomfort. 'Well, I never.' She begins to laugh. Not at Nancy, not at either of them, but it's a proper laugh, full of life and stronger than she's got a right to make by the look of her. 'A whole roast chicken! Who'd have thought it?' She stands slowly. Takes a step towards them and then another.

Miss Jackson is encouraged. 'Would you like a sprout, Miss Divine? A little bit of gravy?'

The Duchess comes to a stop in front of Nancy, who offers her the plate. The Duchess looks down at the chicken. 'Just what the doctor ordered!' she says.

'That's right,' says Miss Jackson. 'It'll do you a world of good.'

The Duchess picks up a piece of the meat, not with her cutlery, like a lady should, but picks it up with her fingers, holding it under her nose and taking in the smell of it till she swoons. 'What *do* they think we're made of?' she suddenly asks of Nancy. 'These little men and boys?'

Nancy just stares, confused.

'Sugar and spice and all things nice,' the Duchess continues. 'Is that really what they think of us?'

Nancy is surprised at her voice which sounds both plummy and common at the same time.

'You can take the plate back to your bed, Daisy,' prompts Miss Jackson. 'Eat it there and save yourself some energy.'

Nancy lifts the plate higher, bringing it closer to the woman's chin. She's desperate to be rid of it.

'Do you know they put mice down to scare Miss Pankhurst when she speaks?' the Duchess tells them, ignoring the plate of food. 'She used to go into towns and stand on a cart to address the people and the little boys brought mice along to put under her skirt. They thought they could scare her away or show her up as a silly little thing but of course, she always made a point of picking the dear things up and handing them back.'

She smiles at Nancy. She's got a lovely smile. Gracious. Like she already knows that this poor girl in front of her could never pick up a mouse. But it doesn't matter. Not everyone can be charming or brave. Not everyone can be confident. She seems to know that Nancy could never be like her. And yet she smiles at her so graciously.

But then the smile disappears. 'Not today thank you, warden.' The Duchess dismisses her. She turns to face Miss Jackson. 'You know our demands.'

Miss Jackson looks like she might slap her but instead, she sets her jaw and walks smartly from the room, leaving

Nancy alone and feeling like a right fool, standing with a plate of chicken and a spoon in her hand as the Duchess walks back to her bed.

'Don't look so worried,' she tells Nancy as she sits on the edge of it. 'I don't expect you'll be needed to help. They'll have come prepared.'

There are footsteps from the corridor and a moment later the procession arrives at her door. The doctor is first into the cell and he goes straight to the Duchess, putting a stethoscope to her heart. Clara is part of the procession too. She collects the chair from the corner of the cell and sets it in the middle of the floor. Mrs Armitage enters with the funnel held high, the rubber tube coiled tight in her other hand. Miss Needler brings the jug with the slop in it. The doctor finishes his examination and declares the Duchess fit enough to be fed.

'Don't stand and stare!' Miss Jackson scolds Nancy. 'Get rid of that chicken!'

'Sorry, ma'am.' Nancy jumps to, putting the plate on the table and lifting both of them together. She hurries out onto the gantry then props them up against the wall, unsure what she should do now but there's no one else out here, no one to ask. She looks back through the door to see Clara and Miss Jackson dragging the Duchess from the bed by her arms.

'I refuse my consent!' the Duchess shouts as they bring her to the chair. 'Let it be known I refuse to give my consent!'

And that's how it begins, the banging of tin mugs on walls and doors. It starts in the neighbouring cell and moves

73

along the corridor, reaching out into the stairs and dropping down onto the floor below, a hollow rattle of mugs that makes such a din, with cries of, 'Shame on you! Shame on you! Shame on you!'

Nancy stands very still in the middle of the noise. All she can see of the Duchess now is her legs, wearing the regulation red and black stockings and a pair of wooden clogs that lift off the ground as they tip the chair back.

Nancy picks up the tray and hurries to the metal staircase that descends to the next floor. She goes down and down, scurrying back to the kitchens where she puts the tray onto the side where she collected it. An open door promises light and fresh air so she hurries outside, breathless, her pulse racing and her mouth dry. She puts her back against the wall, breathing in deeply. And the Duchess walks inside her head. She's there, pacing from one side of her skull to the other, as though she has a perfect right to be there. As though she owns Nancy's thoughts.

How does she do that? How is she possible? How could a woman be . . . like her?

'She says she'll do another bombing soon as she's out.' The kitchen girl is lounging at the kitchen door, watching Nancy. 'Can you believe the cheek of her?'

Nancy believes the Duchess could do anything. 'They won't let her go though. Will they? Not if she did all those things.'

The girl shrugs, suddenly uninterested, and takes herself back inside.

Nancy takes a moment more, and when she's ready she

74

goes back up the staircase to the suffragette wing. She sees the procession of wardens entering another cell on the floor below and the idea comes to her that she might look in on the Duchess one more time, that she might use the spy hole to check on her. She goes to the door, guilty that the Duchess won't even know she's there, but glad to get a chance to look at her again. She slides back the cover and presses her eye to the door, expecting to see the Duchess lying on her bed and staring up at the ceiling as she was before. But the bed is empty and so is the room. Nancy's first thought is that they must have taken her elsewhere. Perhaps they hurt her and she's been taken to the infirmary? She presses her eye to the door again, but this time, instead of the empty room, a flash of pale skin fills her eye, a shoulder and bare neck, so close to the spy hole it feels like a slap in the face. Nancy pulls her head back. Was that her? She looks again, with an urgent eye that darts left and right, following the naked woman as she runs around her cell, a hand held out against the wall to keep herself from falling.

Nancy steps back from the door. She swallows hard, her stomach lurching, unsure whether she should shout for help or deal with it herself. She fumbles for her ring of keys, rattling them in the lock as she opens the door. The Duchess runs past, moving quickly, half stumbling but using the wall to support herself. She looks like a mad woman.

'Stop,' Nancy tells her quietly, unsure she's even said the word out loud. 'You've got to stop.'

The Duchess crashes past again. Her feet are heavy on

the stone floor. Her hair is flowing out behind her and she's breathing hard and fast, her ribs rising and falling like the gills of a fish that's been pulled from water. Nancy moves into the middle of the cell to avoid a collision. Because the Duchess won't stop. The woman spins around her like the rim of a wheel with Nancy at its centre.

'Please!' she says again. She steps forward and stretches out her hand, but she can't bring herself to touch. 'Please. You've got to stop!'

She knows she should catch hold of the woman. She should pin her to the floor and shout for help. It's the only thing that will work. But she can't do it. She can't do anything, though she knows if the two of them are found like this it'll be the end of her. She starts to cry. She becomes dizzy from the turning. Helpless. Like a little girl curled up in bed. She drops to the floor, her legs brought up into her chest. 'Stop it!' she screams. She throws her arms around her head. 'Stop it! Stop it! Stop it!'

Just for a moment, everything disappears. There are no walls or doors. There is no naked woman.

When she opens her eyes, the Duchess is walking. Circling her. She still has a hand on the wall. But she's watching Nancy. *The Duchess* is watching *her*. She comes to a standstill, putting her spine against the wall. Her belly pumps like a bullfrog's throat but she's too breathless to be able to talk.

Nancy raises herself up on one elbow. She sees bruises on the woman's thighs and the top of her arms, fierce patches of purple and red against her pale skin.

The Duchess speaks between breaths. 'You're . . . not . . . supposed . . . to use pity.' Even at this distance, her breath stinks of rotten apples. 'It's unfair.' The Duchess slides down the wall till she sits on the floor with one leg folded underneath her. *'I'm* not supposed to feel sorry for *you*. That's against the rules.'

Nancy stares at the woman in utter disbelief. 'What are you *doing*?'

'It burns off the food,' the Duchess says matter-of-factly then doubles over and retches, her forehead almost touching the floor as she vomits nothing but a line of yellow saliva that dribbles from her teeth.

'But . . . but why are you *naked*?'

The Duchess looks at Nancy as though it is *she* who is peculiar. 'There seems little point in protesting against the Second Division while I'm dressed in their uniform. I'm refusing to wear it.'

Nancy suddenly comes to her senses, remembering who and what she is. This is ridiculous. She has to stand up and she does, composing herself sufficiently to get to her feet. She straightens her dress then puts a hand to the back of her head, checking for the pins. 'Well.' She swallows hard, trying to remember how to use the voice she's practised with Clara. 'Please don't do it again.'

The Duchess tries to laugh but instead, she coughs and coughs and coughs. 'I can't promise,' she says, eventually.

8

Clara runs along Prince Albert Road as quickly as her skirt allows. It's only an hour before the zoo closes and Ted will be waiting. When she arrives, she can't see him. He's not at the gate or sitting on one of the benches at the side of the road and for a moment she thinks he might have got fed up and gone home. It's only when she's almost given up hope that she spots him hurrying toward her.

'There you are!' He gasps for breath when he reaches her. 'There was some sort of accident coming up from town and I sat on the tram without us moving for half an hour. In the end I had to get off and run.' He bends over, holding his side and catching his bowler hat as it drops from his head. 'Blimey, O'Riley! I haven't run like that since I was at school.' He kisses her quickly on the cheek. 'I wasn't sure you would wait.'

Clara laughs at him. 'I only just got here myself. I was late coming out of work.'

'Well that's just as well then.' He takes one last deep breath. 'Come on. We haven't got long if we're going to see anything.'

He buys their tickets at the turnstile. Once inside, they look at a map that shows them where to find the animals.

'I want to see all the African animals,' she tells him. 'All the lions and elephants.'

'We're going that way anyway,' he says. 'But there's something I want you to see first.'

'Is this another of your surprises?'

'Actually it is. It's why I thought of coming here.'

He takes her to a pavilion where camel rides are advertised on a big yellow board. 'There you go.'

He stands back proudly, pointing at one of the big hairy beasts and Clara shrieks, covering her mouth with her hand. 'What makes you think I want a ride on one of those?'

'You did, you silly thing! You laughed at them so much in the cinema. Don't you remember? That's what made me think of it.' He pays the keeper with a shilling piece and pockets the change. 'I thought you'd like to see one up close. You can feed him too if you've got the nerve.'

She takes a handful of corn from the bag the man holds out for her. 'Careful of your fingers, ma'am,' the keeper says with a wink. 'It could have one of 'em off in an instant.'

'Which do you want to keep?' Ted joins in on the joke. 'Better be your wedding finger.'

Clara ignores them. She holds her palm flat and the camel steps closer, sniffs, then snuffles up the corn with a snort, its big black lips leaving slobber on her skin. 'It's no different to feeding a horse,' she tells Ted matter-of-factly, thinking of the rag and bone man's cart that stops outside her house.

The trainer has a stick that he presses to the camel's neck, pulling on the halter to make it kneel so they can both climb up, Ted sitting behind her, pressed close against her back with his arms around her waist.

'Don't worry,' he whispers as the camel rises. 'I've got hold of you.'

The keeper takes them the length of the path and back again, past the hippopotamus and the monkey house, past all the caged animals. Clara doesn't know whether she feels like an African queen or one of the exhibits, what with everyone staring at them.

'What do you think of the camel now then?' Ted asks when they're nearly back at the pavilion.

'They're not as funny when you get up close,' she says. 'Actually, I feel sorry for him.' But then their camel bellows like a fog horn and tries to put its long pink tongue into the keeper's ear and both of them can't help but laugh.

Once they're back on firm ground, Ted takes hold of her hand. He buys a stick of fairy floss and they tear pieces off with their fingers, rolling them into their mouths and smiling, all the strands of sugar disappearing on their tongues. In the lions' enclosure, a single male with a shaggy mane is spread out on a rock while four lionesses prowl down near the bars. Clara and Ted are still watching them when a keeper shouts out that the zoo is closing and they saunter back to the exit.

They take a walk in Regent's Park, following a path that leads toward the setting sun.

Ted points over to a tree, a big old oak out on its own in the middle of the grass, with a canopy that is big enough to hide them in its shadow. 'Come on,' he says. 'Let's stop over there.' He produces a bottle of port from his bag. He's got a couple of glasses in a presentation box. 'Real crystal,' he tells her, flicking at the glass with a fingernail to make it ping.

Clara holds the glasses while he pours. 'Ooh, Ted, it's a good one by the look of it.' She takes a quick sip. 'It is too! You shouldn't have.'

'A little bit of what you fancy,' he says with a cockney grin that he can't quite pull off.

'You shouldn't make a joke of everything,' she tells him. Ted's the only person who goes to the trouble of making her feel special and she doesn't want him to give it with one hand and snatch it back with the other. 'This is lovely of you. Very thoughtful.'

'Here's to you then.' He raises his glass theatrically. 'To the loveliest girl I've ever had the pleasure to meet.'

'You're doing it again!'

'No, I'm not! I mean it. I think you're super. I really do.'

Clara smiles so wide he must see her teeth. And she feels that warmth again, the one that only comes when she's with him. And she knows that she should stop herself. She should have told him by now that this isn't possible. But she doesn't want to. She wants to walk right up to the edge of her cliff and look over. The way she feels now, she might even jump.

Ted leans into her. He puts an arm around her waist and they watch the people walking their dogs under the lamps along the path. At the moments when they don't talk she can hear the monkeys chattering away in the zoo. Soon there is only a little light left in the sky. Ted tops up their glasses. He spreads his coat over the ground, sits down and pats the place beside him. Clara unbuckles her sensible shoes, kicking them off into the grass. She sits down next to him and when he kisses her properly, they lie back against his coat, holding each other tightly, the crystal glasses abandoned in the grass beside them.

In the dark like this, they could be the only people in the park and Clara breathes him in, holds the musk of him there at the back of her throat. Her lips touch the tiny hairs on the back of his neck. When she is this close he smells of soap, all clean and scrubbed behind the ears. A shiver runs across the top of her shoulders. 'It's getting colder, isn't it?' She slips a finger under his jacket, feels for a button on the front of his shirt and pops it open. She sneaks her hand in next to his skin. How can it be that the world stops turning when you touch someone? It shouldn't be possible. But it is. She could stay like this for ever, with a hand upon his chest, feeling him breathe. She's got all the time in the world.

Ted holds her tighter. He puts his tongue a little deeper into her mouth and then undoes two buttons of her coat, not the top two but the buttons immediately up from her waist. He puts his hands inside, resting them on the bottom of her ribcage. 'That's better,' he whispers. 'That's nice and warm.'

She should stop him there. She knows he's waiting to see if she will and she ought to. But she doesn't want to. Not right now. She moves her hand down around his waist, slides a finger along the belt line of his trousers, feeling the rise of his hipbone and the tiny roll of fat that reminds her suddenly of Nancy's baby. She could stop the world too, that little thing. But not for long. And she couldn't do anything to change it.

Ted's palm brushes the top of her breast. He removes a hand and picks at the remaining buttons of her coat. Suddenly he's got clumsy fingers and it feels wrong for such a precise man to be so careless, like he's wearing another man's hands. He slides a leg between hers and edges himself on top of her, the weight of him making it difficult for her to breathe, so that all of a sudden she loses the delight of touching him and being touched. The last person to behave this way was her father and he smelt of soap too.

She pulls her hand from his shirt, shoving his shoulder hard and bringing her thigh up quickly to roll him away.

Ted sprawls out across the grass. 'What did you do that for?' He sits up straight, all hurt and bewildered and breathing too quickly. The two of them glare at each other. 'I thought you wanted to.'

'I did.'

'So what's the matter?'

'I don't know . . . it was too much.'

'It was hardly anything.'

'Too fast then . . . oh . . . I don't know.'

Ted takes a deep breath. He hangs his head. After a moment he slides across to her, putting his hand on her knee. 'I'm sorry. That wasn't fair. But I thought you wanted to.'

'I did,' she says again. She feels as if he's putting her in a box and deciding how to label it but she also thinks she's being unreasonable, that she's to blame, like a child that changes their mind from one minute to the next.

He pulls her coat closed. 'I suppose we shouldn't do something we'll regret.'

'No, Ted,' she agrees. But she wouldn't regret it. Not if things were different.

She feels as if she is being torn in half. All the things she wants are at war with each other. But not because of her. That's what makes her so angry, because all of this is about other people. It's not about her and Ted. It's about everyone else telling them how they have to live. It's not even real. Not something you can touch. And yet it is. The possibility of a baby is about as real as it can get. Just the idea of it is big enough to make her head explode. She puts a hand up to cover her face. 'This is impossible!'

'Don't say that.'

'Well it is, Ted.'

Now it's him that looks like a child. He's suddenly sullen, like a little boy who can't get his own way and doesn't know why. She actually feels sorry for him. And that makes her feel guilty. She puts a hand on his knee, picking at the twill of his trousers.

'I love you,' he tells her suddenly.

'What?'

'I do.'

'What's that got to do with anything?'

'Thanks very much.'

'Well it hasn't.'

Of all the stupid things he could say right now. She could slap him. She really could.

But he won't let it lie. 'Clara, I'm in love with you. I want us to get married. I was intending to wait for my promotion but I've got some money put aside. It's not a lot, not very much at all, but it might be enough. So you may as well know now as later.'

'And is that all you think of me?'

'What?'

She stands up quickly, brushing off her coat by slapping at the front and back of it.

'I don't understand,' he says.

'Where do you think that leaves me? I can be a wife or a whore – oh, and by the way, becoming a mother comes with either of them. Is that all the choice I've got, Ted? Is that all you've got to offer me?'

'That isn't what I meant.' Ted gets to his feet. Now it's him with a hand to his head, holding his forehead as though it hurts. 'It doesn't have to be like that.'

'No. Not for you it doesn't. It's me that has everything

to lose!' She picks up her handbag, puts her hat back on her head. 'I'm going home. This was a mistake. I'm sorry, Ted. I was stupid to have come.'

'Wait!' He begins to scramble about on the ground, putting the port and glasses back in his bag and picking up his coat. 'Wait, Clara! I'll walk you,' he shouts after her.

'I don't want you to walk me!' she shouts back at him.

By the time she reaches the path, he's caught up with her. 'Don't, Clara.' He grabs at the sleeve of her coat. 'Wait for me.'

'Ted, I want to be on my own.'

'But it's not safe at night.'

'Isn't it?' She turns on him again, angrier now than she was before, because although she might blame herself for letting it get this far, it was never a fair choice from the start. All of this, the things she has to do and the way she has to behave. None of it is fair. Not for either of them, but especially for her. And Ted is right. She can't even walk along a street on her own. Because that's the truth of it, isn't it? She can't even get herself home without the help of a man!

What she would give for a bicycle right now, to whisk her away with speed and grace, delivering her safely back home. 'Go away, Ted,' she tells him but when she reaches the road, he's still there, twenty paces behind her.

'I'll just *watch* you home then,' he calls out, holding his hands up to show he daren't come any closer. 'I need to know you're safe. For my own sake, Clara. It's not for you. But I don't want to be up half the night worrying.'

Clara walks on and she doesn't look back again, even though it takes her half an hour before she reaches the prison, all the time reminding herself that she knew this was on the cards. Did she expect the world to fall into place just for her? Did she think Ted was too nice a bloke to want to push it further? But just a little longer would have been nice. He's the only thing in the world outside of work and when she turns around, he's still there, twenty paces behind her, like she knew he would be. She walks back to him.

'I want to apologize,' he says before she arrives.

'Don't,' she tells him. She's calmer now that she's had the space to think. 'It's not your fault. Not really. But I can't keep seeing you, Ted.'

'Don't say that.'

'It's been lovely, Ted. But I was never going to give up my job. I should have made that clear from the start so perhaps I've been leading you on. And you don't deserve that. You deserve someone who can give you what you want.'

'But I want *you*. I know I do.'

She kisses him before he can speak again. Just once. On the cheek. The way they used to a month ago. 'Goodbye, Ted.'

'I'll be here next week,' he calls to her as she walks away. 'Same time as usual. That'll give you time to think about it and if you don't want me here, you'll have to tell me yourself. You owe me that much at least.'

9

Nancy gets up at 4.30 a.m. She washes at her basin and dresses in her uniform, stretching her arms behind her back to fasten the buttons of her dress. She brushes her hair, ties her bonnet under her chin and walks from her cell, locking the door behind her and descending the metal staircase to the hall below.

She finds the dining room half full. At the far end, the kitchen staff are serving breakfast from three large metal dishes with lids to keep them warm. She has a kipper with a piece of toast and pours herself a cup of tea from the large urn. She chooses a place at the table, close to where Mrs Armitage sits gossiping with a couple of wardens that she can't put names to. She lays her breakfast on the tabletop and pulls up a chair. She has only just sat down when Miss Jackson approaches.

'Are you volunteering for us, Miss Cooper?'

'Pardon, miss?'

Miss Jackson comes to a standstill behind her. 'If you insist on working then you should know you won't be paid.'

'But I don't understand, miss.'

Miss Jackson puts her out of her misery. 'It's your day off, Miss Cooper. You shouldn't be here!'

The women at the table stop their conversation and watch them with amused faces.

'I'm sorry,' Nancy apologizes. 'I must have made a mistake.' She stands up, ready to leave the table.

'You don't need to apologize to me, Miss Cooper, and you may as well finish your breakfast.' Miss Jackson takes the chair opposite her own. 'Waste not want not.'

Nancy sits back down when she would rather be away and feel a fool on her own. She can visualize the piece of paper pinned to the notice board with the rota of work. And today is Thursday. She should have known that it was Thursday. But she never expected a day off so soon after starting a new job.

She finishes her breakfast quickly then returns to her room just as the bell goes for the prisoners to rise. She closes the door, takes off her uniform and hangs it up. She sits on the edge of the bed in her petticoat. Outside her door the buckets clang against the gantry rail as the women go to fetch their water. Nancy wonders what people do on their days off. She could go out, but it's still too early. She lies down on her bunk and tries to sleep. After a long while she sits up again, remembering some needlework that needs doing, a button on her jacket that has come loose and is waiting in the pocket. She could do it now. She goes across to the shelf where she keeps her sewing kit, brings it back to the bed with the jacket and is about to begin when she remembers that this is what the prisoners do. They sit and sew at the tables in the hall or in their cells. She lays the jacket aside. But she can't simply sit here doing nothing. If someone were to see her now, to spy on her like she does with the woman in the next cell, what would they think of her, sitting in her underclothes on the edge of her bed and twiddling her fingers? She spots the lipstick on her shelf, the one that Clara bought for her last birthday, and it reminds her that she meant to buy a mirror. She checks the time on her pocket watch. The shops will be open soon enough. She fetches the dress she wore when she arrived. She slips on her hat and gloves. At the prison gates, she half expects to be stopped and sent back, but the woman only passes the time of day with her.

'Off somewhere nice are we?' She gets her to sign in the large green attendance book.

'I hope so,' says Nancy, thinking that if she's back before an hour it will look odd.

When she steps into the rectangle of bright light beyond the open door, the sun makes her dizzy and she pauses, putting up a hand to shield her eyes. She puts the brolly she has brought under her arm, then undoes the top two buttons of her coat. Even the weather is out to trick her today, though to be fair, there are some clouds in the sky, so a small chance of rain. She hasn't gone more than twenty yards when she remembers the purse in her bag. She has no money aside from a few coppers that were there when she packed her suitcase and left home. She goes back inside the prison.

'Forgot something?' asks the woman on the desk and Nancy pulls the same face her mother uses to tell her she's useless. She makes her way to the infirmary, hoping to find Clara, but the place is empty except for a doctor who is young and dapper, his hair greased back to one side in the fashion.

'What can I do for you?' he asks her with a knowing grin. 'Unless you're here to do something for me?'

Nancy tries not to look at him directly. 'I'm looking for Clara. Is her room somewhere here?'

'What do you want with Clara?'

'She's my sister.'

'Clara is your sister? Really? I never knew she had a sister but now that you mention it I can see the similarity.' He looks her over from top to toe. 'Something in the eyes perhaps?'

'Do you know where her room is?'

'I do,' he says. 'But I don't think I can tell you. Not if I don't know what it is about. You might be up to no good.'

And Nancy feels like a butterfly, pinned to a wall and struggling, hoping he'll let her go sooner rather than later because she knows what he's about.

'I need to borrow some money from her.' Nancy regrets it immediately but there's something about men like this. They don't let you breathe. They don't let you think. And they make it difficult to say no.

She tries to make light of it. 'I've been left without a penny till payday.'

'Well never mind. I'll tell her you were looking for her. Actually, no. I can do better than that.' He reaches into his trouser pocket, brings out a couple of shillings and offers them. 'Go on. You might as well borrow from me as from her and anyway, I know where you live. I suppose they have you up on one of the wings?'

'Yes.'

'C wing?'

'No.'

'That's unusual. Normally it's C wing for the new girls. Where have they got you then?'

'D wing.'

'Well then, now I know where to find you if you don't pay it back.' He steps closer, putting his hand in hers, leaving the coins between her fingers.

'Thank you,' she says, retreating, and then at the door, 'I'll pay you back. At the end of the month. Just as soon as I get paid.'

She walks fast along the Camden Road. Too fast, she thinks, telling herself she's meant to be leisurely. She makes herself stop and look in the first shop window she comes to, then finds that it's a butcher's, with posters in the window for Jersey pork, neck bone and leaf lard. Not the sort of shop she had in mind but why shouldn't she look if she finds it interesting? Behind the glass, cuts of beef and lamb dangle from their metal hooks. A neck fillet. A half pound of silverside. Another woman comes to a stop beside her, sees something she likes and goes inside. Nancy notices a string of sausages and thinks that'd be nice, to have some fried up sausages for her supper and she almost follows the woman inside before remembering that she eats in the canteen now and has nowhere to cook them. Still, she feels better for knowing she could've gone inside, that it wasn't for the lack of courage.

She walks on past the Castle tavern and Bessie's needle-makers with its linens and threads. There's a new department store at the next big junction. They'll have mirrors there for sure and she decides to go in, to shop in style the way her sister would. She walks through the splendid revolving doors and stands inside the great hall, marvelling at the noise and colour of the displays. Above her head is a large gilt cage filled with real birds, all of them exotic, with bright feathers of scarlet, turquoise or yellow. There is a pair of elephant tusks, inlaid with silver at their tips and standing upright over a door. It's like another world – or rather that the whole world's been packaged up and put on sale for her delight – and she goes between the counters, looking at jewellery and bottles of perfume and clothes of every style, shape and colour.

She begins to relax enough to watch some of the other women shopping and she notices the shop assistants that serve them. She used to do the same job they do, although not in a big posh store like this one, but even so, she used to be a shop girl. Suddenly it doesn't seem so long ago. Perhaps she could still do it. She'd met a few girls that managed to pay the rent on a room of their own and if her father hadn't taken her wages then she might've thought of it for herself. She finds a mirror that pleases her, a simple handheld glass with a stained oak surround. It would do nicely for her face and hair, so she buys it, even though it costs more than she would normally spend. She puts the change in her purse and wonders what to do next. Have a coffee, she thinks. That's what Clara would do if she were here.

She finds a notice board at the main staircase which tells her there is a coffee room on the third floor and when she reaches it, the place is just right. It's not too busy but not empty either and she is able to take a table by the window where she can feign an interest in the street if she feels at all conspicuous. She imagines she is waiting to meet someone, perhaps one of the glamorous ladies who are shopping on the floor below. Opposite her, another woman sits on her own, so that is a comfort. She wears a large round lemon yellow hat with a twirl of white silk, which reminds Nancy of the women from the Lady Visitors' Association. A tea set is laid out before her and she has a selection of cakes on a tall china stand. The woman catches Nancy's eye and smiles at her. So there, she's not out of place here at all.

The waitress arrives and asks Nancy if she is ready to order. She asks for a coffee and then adds a slice of strawberry sponge cake on a whim. She says yes to cream, thinking of how it would make her mother tut. When her order arrives, she sips at the coffee slowly and eats her cake in tiny mouthfuls, leaving a good amount of time between each, so she can savour the experience.

The woman at the next table smiles at her again then says, 'It looks as though the sun might get the better of the rain today.'

'Yes,' says Nancy. 'Yes, I think it might.'

A little while later, the woman stops the waitress and asks for her bill.

'Me too, please,' says Nancy. The cafe is filling up now with customers looking for an early lunch and the two of them survey the surrounding tables till the waitress arrives and puts a silver plate with a folded bill in front of each of them. Nancy picks up hers and sees the scribbled sum. It's more expensive than she realized and her heart skips a beat as she remembers how much money the doctor gave her and the cost of the mirror. She reaches for her purse, opens it and flicks through the coins. She can feel the colour draining from her face. She hasn't the money to pay her bill. She had forgotten buying the mirror when she ordered the cake and now she doesn't have enough for her bill and she will have to admit it to the waitress and heaven only knows what will happen.

'My goodness! Are you all right?' The woman at the next table leans across to her. 'You look like you've seen a ghost.'

Nancy knows she should smile, that she should tell her she's fine, but she can't connect her mouth with her brain, can't loosen her tongue enough to say anything at all. It's all she can do to breathe as the waitress approaches them again, expecting to be paid.

The woman in the yellow hat stands up. 'I'd like to pay for this lady as well as myself,' she instructs the waitress and flourishes a pound note before leaning down towards Nancy. 'You've been such charming company, my dear,' she tells her. 'Let this be my treat.'

'Thank you.' Nancy actually curtsies when she stands and the woman can't help but let out a little laugh. She taps the top of Nancy's hand.

'It's rare to see someone take such pleasure in a cake. I eat so many of the things that I'd quite forgotten that is the point of them.'

'Thank you,' Nancy says again, turns quickly on her heels and leaves. She feels stooped and shabby as she walks among the fine dresses and suits, thankful that the woman in lemon doesn't follow her and telling herself she won't cry till she's out of the shop. But oh, how could she have been so stupid? Of all the things she could have done in a place like this! She should have known better than to come to somewhere she doesn't belong.

She doesn't dare use the revolving doors again but finds an exit to the side, a normal door that opens and shuts as it should and won't threaten to trap her. Once outside, she runs straight across the busy street, dodging carts and motorcars, then darting down a side street. She wants to get as far away from the department store as she can and she marches blindly, thinking that she doesn't know or care which way her feet take her, though she's not surprised to find herself turning into the Seven Sisters Road. She slows down as she passes the terraced houses on the street where she lived. She is on the opposite side to her father's house and she stops across from its front door and stands there watching the windows for movement.

That woman in the cafe was wrong about the sun. There are clouds in the sky. If anything it's getting colder. She pulls the edges of her coat together. If he comes outside, he'll take her back in with him and she won't resist. She knows it. She thinks she wants it. Wants to go inside the front door. Wants the comfort of familiar things. The chair by the fireside. The smell of stewing beef. He'd be good to her for a time. She knows he would. He'd pamper her, get her mother to be pleasant and stop her nagging. He'd leave her alone for a while too.

She thinks she sees someone at the window, in the upstairs room where she gave birth. She closes her eyes. If he takes her by the arm then so be it. She begins her count to a hundred. When she opens them again it'll all be over. Something will have changed. The rain begins when she reaches fifty. A single drop that lands on the end of her nose. Another splashes on the lid of her eye. There was a time, as a girl, she used to enjoy the rain. She'd throw back her head and open her mouth, laughing. She and Clara, catching raindrops on their tongues.

She opens her eyes again at eighty-seven. No one comes

10

Ted stands as Clara approaches the table. 'I want to apologize.'

'Please, don't. If anything it's me . . .'

'No, it's not. You've got nothing to apologize for.'

'Right then.' Clara tries to smile. She pulls a white wooden chair from the table and sits down awkwardly.

'I'm glad you came.' Ted doesn't dare smile. 'I wasn't sure you would.'

'I said I would.'

'Yes. Well, I'm glad you did.'

Oh dear God! Will they ever stop being polite? If she can't stop herself, they could go on like this for hours. She tries not to talk and looks instead around the tea room. There are white whicker tables with cloths made of pink lace. Each table has a red candle, mounted in a china figure of Cupid, his bow pulled back and taking aim.

'Have you been here before?' she asks him, wondering if this is what he intended.

'I've passed it from the outside but never come in.' He looks embarrassed. 'It has a certain style, hasn't it? We can find somewhere else.'

'No. Really. There's no need.' She turns the figurine till Cupid's arrow points away from them.

'Tell me about your work.' He stuns her. Just with that. Manages to turn on a sixpence to relax her. 'It's obviously important to you and I've never really asked you about it. I suppose I assumed you were only doing it because you had to.'

'I did initially, Ted. I needed to leave home and the job requires me to live in, so it was the best way to do that. I've been there a while now and I'm doing well enough. Actually, I enjoy it. Not all of it and not every day, but I do feel appreciated and I think I'm doing something worthwhile.'

'What sort of women are in there?'

'Do you mean the murderers?'

'No, I didn't mean that. I meant in general. What sort of women end up in prison?'

'You'd be surprised. Many of them can't read or write properly and they're either there because they're drinking away their misery or they're trying to make a living.' She means prostitution. She should speak it, say the word out loud, but she can't, not in front of Ted. He'd only be embarrassed and if he wasn't . . . well . . . The thought that Ted might use a prostitute pops into her head but she shoos it away as quickly as it came. She says, 'Women get much harsher sentences than men.'

'Do they? I'd imagine they'd go easier on them, but if anyone knows it would be you.'

Clara nods. 'Yes. I believe it's true.'

They hesitate, unsure where the conversation is taking them until Ted asks, 'And you can't carry on working if you get married? That's the usual way of things, isn't it?'

'That's right, Ted. I'd have to give it all up and I don't see why I should. Do you?'

'Not if you don't want to.'

The owner comes to take their order. She's an older woman in a red dress made of crepe and lace. She lights the candle in the centre of their table with a flourish of her matchbox then turns the cupid back around to face them. She asks if they'd like to see the cake tray for a slice of something special.

'No, thank you,' Clara says without hesitation. 'We'd like tea for two with a buttered scone.'

The woman scribbles their order onto her pad with a look of disappointment.

'No wonder you felt trapped,' Ted says once she's left the table. 'It wasn't me, then? You didn't think I was ugly or too stupid for you?'

'No, Ted. Never.'

'There was a girl at the bank where I work and she was good at her job too. She used to work on the front desk and she was nice with the customers. She had to leave when she got married. I couldn't see the sense in it. I told her she should take her ring off but it was too late by then and anyway, she said it wouldn't feel right, making out she was something she wasn't.'

'A lot of girls do.'

'Well they shouldn't have to. When she left, it seemed to me we all lost out.'

The waitress returns with a single plate of two scones and a tiny pot of red jam. She puts out cups and saucers and brings their tea in an ornate pot with a separate jug of milk.

Ted does the honours, pouring her cup before his own. 'My mother was very involved in doing good works, the Board of Guardians, things like that. She was intelligent too, the same as you.'

'And you like that in a woman?'

'Of course I do.'

'Some men wouldn't.'

'Maybe not.'

Clara cuts a scone in half and butters it up. 'What else do you like about me?'

Ted doesn't have to think for long. 'I like the way you say what you think.'

'I don't always.'

'You do often enough. And you know what you want too. Like when you kissed me on the bus back from Brixton. Not many girls would have done that. Not the way you did.'

'It was just a kiss.'

'But you took the risk that I might think less of you.'

'It wasn't such a risk. Most men like to be kissed.'

That was a stupid thing to say. It makes it sound like she kisses men all the time. Other men than Ted. And it brings back their trip to the zoo, brings it right here into this silly pink room and Ted must be thinking of it too, because he suddenly hasn't got a thing to say.

Clara looks back over her shoulder where the owner is watching them from behind her counter. She puts her hand out and touches the tips of Ted's fingers. 'I like being listened to. That's one of the things I like most about you, Ted. You let me have some space.'

'Do I?'

'Yes, you do. I feel like I can breathe when I'm with you.' She squeezes his hand. 'But I want to be able to do things with my life, Ted. There's no point being intelligent and not being able to use it.'

'I think you should be able to do what you want, Clara. I don't want to stop you.'

The bell rings on the tea room door as a child enters, a little girl with a bucket of roses, and she nods at the owner and then makes straight for them. 'A penny for a rose, mister?'

'Here,' says Clara quickly. 'I'd like one.' She finds her purse and gives the girl a coin before Ted can get his money out. 'This is for you,' she tells him and he takes the flower, holding the rose up to his nose. 'Do you mind a woman buying you flowers?'

'Not if it's you.'

They get up to leave. At the front desk, Clara asks the woman how much they owe.

'Two and six,' she tells Ted directly.

'I'll pay that.' Clara has her purse out of her bag already and puts her shillings down on the counter, the woman watching her with the face of a gargoyle.

'Are you going to pay for everything?' Ted asks once they're safely outside.

'Did I embarrass you?'

'A bit, if I'm honest. I'll have to be quicker next time.'

'I want to pay my way, Ted. It's important to me.'

'Careful now. I might get used to it.'

'It's not a joke, Ted. If I can't do a little thing like that then I can't do anything.'

'So you want to see me again then?'

Clara breaks the stalk off his rose then slots the flower into his lapel. 'I don't think I can stop myself. But I want it to be different, Ted.'

'Like how?'

'I don't know. I just don't want us to assume anything of each other.'

'In what way?'

'I don't know . . . I suppose I mean taking things for granted.'

'Right,' says Ted, as though he has to make an effort to remember it.

Before they reach the prison, she kisses him lightly on the lips, feeling like they're starting afresh. Like everything

104

is new. And she thinks she understands how sometimes the best thing to do is the thing that makes no sense. And you do it because it feels right. Like seeing a man you shouldn't. Or keeping a baby with its mother when you know all it will do is drag her down.

She feels the need to see Nancy again, to speak of it properly and once she's back inside the prison gates, she takes the stairs that lead away from her own room and up towards the wings. It's getting late but Nancy should still be awake and she wants to apologize, wants to be able to talk about what happened with the baby, to tell Nancy that falling pregnant wasn't her fault.

The stairs up the inside of the wing are empty and quiet and when she reaches Nancy's door, she knocks and pushes at it, walking straight into the room. The first thing she sees is the doctor's long white coat as he turns, startled, revealing Nancy backed up against the wall. The top three buttons of her uniform are undone and a triangle of cloth flaps down to expose her collar bone and the top of her chest.

The doctor backs away from her, buttoning up the front of his coat. He wipes a hand across his greasy hair. 'I came to ask for some money that I'm owed,' he tells Clara stiffly as he walks out of the door.

Clara struggles to make sense of what she has seen. Her first thought is that her sister is up to no good but then Nancy starts sobbing.

'Why do they always pick me?' She wipes her hands on

the front of her dress, rubbing away at something that can't be seen.

Clara goes across to her, takes hold of her arms and brings her hands to a stop. 'It's not your fault.'

'Yes it is. It's like they can smell something on me, like they know there's something wrong with me. But I didn't want to borrow the money. I didn't ask him for anything, he just gave it to me.'

Clara takes hold of Nancy's head and kisses her brow. 'How much was it?'

'A couple of shillings. It was only till the end of the month.'

'I'll give it him back,' she tells her. 'I'll do it now and tell him that's an end of it.'

11

It takes five of them to hold the Duchess down and Nancy is glad she's not one of them. Instead, she must administer the slop and she stands a few feet away from the chair, holding the large white jug, trying to convince herself this is the right thing to do.

Miss Jackson has a free hand. She puts a finger hard against the gum, her thumb pushing the top lip up against the nose so the doctor can see for himself. 'Here.' She points to a gap in the teeth, a place where they don't fit tight when the Duchess clenches.

The doctor leans in closer. 'Thank you, Miss Jackson.' He walks back to the table by the door and returns with the clamp. 'Miss Cooper?' He addresses Nancy directly. 'If you are going to learn the procedure, you need to watch what is happening. This is your first time, isn't it?'

Nancy lifts her eyes from the floor, feeling like a child caught out in the classroom. 'Yes, sir.'

'Well then, you must pay attention.' He decides to make a lesson of it to punish her. 'We'd prefer to feed her with a cup, Miss Cooper, but she's still too strong.' He stands close to the wardens who hold the Duchess to the chair, one for each limb. Miss Jackson stands behind with her hands across the face, exposing the Duchess's teeth as a thin white line between her fingers. The Doctor holds the steel clamp against them, finds the space between the teeth then pushes the edge of the metal slowly but firmly between them. 'There we are,' he says, sounding as though he's just given her a spoonful of syrup.

He turns the screw to widen the clamp and the tendons in the Duchess's throat become tight as she resists. She tries to scream, but her throat can't manage without her mouth, so she produces a long, low moan which is cut short when she chokes and swallows. The doctor continues to turn the nut on the clamp until her teeth are an inch apart. 'That should do the trick. Now, let's be ready with the pipe.' He holds her tongue down flat with a wooden spatula. Miss Barraclough hands him the free end of the tube and unravels the rest till the funnel is in reach of Nancy. 'By using a pipe we can administer food deep into the gut.' He slowly pushes the tube down into the throat.

The Duchess shudders and rises an inch from her seat.

'This way, when she vomits, she will still retain at least some of the liquid.' He puts his face close to her mouth, peering in between her teeth. 'I think we are ready. Lift the jug please, Miss Cooper.'

Nancy does as she is told, raising the jug to pour the slop into the funnel, hoping she doesn't go too fast or too slow and glad the wardens have their hands over the Duchess's eyes because she couldn't bear to see her watching.

The Duchess shakes against the frame of the chair and rises again. The wardens tighten their grip, bringing her back into her seat while Miss Jackson steps forward, readying a bowl for the vomit when the tube is withdrawn.

'There now,' says the doctor. 'No harm done this time.' Though he knows there might be. A misdirected tube that delivers slop into the lung will most likely kill her. He pulls the tube out briskly, like reeling in a fishing line, and when it is done the wardens release their hold.

The Duchess makes the sound of a cat spitting up a hairball. Nancy hurries outside and puts the jug on the trolley then waits by the door, glad to be out of the cell. Miss Denton arrives with the chair and wipes it down with a cloth that she wets from a bucket of water positioned in the corridor. Miss Barraclough sluices through the tube then wipes the funnel with a cloth. The women follow the doctor from the cell then accompany him to a cell on the floor below, where they will perform the same process on an elderly woman who is confined to a bath chair.

There are nine other suffragettes to force-feed that morning and Nancy lifts the jug for all of them. Each time the jug seems heavier until she realizes that it is not the jug getting heavier at all, but herself. Something inside her is hardening and dropping like a stone to the pit of her stomach. She tells herself that it's the women's own fault. All this unpleasantness is brought upon themselves. But she knows that she's lying. She has always had a second sense when it comes to deceit.

In the evening, she forces herself to visit the common room where the fire is lit and they have a piano, a little upright, which a few of them play. Sometimes there's a singalong, though it doesn't do to hope for the sort of song you might hear in the music hall nowadays. That wouldn't be proper.

Tonight though, there's no one at the piano. Instead, Mrs Armitage is holding forth about 'them not being women at all'.

She sits at the table with some knitting, her needles clicking aggressively. 'If God had meant for us to be equal he'd have made us all men.'

There are some nods of agreement, though not by all. The hunger strikes are upsetting everyone, but then again, there's not a woman here who's not felt thwarted or cowed at some time in her life.

'I'd let them starve to death,' Mrs Armitage announces, still far from finished. 'I would. If that's what they want to do then I'd ship them out in boxes. Serve them right too. Whatever next? Holding His Majesty's government to ransom. What's the world coming to?'

Nancy lets herself out of the door before she's been noticed. That woman's got a mouth on her for sure, she thinks, but then remembers that is one of her father's favourite phrases and it makes her want to spit and rinse her mouth out.

She goes back onto the prison wing that holds the suffragettes. Everything is quiet. Everything is still. She looks for the starling as she climbs the metal staircase to the top floor. The spy hole in the Duchess's cell door stares at her without blinking. When she puts her eye to it she can see her shape beneath the blanket on the hard plank bed. She stands a long while watching, breathing as quietly as she can, a patch of moisture forming on the painted wood close to her lips. But the Duchess doesn't move at all. Nancy gets it into her head that there might be something wrong. It's not right to sleep as still as that. So she reaches for her keys, thinking it would be best to check. She unlocks the door then closes it behind her. Now that she is in the cell she can hear the Duchess breathe. And it feels comforting to be close to her.

In the morning, Miss Needler comes to find Nancy in the common room and tells her that for the time being, she will work exclusively on the suffragettes' wing and does she mind doing it, because there's a lot that do and it would be better if she says so now rather than gets all upset about it. Nancy can't help but smile, thinking she will be able to see the Duchess whenever she likes. She says that no, she doesn't mind at all.

At the Duchess's door, she knocks before she enters. 'Good morning, Daisy,' she says, pleased that Miss Needler allows the informality of names when they're alone with a prisoner, as a sign of respect for them being here out of conscience, though don't let Miss Jackson hear you say that.

The Duchess turns her head, blinking towards the open door. Nancy picks up the loaf and butter from the floor and replaces them with fresh ones.

'I have to ask if you will eat today.'

'I would like to request a pen and paper. I've been thinking I should write to the Home Secretary about my treatment here.' She lifts herself upright and brings her legs around, pulling up her nightdress and pointing at a semi-circle of bruises where a warden has gripped her too tightly.

'I shall have to ask if it's allowed.' Nancy holds the stale bread roll close to her chest.

'Well then, I shall have to wait. But I'll be making sure the doctor keeps a record of these in his notes.'

'And will you be eating today? I've been told I have to ask.'

'And I don't intend to dignify that question with a reply.'

'I'll tell her no then, shall I?'

The Duchess lies back on her bed and closes her eyes.

'I wish you would, miss. Everyone's got to eat. You could do yourself real harm if you go on like this.' She expects a tongue lashing, so when the Duchess stays silent, she feels bolder. 'I wanted to ask why you do it, miss. Why do you starve yourself like this? I'd like to understand.'

The Duchess raises an eyebrow and opens one eye. 'We are involved in a struggle to get the vote for all women. You included.'

'I don't see how it'll make much difference.'

'Then you don't know how the world works.'

'Plenty of men can't vote.'

'That doesn't concern me.'

Nancy looks perplexed. She doesn't understand. She's never been any good at teasing out an argument and anyway, Clara could always best her.

The Duchess suddenly rounds on her in frustration. 'You misunderstand the problem, if you don't mind me saying so.'

Nancy doesn't mind. She's used to being told she's in the wrong.

'Men are deemed inferior only on account of their wealth or status, a situation which they might do something about, whereas a woman is held to be inferior on account of her sex and nothing she can do will change that and so we must directly challenge the system of men that wield power over us.' She lifts a hand to her eyes, squeezing at her temples as though the train of thought is giving her a headache. 'You should read a book about it. Or better still, buy one of our newspapers.'

'Yes, miss. Thank you for giving me the time to explain.'

Nancy locks the door as gently as possible on the way out.

12

Clara is on her knees. She has her hands around an ankle and a leg of the chair. Her sister stands behind the chair, clutching at a forehead, her fingers covering the eyes. Clara can smell the polish of her sister's shoes but her view of Nancy is obscured by the skirts of Miss Barraclough, who has a grip of the woman's arm. The only face Clara can see is Miss Needler's who kneels opposite, securing the other leg, but her eyes are tight shut, like she's concentrating very hard on not being there at all.

The Duchess is weaker now but the chair still shudders as the tube is fed down. Clara tightens her grip and puts her weight against the woman's leg. Nancy steps on Clara's foot. Clara nudges it away then tries to tuck her foot under her other leg, only she can't shift her weight and hold the Duchess at the same time. Nancy steps on her again, this time pressing down hard with her heel, so Clara thinks she must be doing it deliberately. She glares up at her sister, though neither of them can see the other's face. While the tube is withdrawn the Duchess shudders uncontrollably and Nancy rakes the buckle of her shoe down the back of Clara's calf. This time she retaliates, letting go of the ankle and pinching Nancy's shin through her stockings. If her sister wants to be like that, Clara can give as good as she gets.

Later, when she's getting changed to meet Ted, she discovers a thin red graze where Nancy left her mark and her temper flares at the injustice of it. She steps into her new beige skirt, bought from a catalogue and recently delivered to the post room, then buttons up her favourite blouse, the one with a frill that runs from her neck to her navel, but she leaves her legs bare, putting her stockings in her bag so she can show Nancy exactly what she's done.

'Are you going out?' Nancy asks as soon as she comes through her door.

Clara lifts the skirt to her knee, twisting her leg to show Nancy the graze on the back of her calf. 'What makes you think I deserve that?'

Nancy shrugs weakly and looks at the floor.

Clara spits on her finger then runs it along the sore red line. 'You always were spiteful. If you're not careful they won't give you this job. Don't think you'll get it just because of me and don't say you don't want it either, because you'll end up in here one way or the other.'

'Don't say that.'

'Well, it's true, isn't it?'

'I shouldn't have done it. I'm sorry. But I was upset. It's such a horrible thing to force food down them.'

'And what makes you think I'm to blame?'

'I don't know. I suppose I wouldn't be here if it wasn't for you.'

Clara bites her tongue. She raises a hand to her head, and pulls a pin out of her hat before replacing it exactly as it was. She sits down on Nancy's bed then takes the stockings from her bag, shuffling the first onto her hand till she has her thumb inside the toe. 'This is a good job, Nancy. I've told you that before.' She slips off her shoe and pulls the stocking over her foot, easing it up around her calf. 'You can't take it for granted. And you can't punish me, either. None of this is my fault. If you don't like it then you can leave. You'd do well to remember that.'

'You look nice.' Nancy sits beside her sister. She has always found a way of slipping under Clara's guard. 'I like your skirt. It's new, isn't it? Are you going somewhere special?'

'I am if you must know. I've got a fella. He's looking after me.'

'How can you?' Nancy asks pitifully.

Clara hasn't told a soul about Ted and she'd rather Nancy didn't know but now her spite has caught her out, so she'll have to live with it. 'You could do with getting out too,' she says and rolls the other stocking onto her hand. 'A change is as good as a rest. You know that, don't you?' She finishes with her stockings and stands, pulling her skirt back down over her knees. 'And not a word of it to anybody in here. Do you understand?'

'What if you have a baby?'

'I won't.'

'I did.'

'That was different.'

'How was it you didn't have a baby too?'

Clara uses Nancy's mirror to check her face. 'I suppose I was lucky.'

'You've always been luckier than me.'

Clara feels a sudden shame at having abandoned her sister, of leaving her in that house with him. 'If we'd run away, we'd both be on the streets. You know that, don't you? That's why I had to get myself sorted first. You do understand that, don't you?'

Nancy has taken hold of a piece of her skirt that she twists between her finger and thumb. 'Did she go somewhere good?'

'I think so.' She takes hold of Nancy's hand. 'You can't see her, Nancy. You know that, don't you?'

'I don't want to. Wherever she went, she's better off without me.'

And Clara knows that's not true. That it's the other way around. Nancy will be better off without her baby. That's the pity of it. And there was nothing else to be done if she was going to save her sister.

13

The Duchess speaks with her eyes closed. 'You are the only one who knocks on my door. Do you know that?'

Nancy is glad she's noticed, proud to be marked out from the others. She replaces the loaf and butter on the floor. 'I only do it if I'm alone.'

'And never when you watch me through the spy hole.'

Nancy startles and then swallows. 'How would you know if I did that?'

'I can't imagine how you could resist. I wouldn't. Obviously I'm used to far bigger audiences, but I'd be upset if no one was watching me at all. Please say you do. I'm not doing this for nothing.'

By now she should be losing some coherence in her thoughts and speech. Nancy has spoken to others who have been on hunger strike for less time and are incapable of stringing a sentence together, but although she often speaks slowly, the Duchess is always lucid.

Nancy takes her opportunity to confess. 'Sometimes I do. I have to keep an eye on you.'

'Well, I am glad, though I have never played a less glamorous role, I can assure you.'

In the last few days her hair has lost its shine. Her skin has taken to wrinkling, at the edges of the eyes and the knuckles of her hands, like little cracks in her composure.

'What's it like to walk on stage in front of all those people?'

The Duchess finds the energy to lean up on an elbow, her eyes still able to sparkle. 'My dear, there is no greater thrill than to walk out on stage. To act is to be alive, to risk everything on the moment, fearing the boos, hoping for the adulation.'

'I don't believe you have ever been booed! No one would dare!'

'I have had to learn my trade like everyone else. But to be on a big stage, to know that whatever you do next will make people gasp or cry or cheer you to the rafters. There is no better way to live, I can tell you that.'

Nancy imagines herself walking out into the limelight and a shiver runs up her spine. 'It's not for everyone.'

'I can't imagine why. Well, perhaps not. Where would we find an audience if all of us were actors?' She lays her head back down. 'I won't be eating today.' She folds her hands and lays them across her chest.

'I wish you would.'

'Do you?'

'I don't want to see you getting worse. And heaven knows where it will end. Please would you try? It'd put my mind at rest.'

'You are quite the most courteous warden we have here. But politeness will get you nowhere. As a woman you should know that.'

Nancy tries to impress her. 'I'm not polite to everyone.' She feels sure of it, though she can't remember the last time she told someone what she really thinks, except for Clara. If she gets to be on stage at all, it will only be as an extra, as a walk-on part who does as she is told.

'I'm sorry,' she whispers.

'Pardon?' The Duchess raises her head again and looks at her squarely.

Nancy looks the other way.

'You apologized,' the Duchess tells her. 'I heard you.'

'Yes.'

'What for?'

'I have to help when we feed you and I wanted to apologize.'

'Well I don't accept it.'

'No. I don't suppose you do. But I didn't want you thinking . . .'

The Duchess lifts a finger in the air. 'Deeds not words! It is what you do that matters, young lady. Not what you say. All the good words in the world won't change a thing. One must take to the stage and act or you will forever live a lie.'

Nancy feels immediately guilty. That her life is not her own. That she does what is expected of her.

The Duchess closes her eyes, bringing an end to their conversation, but Nancy remains for a moment longer, wondering how she must look to the Duchess when she stands here in her prison uniform, so desperately in need of approval. What must a woman like this think of a girl like her? It's no wonder the Duchess pities her. And that's the best she can hope for.

In the afternoon she finishes her shift early and has some free time before supper. She determines to go for a walk, nowhere in particular, but she feels that she should get into the habit of going out as often as she can. The discipline of fresh air will be good for her and anyway, it will keep Clara from badgering her.

Outside the prison gates there is the usual suffragette protest. A cart and horse stand by the kerbside, decorated by a banner that reads *Fight On and God Will Give the Victory*. Gathered beside it are a group of women with sashes of green, mauve and white. They have placards saying *Votes for Women*. Nancy puts her head down and walks more quickly.

'Copy of *The Suffragette*, miss?' The newspaper seller who addresses her stands apart from the others, holding the paper up to show off the cover.

Nancy glances her way and glimpses an image of the Duchess on its front page. She carries on walking, wondering what the newspaper has to say about her. When she finds a park, she walks the path that runs around the outer rim, arguing with herself about whether she should buy a copy. After all, it's not against the law, so why shouldn't she? It's up to her what she chooses to read.

The woman is still there when she returns. She is younger than the others, closer to Nancy's age and pretty. Nancy slows her walk. She smiles awkwardly. 'How much?'

'A penny, please.' The woman offers her a copy from the top of the pile.

Now that Nancy sees it clearly, she can tell the picture was taken during a performance of a play. The Duchess is standing on her own at the front of a stage, holding her arms out to the audience. Nancy reaches into her bag, finds her purse and fumbles with the clasp. She notices a badge on the woman's coat from The Actresses Franchise League and without thinking, points to the picture of the Duchess. 'Do you know her?'

'Oh yes, we all know Daisy.'

'Me too,' says Nancy and then realizing she needs to give the woman an explanation adds, 'I work at the prison. I suppose I get to see quite a lot of her.'

The woman looks at her suspiciously but then she says, 'Tell her you met Ada. She'll know who you mean. Tell her Lily got the part of Ophelia at the Garrick. It'll make her laugh.'

Nancy nods, folding the paper and stashing it quickly away inside her bag. When she is back in her room, she takes the paper out and reads the caption under the picture. *Daisy Divine Leads Hunger Strike in Holloway.* She is disappointed that the story tells her nothing she doesn't already know, that it's not really a piece about Daisy at all. She flicks through the pages, looking at the announcements for meetings in town halls or debates on the role of motherhood, a whole new world that she never knew existed. She finds the ideas exciting but scary too. Like a dare or a forfeit. Like standing on the edge of a cliff and wondering what it would be like to jump.

She puts the newspaper under her mattress, suddenly afraid that someone will discover it and know her thoughts, but however long she sits and sews, she can't ignore it being there, nagging at her to look again. She tries to sleep then finds she can't. When it is late and the prison is still, she gets up and dresses in her uniform. She will give the newspaper to the Duchess. Make a gift of it. Daisy will appreciate the small act of defiance.

She takes the newspaper from its hiding place, rolls it tight, then lifts her dress and slides it into the top of her stocking. If she is quiet, she can slip into the cell unnoticed and leave it under the bed while the Duchess sleeps, then 'discover' it in the morning when she comes to change the food. She turns the key in the lock as quietly as she is able, enters the cell and presses the door closed.

'Ah, my little mouse.'

The shock of a voice makes Nancy jump.

The Duchess is wide awake and watching her in the

dim light. 'Here you are again, come to check on me.'

'Not to check on you.' Nancy steps forward from the door. 'I've got something for you.'

The Duchess waits and Nancy, embarrassed, turns her back, lifts the front of her skirt and retrieves the newspaper. She unrolls it as she steps closer to the bed. 'It's a copy of *The Suffragette*. I thought you'd like to read it. There's a picture of you on the front page.'

The Duchess takes hold of it and squints. 'I can't make anything out in this light.'

'Wait a moment.' Nancy goes back out into the corridor, takes down one of the lamps that hang outside and brings it back. 'There now.'

The Duchess looks at her picture but is unimpressed. Nancy supposes she must be used to seeing herself in print all the time.

'I thought you might like to read the whole thing. Catch up on some news of your friends.'

'I would. Thank you.' The Duchess turns to the second page and squints. 'My eyes are too weak. Would you stay and read it to me?'

Nancy glances back to the door as she fetches the chair from the corner of the cell then sets it down at the head of Daisy's bed.

'You must tell me your name,' the Duchess says.

'Nancy, miss. I'm Nancy Cooper.'

'Well, Nancy Cooper, I would be very pleased if you would read to me.'

'I'll only read a page of it. I can't be here long.' She folds the cover back and begins with a news story on the second page. '"A serious outbreak of fire was discovered at Alstone Lawn Manor, an unoccupied house at Cheltenham, in the early hours of Sunday morning, December 21st. The fire brigade was promptly summoned, and succeeded in saving the house from complete destruction, though damage to the extent of about £400 or £500 was done. Suffragette literature was found near the building, and later in the day two women were arrested and were charged before the local bench."'

The Duchess chuckles. 'I know who that'll be.'

'Well please don't tell me. I'd rather not know.' She chooses a longer piece, a letter written by Christabel Pankhurst. She clears her throat. '"The Prime Minister has announced that in the week beginning January 20th the Women's Amendments to the Manhood Suffrage Bill will be discussed and voted upon. This means that within a few short days the fate of these Amendments will be finally decided.

'"The WSPU has from the first declined to call any truce on the strength of the Prime Minister's so-called pledge, and has refused to depend upon the Amendments in question, because the Government have not accepted the responsibility of getting them carried. There are, however, some Suffragists – and there might be some even in the ranks of the WSPU – who hope against hope that in spite of the Government's intrigues an unofficial Amendment may be carried. Feeling as they do, these Suffragists are tempted to hold their hand as far as militancy is concerned, until after the fate of the Amendments is known.

"'But every member of the WSPU recognizes that the defeat of the Amendments will make militancy more a moral duty and more a political necessity than it has ever been before. We must prepare beforehand to deal with that situation!'"

Nancy wishes she had chosen a different piece, something that didn't so obviously compromise her position or put words in her mouth that she would rather not speak. And yet there is a thrill in saying them. She carries on . . .

"'There are degrees of militancy. Some women are able to go further than others in militant action and each woman is the judge of her own duty so far is that is concerned. To be militant in some way or other is, however, a moral obligation. It is a duty which every woman will owe to her own conscience and self-respect, to other women who are less fortunate than she herself, and to all those who are to come after her.

"'If any woman refrains from militant protest against the injury done by the Government and the House of Commons to women and to the race, she will share the responsibility for the crime. Submission under such circumstances will be itself a crime.

"'I know that the defeat of the Amendments will prove to thousands of women that to rely only on peaceful, patient methods, is to court failure, and that militancy is inevitable.'"

When she finishes, Nancy stands immediately. 'That's enough of that for now.'

'She is quite a woman, isn't she?'

Nancy folds the newspaper in half and slides it under the mattress.

'You can't leave it there,' the Duchess tells her. 'It'll be discovered as soon as they change my sheets.'

Nancy retrieves it and looks around the bare cell, not knowing what to do with it.

'If you tear each page out you could fold them between the pages of my books. *The Perfect Home and How to Keep It* will do. I don't think anyone has ever read it.'

Nancy does as she is told, placing the newspaper flat out on the floor and ripping the pages carefully along the crease till she has the sheets separated. She folds and presses them into the volume, placing the book back in the middle of the shelf so that the others keep the edges pressed together.

'You must come and read to me again,' the Duchess tells her. 'I rather like it.'

'I shall try,' Nancy promises.

When she reaches the door she remembers her message from the newspaper seller. 'There was something I had to tell you. Ada said to let you know Lily got the part of Ophelia at the Garrick.'

'Ada Wheatley?' The Duchess is suddenly all ears. 'She told you that? How?'

'She was outside the prison selling papers. It was her I bought it from and she told me to say she is thinking of you.'

127

'Did she? Well I shall think about her too.' The Duchess lays her head back on her pillow, crosses her hands on her lap and closes her eyes. 'Lily won't be any good,' Nancy hears her say, before she shuts the door. 'Not as good as me.'

14

There are ten suffragettes on hunger strike. Ten women who have lost the strength to stand on their own two feet and so, every morning, ten prisoners from the third division are escorted onto the wing to scrub the floors of their cells. They seem happy enough to do it. It brings some variety to their day and they do a better job of it than some of the suffragettes who are not used to the task. Daisy is the exception. She knows how to clean a floor all right and she tells the poor girl so.

'You need to be more thorough than that. There's a space by that wall that needs special attention. And use plenty of carbolic, would you? I have to live with the smell of vomit and you never get used to it.'

Nancy stands at the door to supervise. 'That's enough talking now,' she tells them.

The prisoner looks up from the floor, shifting on her hands and knees. 'I didn't say a word, miss.'

'Then make sure you don't start now.' She walks over to the bed, leaving footprints on the wet cell floor.

'Look what you did, miss.' The woman crawls across and scrubs away the marks.

Nancy wants to be nearer the Duchess. She can feel the closeness of her in the bed behind, a kind of radiance that warms the base of her spine. She would rather they were alone together. 'That will do for now,' she tells the prisoner who shuffles backwards to the cell door, dragging the bucket with her. Nancy has her hands clasped behind her back in the way that wardens are instructed to stand and when the Duchess touches her skin she half expects it. She curls her fingers, finds the hand gone and a knot of something left in her palm. She keeps her fist closed around it.

'Go and empty your bucket in the slop room,' she tells the prisoner who stands, picks up her things and rattles off down the gantry. Only then does Nancy open her hand. In her palm is a twist of paper that has been folded into thin pleats. 'What is this?'

'A message,' the Duchess tells her. 'Not for you. Give it to Nelda.'

Nancy quickly closes her hand. She walks across the wet floor, checks the corridor, then steps back inside the cell, pushing the door shut. She opens her fist again, hoping it might be gone but there it is, a little scrap of paper that fits in her palm like a fuse.

'You gave me a message,' the Duchess reminds her. 'This is no different.'

Oh, but it's a lot different. It's a lot different and they both know it.

Suddenly Nancy wants to be as far away from the Duchess as possible. She walks quickly from the cell without saying a word. She goes to the top of the staff stairs then stands with her back to the door, knowing that it's a safe place to look at her hand again. There it is. The message. She turns the knot in her hand, spots a page number on the edge of a crease and thinks it must be from one of the books. *The Narrow Way* perhaps? But how did she find a pen? She tucks the message up into the sleeve of her dress, putting it out of harm's way so she can think clearly, try to calm the panic till she decides what to do.

What could be in the message? It could be anything. A message of friendship. A shared joke. An observation. Or it could be something important. A secret. Or a plan. She could read it. She levers the paper out again with a finger, feels how tight the knot is, then tucks it back into her sleeve, telling herself it's better not to know. Better to be ignorant. And not get caught. Above all else she must not get caught. So she must do it quickly. Whatever she decides. Either get rid of it or deliver it. But do it quickly.

Nelda has a cell on the floor below and Nancy goes there straight away. She checks on the prisoner through the spy hole. She is there alone, sitting in a chair, reading a book. Nancy opens the door. Once inside, she moves quickly, taking hold of the woman's hand, putting the message in her palm, then leaving without a word.

'There,' she tells herself once she's well away and glad to be rid of it. 'It's done and over with.'

She goes back to her work, supervising the women on their way to chapel, taking the roll call from another van that disgorges women onto the steps of the yard. Nothing is different. No one comes for her. So that is that. A favour for someone who can't do it themselves. Like reading a letter to a prisoner. And now it's finished with. So what of it?

Another knot of paper. This one put into her palm when she least expects it, in a moment, out in the exercise yard, when she thought she stood alone.

'For Daisy,' says the voice in her ear and Nancy turns in time to see the face of the woman as she walks away. She doesn't even recognize her! She feels abused. Someone else, someone she doesn't even know, now has a hold of her secret and she wonders who else knows. Who else is making plans for her? Who else is talking about her?

She tucks the message up into her sleeve then takes a short walk along the bottom of the high brick wall, watching the face of Mrs Armitage who stands on the other side of the yard. She can't have noticed anything amiss or she'd be striding across the yard to sort it out. But Nancy is still terrified and she has good reason. This is out of control. And that Mrs Armitage is a sly one. She won't be fooled for long.

At the first opportunity, Nancy darts into a lavatory. So here she is again, with her back to a door and breathless. And it won't stop here. If she delivers this, there'll be another. Better to throw it straight down the pan and flush it away. Better to stop this nonsense right now. Say enough is enough.

But she doesn't.

The message in her hand has a line that goes straight to the Duchess. It connects the two of them. Makes Nancy special. Flushing it away would be as good as turning her back on her. And if she doesn't deliver, then she's no different to any of the other wardens. Deeds not words. That's what makes a person. So if she doesn't want to be herself, if she wants to be like them . . . Well, it isn't enough just to think about it.

So she'll deliver the message. And afterwards, once it's been done, nothing more need be said because Nancy will belong to her. That's the choice she is making this time. She'll belong to all of them.

'What did it say?' Nancy asks the Duchess.

'Didn't you look?'

'I wouldn't do that.'

The Duchess is lying on her bunk, staring up at the ceiling. 'These notes, they're not so important.'

'Then I don't know why I'm bothering to deliver them. If I got caught, I'd lose my job. They'd probably lock me up in here with you.'

'I do appreciate that.' The Duchess chooses her words carefully. 'Then let's say, they're *significant*.'

'Probably just as well I don't know.'

The Duchess puts her hands together on her lap. When

133

she opens them, there's another message, another twist of knotted paper in the palm of her hand.

Nancy ignores it. She walks across to the shelf and picks out *The Narrow Way,* flicks through the pages till she finds a torn edge then holds it up to show the Duchess. 'I still haven't worked out how you have a pen.'

'It's a pencil.' Daisy has closed her hand again, concealing the message. She must be conscious that anyone could be observing them from the other side of the door. Normally she would close her eyes too. Everything she does these last few days is slow and deliberate. But she waits for Nancy, watches her, and Nancy swoons in the privilege of her gaze. When she comes back to the bed, Daisy opens her hand and Nancy takes the message.

'For Constance,' Daisy tells her.

'That's the new girl?' Nancy says. 'Only came in yesterday?'

'I'd like her to receive it quickly.'

'So it's important?'

'It's significant.'

'If I can, I'll wait for a reply.'

The Duchess rewards her with a smile, acknowledging the commitment. 'That would be very much appreciated.'

Constance is not much older than Nancy is herself. She takes the message, unties the knot and twists the paper till it unravels in her fingers. She holds it close, squinting to read it while Nancy watches her face, looking for a clue to the nature of the message and jealous that she doesn't know.

'I'll wait for a reply,' she tells the girl and then adds, 'Do it quickly.' It feels good to give Constance an order.

Constance lifts the bottom of her dress and fiddles with the hem, carefully easing an inch of pencil lead from the lining. She leans on *The Narrow Way* to write but after a few words she pauses, perhaps conscious that she is being watched by a warden.

Nancy shrugs. 'If I want to read it I will.'

Constance continues to write. She twists and ties the paper into a knot. Nancy has the message back with the Duchess before the half hour is up. She has to wake her from sleep but Daisy doesn't mind. She knows Nancy has done well.

'You're quite the little postman,' she tells her before her eyes fall shut again.

15

Clara sits at her desk, spreads the staff rota out in front of her and flattens the piece of paper with the palm of her hand. Her new office is small but orderly. There are two wooden filing cabinets, a set of shelves with manuals on procedure and a drawer containing paper clips. The room has none of the comfort of Miss Hardgrave's office, but it has a door that she can shut and a secretary in the office opposite, who will take dictation. Clara is thrilled with it.

That morning, she had gathered the wardens together and told them there would be changes to their roles and duties. She knows them all – their strengths and weaknesses, their little habits – and she knows she can improve them. A little tinkering is all it will take to leave them in no doubt who is in charge. She takes a pencil from the pot and begins a list of names, their current work and the jobs she has in mind to give them.

A knock at the door interrupts her. Miss Barraclough enters without waiting to be asked. 'You need to come quickly, ma'am. There's an emergency up on B wing.'

Clara stands quickly, the pencil still in hand. 'What sort of emergency?'

'One of the suffragettes has barricaded herself in her cell.'

'Which one?'

'424. Constance Rigby, her name is, ma'am. One of the new girls.'

When Clara reaches the wing, whistles are being blown and there are running feet upon the staircase. A line of prisoners are being escorted from the exercise yard and locked in their cells. Clara finds a crowded gantry, a line of wardens leading away from Constance's door.

'She won't budge,' Miss Needler tells her. 'She has used the planks from her bed to wedge the door quite tight and we can't move it an inch.'

Clara puts her eye to the spy hole but finds it covered. 'What is she doing in there?'

'We can't be sure, ma'am, but she has been spotted from her window.'

'And?'

'She is naked, ma'am. Naked and singing the *Marseillaise*.'

The Governor arrives with Miss Hardgrave. Clara steps forward intending to give them what little information she has but the Governor ignores her and puts his eye to the spy hole. He casts a worried look back at the Matron. 'Do we know what she wants?'

'Votes for women, sir,' Miss Hardgrave answers him calmly.

His face darkens. 'And how exactly does she propose I give her that?' He raps his knuckles against the hard wood. 'This is the Prison Governor!' He puts his mouth close to the door. 'I have to warn you of the very serious consequences if you do not allow this door to be opened.' He mops his forehead with a clean handkerchief that he takes from his top pocket as he waits for a reply. When none is forthcoming he steps back from the door and thinks for a moment. 'We'll be patient,' he tells Miss Hardgrave. 'She'll come to her senses once she's cold and hungry. That's when we'll really see what she's made of.'

He leaves as quickly as he arrived, passing back along the gantry as the prisoners smash the windows of their cells, sending shards of glass to splinter and crack in the concrete yard below.

Clara desperately wants to cover her ears. Since she was a little girl she has always been upset when something gets broken.

Miss Hardgrave raises her voice above the din. 'Leave a single warden outside the door and come at once if anything changes.'

'Yes, miss.'

She chooses Miss Needler once the noise has subsided. 'Send for me at once if there is any change.'

Two hours later, the Matron knocks on Clara's door. 'I have some news for you on the situation. It seems the

Governor has been advised to restore order as soon as possible and so a team of men will arrive shortly. Please would you show them to the cell and assist them with anything they need?'

'Yes, ma'am. Should I let you know when they arrive?'

'That won't be necessary. I have other business to attend to. You simply need to do as they ask.'

When they arrive there are seven of them waiting just inside the main door. Two of them are policemen in uniform. Four are roughly dressed in cheap woollen suits and flat caps. They have large canvas bags of tools by their feet. The man in charge, perhaps from the Home Office, stands apart from the others, drumming his fingers on the top of the front desk. Clara is unsure whether she should shake his hand and falters as she approaches.

'You must be the men,' she tells them.

'We've come about the spot of bother.' The man in charge is bright and breezy. Clara wonders what he finds amusing. 'We'll sort it out in no time for you, don't you worry.'

'This way, then.'

'We'd like to begin in the yard if we may.'

Clara finds the idea strange but she takes them quickly to the yard without asking for an explanation. She finds four other men already outside. They have a wagon and a hose that they have unrolled and left upon the ground like a long pink worm. The sight of it makes her swoon. The thought of what they mean to do and the possible repercussions. She tries not to panic and thinks of sending for Miss Hardgrave, but then she thinks that Miss Hardgrave must have known what was going to happen and told her to take care of it.

'Bit of a deterrent.' The man interrupts her thoughts. 'We don't want anyone else getting the same idea, do we?' He looks up at the side of the building. Every one of the windows is smashed and gaping. 'That's a bit of a mess, isn't it? Which one is she in?'

Clara tries to clear her head. She points to the fourth window from the left. 'It's that one up there on the fourth floor.'

'Right then. We better get inside, hadn't we?' He points to the men who will handle the hose. 'I'll send a runner down as soon as we are ready to begin.'

Clara leads them back inside and along the corridors till they reach the wing and take to the stairs. Most visitors to the prison are anxious and quiet and Clara usually makes a point of reassuring them, of making the place feel as normal as possible. But this is different. The men are easy going. Casual. They bring with them an assumption that they are in charge, that they have taken over, and have nothing to worry about. Clara feels complicit in the invasion.

Miss Needler waits for them at the door of the cell with a look of apprehension. 'Is it true?' she asks in a whisper, her hand pressing on Clara's arm, trying to guide her away from the men who have opened their bags, bringing out hammers and chisels and long iron bars with claws at each end. She stands directly in front of Clara's face. 'There's no need for it. You do know that?'

Clara takes her to one side. 'These men have been sent from the Home Office. It is not our decision to make.'

The men begin to feel around the frame of the door, looking for its weakness, pressing their fingers gently into the gap between the door and the frame. One of them nods. 'It'll give. Shall I tell the boys they can start?'

'Miss Needler, would you accompany him, please.' Clara wants to be rid of her. 'You will need to manage the locks.'

Miss Needler does as she is told but the other suffragettes must have spotted the hose in the yard below because they are rattling their mugs against the bars on their windows shouting, 'Shame on you!' and Clara thinks that Constance must be hearing it from the other side of her door, must be wondering what is about to happen, perhaps moving away from the door toward the window.

'We better stand clear,' the man from the Home Office tells them and the men move to either side of the door and wait for the water. Clara stands with them, her back against the wall, still feeling that she should say something, that she should try and stop what is about to happen but knowing that she won't. That she doesn't know what she can do.

The water arrives with the violence of a clenched fist. It beats the wall like a drum and hisses at the bars of the window. Clara holds her breath, trying not to think what it must be like to be in there, to be a woman trapped crouching against a wall and battered by the force of it. Water trickles from the crack beneath the door, then quickly becomes a steady stream that seeps beneath the boots of the men and drops through the metal grille to fall like rain into the hall below.

The water stops. For a moment there is silence.

The men put their hands back against the door.

'Here.' One points toward the bottom and another puts his wrench into the gap, leaning back with his weight till the wood cracks and splinters, opening it an inch and then another till something gives way and the bottom of the door juts out from the frame like a broken bone. Water swoons from the open hole. The man puts his arm in, feeling for something, then yanks at a plank of wood which he pulls out like a rotten tooth. The men put their shoulders to what remains of the door and burst through. A few moments more and they emerge dragging Constance by her arms. She looks small as a child – all naked, wet and blue – and the men lay her down on the deck of the gantry then stand back, unsure what they should do next, looking like fishermen who have pulled something unrecognizable from their nets.

Miss Needler hurries back along the gantry. 'The shame of it,' she mutters as she crouches over the girl. She looks up angrily at Clara. 'Get me a blanket.'

And Clara does as she is told.

16

The Duchess smells of a delicate corruption. It is almost nothing, a hint of something rotten in the cell, as though someone has hidden an apple beneath her mattress and left it to rot.

Nancy leans close to her ear. 'Wake up.' She can see the Duchess breathing and her forehead is clammy, so Nancy knows she's alive. But she won't open her eyes. 'It was you, wasn't it? You gave the order for Constance to barricade herself in her cell. You did, didn't you? And I delivered it.'

The Duchess moistens her lips with the tip of her tongue, 'I'm so very tired today,' she whispers.

'Why won't you look at me?'

'If only you knew the weight of an eyelid,' the Duchess tells her slowly, each word of it an effort.

This scares Nancy. It is not like the Duchess to give in, to lack any sort of spark, and Nancy realizes she's been lying to herself about the seriousness of the situation. The Duchess, it seems, is not unlike everyone else. If she doesn't eat, she will die. But this change in her has been so rapid, it can only have been will power that kept it from her for so long. Nancy puts her hand behind Daisy's neck. Moves her head gently, easing the skin behind her ear with the edge of her thumb to soothe her.

Miss Needler arrives with the doctor, a senior physician who trades an expression of concern with authority.

'Sit her up, please.'

Nancy puts her hand down into the pillow, slipping her fingers under a shoulder and across the bones of her neck till she is cradled. She lifts the Duchess up, placing the pillow in the small of her back. On the sheet there are strands of hair that have come loose in the night. The Duchess doesn't struggle. They feed her from the bed, tipping a cup against her lips, a little at a time, the way you might feed a kitten or a baby and she no longer clenches her teeth or tries to resist. Nancy wishes she would. She wants a doctor to come with a clamp as it used to be, because the Duchess without defiance isn't the Duchess at all and because if she had the strength left to struggle then this wouldn't be such a grave undertaking.

'Not too much now.' Miss Needler wipes at Daisy's cracked mouth with a cloth, as gentle as she can be.

The Duchess vomits and coughs. So there are signs of life, signs of defiance from deep inside the gut where she has retreated to make her protest. Nancy picks off the hairs from the sheet before she lays her flat again.

The physician places a stethoscope to her heart. 'Has she kept anything down in the last two days?' He presses a hand against her liver and her kidney, all the organs that might fail her. He feels the glands under her chin, then tells Miss Needler this woman is the worst of them, the first that might die. He checks his notes. 'She has some sores, apparently. Could you turn her for me?'

'We're going to turn you, Daisy,' Miss Needler says loudly, as though the Duchess is somewhere far away and not lying there in front of her.

She grips her hips and Nancy slides a hand under the shoulders and they turn her on the count of three. Miss Needler eases the nightdress up and over her legs, her hips, the rib cage, all of them bones where the flesh is stretched to a grimace. Nancy is shocked by her frailty but not by the nakedness, remembering how she shed her nightdress the night she gave birth. The sores follow Daisy's spine, three of them the size of a fist and open, another two that are half the size and still to burst. The smell is faint but present, a mix of pus and ointment, of corruption and cleanliness.

The physician nods. He makes another cursory glance at the notes on his clipboard as Miss Needler replaces her nightgown. 'Feed her from the cup on the hour. Swab her wounds every two. The danger of her condition cannot be overestimated.' He adds his instructions to the notes. 'The Home Secretary must be kept informed. I will send a report immediately.'

A nurse is brought from the infirmary to sit by her bed. Nancy resents the woman immediately and Miss Needler must notice because she says, 'Come along now,' and leads Nancy from the room. Once outside, she holds her by the shoulders. 'Are you all right?'

'What will become of her?'

'That's not for me to say.'

'There must be something they can do now that she is so weak. Can they give her something?'

'There's nothing to be done that we haven't been doing. Otherwise, we wait and watch.'

'But she might die, miss. The doctor said as much, didn't he?'

'We can only hope that it doesn't come to that. In the meantime we must carry on with our work. There are prisoners that need bathing. Please will you see to it?'

Nancy does as she's told, collecting three women from their cells and escorting them down the stairs, through the iron grille and along the corridor that leads to the bathing area.

'You may talk quietly,' she tells them as they begin to undress and then she goes into the stalls, putting in the plugs and running the taps on each bath. One of them is middle-aged and softly spoken, perhaps a nurse or a teacher, and there's a young woman from the cotton mills in Lancashire and a woman who obviously comes from one of the finer homes of London or Surrey. All of them are new here and not on hunger strike, perhaps due to their age or circumstance or the brevity of their sentences. Nancy allows them ten minutes in the hot water although she paces outside their stalls, barking instructions on the benefits of carbolic and the use of a loofah, as she has been taught to do. When they are finished, she escorts them back to their cells and locks their doors. After the last of them is in, she looks up to Daisy's door and sees Miss Needler and Miss Barraclough hurrying inside.

Nancy takes to the stairs, climbing faster than she might, wondering whether there might have been a change with the Duchess. She runs along the gantry and bursts in through the door. The bed is empty. The Duchess has gone.

Miss Barraclough is rolling up her mattress to stow it away behind the door. A pile of sheets lie crumpled on the floor beside her nightgown and prison uniform. Nancy puts her hands to her mouth.

Miss Needler comes across to her immediately. 'She is not dead, Miss Cooper, if that's what you're thinking.'

Nancy manages to breathe again. 'Then where has she gone?'

'She was released by order of the Home Secretary, taken to the prison gates and collected there.'

'By who? Who collected her? Does she have family?'

'I do not know, Miss Cooper, but it is usual for the suffragettes to collect the prisoners themselves. She will be well looked after, so please don't look so worried. They have acquired a great deal of expertise over the past few months.'

'But she still might die, miss. She could, couldn't she?'

'She might, Miss Cooper. But not in prison.'

Nancy feels hollow. There's a part of her that's always been missing, a dark hole that has always been there. Her baby might have filled it. In those moments when she held her, Nancy felt that she might. But the release of the Duchess is another loss. More empty space inside her. Digging deeper. Like a dark well that descends from her mouth to her bowels, dank and dripping, and she knows there's nothing to be done that will make it disappear.

She finishes her shift, going through the motions till the hours are ticked off and she can escape back to her room. But sitting on her bed alone, she only feels worse, trapped like the starling in the rafters, feeding on crumbs of comfort. Miss Needler said they will look after her well. Miss Needler said she may not die. But Nancy can't imagine getting up and going to work tomorrow without seeing the Duchess. Without her being in the prison at all. So she may as well be dead, because Nancy has seen the last of her, that's for sure.

She goes back to Daisy's cell, finds the door ajar and goes inside. Nothing remains of her. The room has been cleaned so thoroughly that even her smell has gone. Nancy feels scrubbed and scoured away. As if she has been rubbed out. But there might be something. She goes over to the book-shelf, takes hold of the book where she hid the newspaper and finds the pages still inside. She pockets them quickly, takes them back to her cell and opens them to read. When she has finished, she reads them again and this time all she sees is the same phrase, repeated everywhere in black and white, the very same thing the Duchess told her.

Deeds not words.

17

Clara notices that Nancy is missing when the wardens gather for the morning roll call. She waits an extra moment before she calls them into line, hoping her sister will spare her the embarrassed silence of being absent when her name is called. She chooses Miss Needler to go in search of her and she reports back that Nancy is not in her room nor any of the bathrooms. There is no sign of her.

Clara goes straight to Nancy's room to see for herself. She notes the uniform still hanging on the back of the door. Nancy's change of undergarments are still in the holdall that she uses to store them. Also, the mirror she bought herself is there on the shelf beside the books. So it appears she didn't plan to leave. But then Nancy doesn't plan things. She always lacked the self-possession it requires. It would be just like her to walk out of the door and never come back and she wouldn't have put a thought into it. She never has.

Clara stands in the middle of the room, annoyed that she can't piece together the clues that must be here. And then she worries for the lack of them. What if something has happened to Nancy? What if this isn't her choice at all? But now she's being silly. Things like that don't happen as often as one thinks. It is far more likely that she has had enough of this place and gone back home. Yes. That is the more likely explanation. And if that's how it is, Nancy would be too ashamed to tell her. Or too frightened of her. Clara wonders whether she should go home at once and fetch her back but much as she dislikes the thought of telling Miss Hardgrave, she decides to do so at once, the same way she would if it were any of the other wardens.

Even so, she hesitates before knocking on Miss Hardgrave's door. She has only ever brought efficiency into this room, a willingness to please and a desire to impress. However much she pretends that Nancy is simply another member of the staff, the association with herself will be made, though never mentioned. The way it was with the baby. Both of the sisters tarred with the same brush.

Miss Hardgrave is surprised to see her. She is still easing her way into the day, the top button of her dress undone and the door to her apartment left open so that Clara catches a glimpse of her breakfast laid out on a table beside a copy of the morning newspaper.

Clara apologizes for the early intrusion then gets to the point quickly. 'I've come about my sister. It appears she is missing.'

'Missing? Since when?'

'Probably last night. Sometime yesterday, certainly. Her bed hasn't been slept in.'

Miss Hardgrave keeps a calm face. 'And you have no idea of her whereabouts?'

'No, ma'am.' Clara can feel her cheeks redden with the admission of her failing.

'Is it likely that she met with someone last night and didn't come home?' Miss Hardgrave's hand goes to her neck, fastening the loose button. Clara thinks she is trying to sound matter-of-fact but there is something in her tone that is almost excited. 'Does she have a young man?'

'No,' Clara answers instinctively, though she hasn't even thought of the possibility. 'No. I'm sure of it.'

'In the circumstance it seems the most likely event. These things nearly always come down to affairs of the heart and a weakness of the flesh. It is not the first time one of our girls has gone missing and it won't be the last. Have you checked her room?'

'Yes, ma'am, but I couldn't find any clue as to where she might be.'

'No note for you?'

'No, ma'am.'

'Nevertheless, I would like to see for myself.'

The Matron's search of Nancy's room is slow and thorough. She makes a point of touching all of Nancy's things, the way a clairvoyant likes to make a connection with the dead. She looks at her own reflection in the mirror that

Nancy bought from the department store. 'It's puzzling that she hasn't taken this.'

'Should we contact the police?'

The Matron shakes her head dismissively. 'Not for three days. They won't take it seriously before then and anyway, there's little they can do except check the mortuary or the hospitals and we can do that ourselves.'

Clara can't help but look shocked. 'Do you think I should?'

'No, Miss Cooper, I don't. We have never needed to before. Affairs of the heart nearly always reveal themselves sooner rather than later and it is rare for them to reach a happy conclusion. Promises will be made and broken. Mistakes will be made. I expect we shall see your sister again very soon.'

She lifts the mattress to look beneath then goes to the books, picking up each of them in turn and flicking the pages with a stiff thumb. The folded sheets of newspaper fall out onto the bed.

Miss Hardgrave unfolds one, gives it a quick glance, then hands it to Clara. 'The picture is of Daisy Divine. I'm sure you recognize her. We released her only yesterday.'

Clara can feel herself being studied as she glances at the page.

'Does she have strong views on the suffragettes, Miss Cooper?'

'Not that I know of.'

'And yet she has their newspaper hidden away? Well,

perhaps it's just coincidence. We shall have to wait and see.'

Clara decides that if nothing has been heard by the end of her shift, then she will go back home to see if Nancy is there. She takes the time to walk, instead of taking the tram. When she finds the front door locked, Clara knocks and waits rather than search for the key in her bag.

Her mother opens it after a few moments. 'Oh, it's you. You don't normally knock.'

'You've taken to locking the door.'

'Yes. Now there's less of you in and out.'

'Can I come in?'

'Is that Clara?' Her father's voice from the parlour. 'Let her in then. Don't leave her standing on the doorstep.'

She steps inside to find him standing awkwardly, not knowing what to do with his hands.

'It's been a while,' he says. 'What is it? Couple of weeks?'

'It must be that.'

'Well never mind. Sit yourself down.' He nods at the chair opposite his own. 'Bring us a cup of tea, Mother.'

'Is she stopping?'

'Course she's stopping. Long enough for a cup of tea at least.' He nods for Clara to sit. 'She needs to tell us her news.'

Clara sits in her mother's chair. A place by the fire. Usually, if she sits in this room at all, she will drag a chair in from the kitchen rather than deprive her mother of her place, but she hasn't the heart to argue with him today and anyway, she won't be stopping long. It's obvious that Nancy isn't here or he'd be gloating.

She resents her sister's selfishness for bringing her home. 'I was passing. So I thought . . .'

'You're looking well,' he tells her. He looks sheepish. Uncertain how he should continue now that he has shown her some affection. 'Are they keeping you well?'

'Well enough.'

It's strange how this can be, coming home to find him welcoming her and hanging on her every word. She forgets he can be like that. That it all gets mixed up with him. That everything is confused. There have been times when both sisters thought they were his favourite or times that it was the other and not themselves.

'So what's your news?' he asks again.

The fear of telling him hangs heavy in the back of her throat, the dread of every eldest child at losing a sibling. All those years of looking after Nancy have marked her out, made her sensible and safe. She decides that it can wait. There's no reason they need to know right now. One way or another, Nancy will turn up out of the blue and she can tell them then if she has to.

Her mother brings a pot of tea with two cups. She says she'll have hers in the kitchen and takes herself away. In many ways, Clara resents her more than him. For making a mother and wife of her before her time.

'I've got a promotion,' Clara tells him, thinking she may as well impress him now that she is here. 'They've made me the Supervisor so now I only have to answer to the Matron.'

'No surprise there. You've always been good at telling people what to do.'

'It'll mean a bit more money.'

'Quite right too,' he says. 'You've been working hard for it. Least, we never get to see you.'

'No rest for the wicked.'

'You'll be able to keep an eye out for your sister then. Make sure she gets the decent jobs. I suppose she'll get a pay rise soon enough as well.'

'I doubt that. You know the way it is.'

She makes her excuses as soon as her teacup is empty.

At the door, as she is about to leave, he says, 'It'd be nice to see her. Tell her she needn't be a stranger.'

And she thinks he looks defeated, as though he has lost something of value and is unsure where to look for it.

She takes the tram back to the prison and uses the journey to convince herself there is no point in worrying. Whatever Nancy is up to, she's likely to have brought it on herself and it won't do Clara any good to spend her days wondering where the devil she is.

On the morning of the third day a letter arrives for her, a postmark from Mount Pleasant, though that doesn't tell her much. Nancy says she is safe. That she's being looked after and that Clara needn't worry.

So not dead then.

18

Clement's Inn it said. The address given for the newspaper. Nancy stands at the reception desk. On the counter there are boxes of badges and medals on green and purple ribbons.

A young woman smiles up at her. 'Can I help you?'

'I've come . . . I've come to see Miss Daisy Divine.'

'I see. Do you have an appointment?'

'I have a message for her.'

The woman nods. 'One moment. I'll see if there's someone who can help.'

In the office behind the reception there are six desks, each with a woman working at them. Some are clattering away on typewriters, others speaking on the telephone. The woman walks across to the far corner where an older lady sits at a proper table, large enough for the piles of papers spread out in front of her. Behind her chair, a giant map of the country is hung from the wall, with bright red drawing pins spread across it in clusters.

The receptionist addresses her, listens to the response and then comes back to the front desk. 'I'm afraid you've already missed her. She was released from prison around midday. She did come here for a short while but she is not here now.'

Nancy panics, all her bravery disappearing at the very first hurdle. 'Could you tell me where she is?'

'Perhaps you could leave a message with us to pass on to her?'

Nancy shakes her head. 'It has to be delivered in person. Can you tell me where I can find her?'

'I don't believe so.'

Nancy doesn't move from the desk. 'But someone must know where she is. It's really very important.'

The woman looks perplexed. 'One moment.' She heads back toward the map, speaks to the same woman and then returns to Nancy. 'Please come inside and wait.'

Nancy is shown through into the hallway and given a seat next to a stack of newspapers that are bundled up and tied with string. After a few moments, a woman arrives from the front door, hefts four of them onto a trolley and leaves by the way she came in. The whole building is a hive of activity with women coming and going. From her chair, Nancy watches them, a woman turning the handle of a desk duplicator in the room opposite, the freshly inked handbills dropping down into the tray below.

'Good afternoon.'

Nancy looks up to find two women standing over her. They are older women, well spoken, and they seem to her very grand indeed.

'I understand you have a message for Daisy Divine?'

'Yes, ma'am. Can you take me to her?'

'I'm afraid that's not possible.' The woman has a warm and gracious smile that makes Nancy believe she would if she could. But if this woman doesn't know where Daisy is then someone must.

'Do you have a letter I might give her?'

'No, ma'am. It's a message. Tell her Nancy needs to see her. I need to meet with her urgently.'

'So it's important?'

Nancy nods. 'Tell her it's significant.'

'And you won't allow me to pass the message on?'

'No, ma'am. I do apologize but I have to see her myself.'

The second woman interrupts with some impatience, leaning into Nancy with a pointed finger. 'Do you know who this is? You're speaking to Mrs Pankhurst herself and if you can't trust *her* with a message, then I doubt that it's of any significance at all.'

Nancy takes a deep breath, suddenly recognizing Mrs Pankhurst from the photos in the newspaper and ashamed that she didn't do so from the start. But she sticks to her guns. 'I have to see the Duchess myself,' she says, thinking what they might do in her situation, what a suffragette would say in the same circumstances. 'And I'm not prepared to leave here till I do,' she adds, barely believing the words that come out of her mouth.

'Very well.' The women leave her without a word of what they will do or what she should do herself.

Nancy sits where she is for another hour. She begins to feel angry and helpless. What if she's been forgotten or ignored? Will she really refuse to budge when it's time for everyone to leave the building? And where will she go? She won't go back to her parents. She is certain of that. So she will have to go back to the prison. There is nowhere else to go.

Someone taps her shoulder, another young woman who says she may as well make herself useful if she's going to be here for a while and she takes Nancy into the post room and puts her to work licking stamps and sticking them onto envelopes that she fills with canvassing cards and leaflets.

It takes another three hours before another woman appears, putting her hand on Nancy's shoulder to draw her attention. 'Would you come with me?' She takes Nancy out into the hall that leads to the front door. 'Do you have an umbrella?'

'Where are we going?'

'You wanted to see Daisy?'

Nancy nods.

The woman snatches an umbrella from the stand by the door. 'You better take this then. It's raining and we've got a way to go till we get there.' She takes a good long look at Nancy, as though she can't decide what to make of her. 'You're lucky she wants to see you. The state she's in, she shouldn't be doing anything but sleep.'

She accompanies Nancy on to the omnibus but she doesn't ask questions, hardly talks to her at all. They alight in Kensington and walk along a road that passes Holland Park. Nancy hasn't been to this part of London before. She's never had a need to. The road is quiet, with large white houses set back from the pavement by pretty front gardens. They turn into another road where the houses aren't quite so grand, though they are large enough, with patterned tile paths that lead to their front doors.

'Is this where Daisy lives?' Nancy asks.

'Daisy? Live in a place like this?' The woman snorts in disbelief. 'I don't think so. It's a safe house. Run by one of our friends.' She points across the street. 'It's that one over there.'

They cross the road, walking round a parked motorcar where a man leans against a lamppost, reading a newspaper.

At the front door the woman pulls Nancy closer. 'See that man stood outside?' she whispers in her ear. 'Police!'

Nancy daren't look around. 'How do you know?'

'Isn't it obvious?' The woman rings the doorbell and Nancy finds the courage to sneak a quick glance over her shoulder. It isn't obvious to her.

The door is opened by a maid who shows them through the hall and into a drawing room where an older woman sits by the fireplace in a high-backed chair. She has white hair held up by a silver clasp and her dress, though plain and practical in its design, is certainly not poor.

'Ethel Birnstingl.' The maid introduces her.

The woman stands and offers a hand. Nancy shakes it, noticing the badge the woman wears on her dress. It has circles of green, mauve and white, the colours of the suffragettes, but with strange lettering. Is that Jewish?

'Nancy Cooper, ma'am,' she says as bravely as she can. 'Glad to meet you.'

'Daisy tells me you're a prison warden at Holloway.'

'That's right, ma'am. Well at least I was but . . . well, now . . .' She trails off, realizing how silly she must sound to a woman like this.

The woman looks her up and down. 'You must have some nerve coming here,' she says in such a way that Nancy can't tell whether it is a criticism or a compliment.

'Is she here?' Nancy is impatient. 'Can I see her?'

'She's sleeping. And on no account will I allow her to be woken. However, she expressed a desire to see you. Please, take a seat. You can wait. I'll have the maid bring some tea and cake.'

The woman takes Nancy's travelling companion out into the hall, closing the door behind them. Nancy can hear them talking quietly as they move into the opposite room. The room in which she finds herself is comfortably furnished with large loungers and chairs. There are shelves full of books on either side of the fireplace. On the walls there are landscapes, paintings of mountains or trees, though Nancy thinks they're not from this country but from somewhere on the Continent. At the rear of the house she glimpses a pretty garden through the French doors. She sits down in a chair, choosing the one furthest from the fire. In her own house, the chair nearest to the fire was her father's place and she would have been shouted at and turfed out. On the coffee table by her knee is a copy of a magazine called *The Freewoman*. Nancy picks it up and flicks through the pages. She stumbles on an article about the virtues of free love and not knowing what is meant by the term she begins to read.

By marriage the man secures the exclusive right to the woman's body and by it, the woman binds the man to support her during the rest of her life . . . a more disgraceful bargain was never struck.

She puts the magazine straight back down.

After a few moments, she hears the front door open and then close. Through the front bay window she catches sight of the woman from Clement's Inn walking away from the house. Tea is brought to her on a silver tray by the maid. Nancy accepts a cup but leaves the thin slice of cake, despite being hungry. From the hallway, the grandfather clock nags at her, reminding her of the prison and the shift she'll be expected to work first thing tomorrow morning. They might have missed her by now. They may be wondering where she's got to. She thinks of Clara, brought into the Matron's office for a quiet word.

It is dark outside by the time Ethel Birnstingl returns. She

163

walks across the room and draws the curtains across the large bay window.

'Come with me,' she says.

She leads Nancy out of the room and up a flight of stairs. They walk along a hallway lit by gas lamps, one at the top of the stairs and a second near the window at the far end. Miss Birnstingl stops outside a bedroom door, knocks and then enters, leaving the door open for Nancy to follow. The room has a double bed with blankets and a pretty quilted bedcover in blues and greens. There is a warm fire in the grate. And sitting up in the bed is the Duchess, waiting for her on a mound of pillows, her face still grey and the skin still shrunk on her bones. In fact, the comfort of the room makes her appear in worse health than when Nancy last saw her. And her eyes are still closed. For all Nancy knows, she could still be asleep, because she gives no acknowledgement of Nancy even being there.

Ethel Birnstingl turns to Nancy. 'You have a message.'

Nancy looks from Ethel to Daisy and back again, the fingers of her hands twisting together and separating.

'I shall be in the hall,' Ethel says reluctantly, though she closes the door behind her.

Nancy sits on the very edge of the bed. If Daisy can't look at her then at least she'll know she's close by. She thinks of holding her hand but doesn't dare. Now that she's here, she's unsure what to say and she struggles to find the words that might fit best. Eventually she says the only thing she can think of. 'Please don't make me leave.'

Daisy doesn't move.

There is a bowl of thin broth on a bedside table and Nancy takes hold of it. 'You should eat,' she says. She lifts a full spoon to her own mouth and blows on it. 'I came here to look after you.' She brings the spoon close to Daisy's mouth. 'Food every hour and your sores dressed every two. That's what the doctor ordered. I heard him.'

The tip of Daisy's tongue appears between her lips but then vanishes.

'Come on. You can do it. Not like you to give up now, is it?'

Daisy opens her mouth just a fraction and Nancy puts the spoon to her lips, dribbling the broth slowly. A muscle moves in Daisy's jaw and then another in her throat. Nancy returns the spoon to the bowl, fills it and blows till it's cool. She tries again but this time Daisy splutters and coughs, her head twisting back into the pillow, the broth smearing across her chin and Nancy jumps up from the bed and opens the bedroom door.

'A cloth, please, quickly.'

Miss Birnstingl walks into the room, picks up a cloth that is folded over the bedstead and holds it to Daisy's mouth. 'We can manage quite well without a nurse, Miss Cooper. If that's the only reason you came then you will have had a wasted journey.' She scowls at Nancy impatiently. 'Would you mind waiting downstairs?'

Nancy leaves the room but she can't bring herself to go downstairs and stands instead in the shadows at the far end of the hallway, wondering what Miss Birnstingl might be doing in the room, wondering whether they are talking and what they might be saying. From the window she can see the policeman in his bowler hat and raincoat, still standing upright against the lamppost. He looks up at the house, perhaps seeing her silhouette, but then goes back to his paper. Miss Birnstingl comes out of the bedroom. She closes the door behind her and Nancy thinks that'll be that, that she'll be asked to leave.

'Come with me,' Miss Birnstingl tells her quietly and as they descend the stairs she says, 'Miss Divine has asked that you remain with us for the time being and I have reluctantly agreed. I shall ask the maid to make you up a bed in the room next to hers.'

19

Clara allows herself the task of delivering the prisoners' post. There's never much of it, a small bagful of letters each day that she sorts out on the post room table, placing the envelopes in order then going through them with a pen, crossing out the names and replacing them with cell numbers. Every morning brings someone new to her. A prisoner who never usually receives word from the outside world is suddenly surprised at the sight of an envelope. These are the letters that normally bring bad news. This morning it is 347. She makes a point of remembering her name.

The woman rises from her knees when Clara enters her cell. She puts the brush back into the pail, leaving her floor half scrubbed and glistening in the small square of light that falls from her window.

Clara already has the letter in her hand. 'This is for you.' Maud Maguire, she remembers. Cell 347. Maude Maguire.

The woman hesitates, looking like the envelope might bite her. She takes it quickly, snatches at it and turns it in her hand. She gives it back. 'Miss?' she says. 'Would you read it to me, miss?'

This is not unusual and it's the part that Clara likes the best. She goes to the door, shuts it softly then walks to the bare planks of the bed and sits on the edge of them.

'Do you know who it is from? Is it someone special?' She uses the same tone of voice when Nancy needs comfort or good advice. Like a big sister should. Like her mother spoke to her before Nancy was born. 'Come and sit down.'

The prisoner sits beside her. Not too close but not far away. 'It'll be him.' Her eyes focus on the scratchy shapes of ink where Clara has scribbled out her name. 'There's no one else it could be.'

Clara runs a nail along the top of it and takes out the single sheet. She looks immediately for the name at the bottom as she unfolds it. 'It's signed from Jim. Is that your husband?'

'Yes, miss.'

'He has decent handwriting. What does he do?'

'Nothing,' the woman says bluntly. 'Not worth speaking of. He'll have got someone to write it for him.'

Clara nods. She holds the paper a little further from her eyes. '"To Maude". Well, let me see what he says.' She has developed a knack of taking in the page at a glance then reading between the lines, leaving out a little of the truth for the very best of reasons. '"When are you coming back? Do you know yet or haven't they told you?"' She skips a line or two as she paraphrases. 'We're missing you. Shirley will have to go out to work if you don't come soon.' She lowers the page. 'Who is Shirley?'

'That's my daughter.'

'And how old is she?'

'Nine.' The woman stares hard at the letter as though it holds a picture of the child.

'And the work he speaks of? Is that the same as yours?'

'Yes, miss.'

Clara nods, knowing that the woman's offence is prostitution. She returns to the letter, paraphrasing the little that remains. 'He says that Bob has hurt his leg. He doesn't say how but I'm sure he would have given you more detail if it was serious. He signs it, "With love, Jim."' She turns the letter over, allowing Maude to see the empty underside. 'I will check your release date with the Matron and see whether you might be eligible for an early release.' She stands and walks to the door, pleased that her promotion offers her the opportunity to do some good in the prison. 'Once I've done that I can write you a reply.' She straightens the front of her dress where her sitting has creased it. 'Now please carry on with your work.'

Miss Hardgrave does not produce peppermints but allows Clara some time without an appointment. 'What can I do for you?' She offers Clara the seat opposite her own.

'I have checked the records for prisoner 347, ma'am, and she still has two months remaining of her sentence. I would like to recommend her for early release.'

'On what grounds?'

'Well, her behaviour has been good but also I have concerns about her situation at home.'

The Matron raises an eyebrow. 'What concerns you in particular?'

'It arises from a letter that I read to her, a veiled threat from her husband that he would force their daughter into prostitution if she does not return home soon.'

'I see. And you think this constitutes good grounds to end her stay with us?'

'Yes, ma'am. I think it does.'

'And so you would encourage the wife to return to prostitution in order to save the child?'

'I only mean that . . .'

'Wouldn't it be better to alert the constabulary to the possibility of the man's crime?'

'Well, yes, ma'am . . . but then the child . . .'

'Would perhaps be better off in an orphanage?' Miss Hardgrave touches the cross that she wears at her neck. 'These are difficult decisions, Miss Cooper, but thankfully, not ours to make. The longer she spends in Holloway, the more likely it is that we might have some influence on the decisions she chooses to make once she leaves us. If she can see the error of her ways then she might yet save herself as well as her child.'

'Or both may be lost.' Miss Hardgrave does not contradict her and Clara, feeling bolder, says, 'It sometimes seems to me that the women here are doubly punished.'

The Matron gives a little nod. 'There is some truth in that. The burden of suffering has always fallen more heavily on a woman.'

Clara senses a chance to impress. 'I have often noted that their sentences, compared to men, seem unfair. For example, a woman found guilty of being drunk and disorderly will be given a six-week sentence when for men it is one. I even read recently of a man who threw a set of tongs at his wife, killing the baby she was holding accidentally. He got four months, whereas we have a woman upstairs serving three years for stealing a gold watch.'

'Perhaps the two don't stand comparison?'

'How so, ma'am? Surely we are all equal before the eyes of the law?'

'On the face of it, I do agree, these things seem unfair. But it also goes to the very heart of why we are here, Miss Cooper. A woman's crime, whatever it may be, is always the more serious because it is against her nature. While it is true that for every woman who prostitutes herself, there are many men who pay for her services, we should remember that it is in the man's nature to behave that way. He is, above all things, a base creature, only capable of good once his worst impulses have been curtailed. And that can only be done if women are the torchbearers of virtue. This is where, in my opinion, the suffragettes are correct for exposing the shameful rules that forbid women to occupy positions of influence. The more influence women can gain over men the better we shall all be. But we should not allow the

171

struggle for women's rights to become an equality of the lowest common denominator, Miss Cooper. When a woman breaks the law, she also commits a crime against nature. She transgresses doubly. Do you see? And so it is appropriate that her punishment is more severe than a man's.'

Clara feels betrayed. She was sure the Matron would agree but she seems to have taken the woman's plight and twisted it into something else. 'You make it sound like a war, Miss Hardgrave.'

'Perhaps it is. And the women in Holloway are turncoats, Miss Cooper. They are traitors to our cause, to be pitied perhaps, but never given in to. Or else we shall all be lost.' She watches Clara's face closely, sees the difficulty she has accepting the argument. 'Perhaps you have got a little too close to 347?'

Maude Maguire. The name comes to the tip of Clara's tongue.

'Perhaps I have, miss. But it is only for a want of doing good.'

'Quite so.' Miss Hardgrave smiles forgiveness. 'There is always one of them that gets under the skin sometime or other.'

'I have noticed that many of the women have difficulty with reading. Perhaps I could try to introduce some more structured learning for them. It might help them understand their choices more fully.'

'Perhaps it would. Or it might seem to be a reward for their crimes. Those of their position outside of this prison will rarely receive such an opportunity.' Miss Hardgrave's eyes flick to the door behind Clara, indicating that their conversation is now at a close. 'I am glad to have been of help.'

But Clara thinks she's been no help at all. Not to anyone.

20

Nancy wakes to sunlight. For a moment, she wonders where she is. This is not her prison cell. It's more like home, but not like home at all. Beside her on the bedside table is a china figure of a ballerina. Above her head there are shelves full of books. A picture of a woman in a bright blue hat hangs above the tiny fireplace and in the corner of the room is a table scattered with the scores of Mozart and Brahms.

Nancy gets out of bed. Her window looks out over the garden where the lawn glistens in the morning sun. She finds a bowl and a jug of fresh water on the dresser and makes herself presentable before she goes in search of the bathroom.

When she comes back out into the hall, the maid is bringing a tray upstairs. Miss Birnstingl is only two steps behind her.

'Good morning, Miss Cooper. I trust you slept well?'

'Yes, thank you.'

Miss Birnstingl opens the door to Daisy's room, allowing the maid to enter.

'Excuse me.' Nancy takes a step toward the door. 'Might I be allowed to see Miss Daisy?'

'Not at the moment, no.'

'I could help.' Nancy glimpses the top of Daisy's head over Miss Birnstingl's left shoulder.

'There is tea on the dining room table. Go down and help yourself. Breakfast will be served shortly, just as soon as we have finished here.'

Nancy does as she is told. In the dining room, two places have been laid at opposite ends of the table. Nancy pours herself a cup of tea from the pot and takes the furthest chair. After a few moments, she hears the maid on the stairs then watches her walk past the doorway. The girl is the same sort of age as herself and Nancy wonders what it must be like to work in this house and be close to these extraordinary people. Perhaps she could find a job like this if she needs to. A clang of pots comes from the kitchen as the maid puts something on the stove. A few moments later, Miss Birnstingl descends the staircase, walks into the dining room and takes the seat opposite Nancy. She tucks a napkin into the neckline of her dress. The maid appears, bringing boiled eggs, one for each of them, in little yellow egg cups. A slice of buttered bread is cut up into soldiers. Nancy unfolds her napkin and tucks it into the neck of her dress just as Miss Birnstingl has done. She finds the silence unnerving. A little conversation might make the breakfast easier but she doesn't know where to begin until she notices the badge on Miss Birnstingl's dress, the same one she saw yesterday.

'Um, excuse me but . . . that badge you are wearing . . .'

Miss Birnstingl looks startled, as though she has forgotten Nancy is there at all. 'Excuse me?'

'Yes. The badge on your dress. It's Jewish writing, isn't it?'

Miss Birnstingl cracks the top of her egg with the back of her spoon. 'It's Hebrew, yes.'

'And that says "Votes For Women", does it? In Hebrew?'

'It does.'

'How does that work then? I mean for the Jews.'

'It works exactly the same as it does for everyone else.'

'Yes. Of course.' Nancy feels like a fool. She had been thinking of the synagogue near her home and how it had two entrances, one for the women and one for the men. But she hadn't meant to cause offence. She wants to apologize and start all over again but the chances are she'd only dig herself deeper. She uses her fingers to peel a section of the shell from the top of her egg.

'Our mission is not to tear down our institutions, Miss Cooper, but to change them for the better,' Miss Birnstingl tells her quite suddenly.

Nancy thinks the woman's eyes could wither a small fruit tree. Miss Birnstingl scoops the top of the egg onto her spoon and holds it to her mouth and then, in exasperation, asks, 'Miss Cooper, do you know anything at all of our cause?'

Nancy lowers her head, just like the prisoners would do when she asked them a question that didn't need an answer. She feels she doesn't know much about anything. All she knows is that she's never met a woman like Daisy, or any of the other suffragettes come to that, and if this is what it takes to be like them, then she'll learn everything she has to.

The two women scrape at their eggs in silence.

'Tell me about the wardens where you work,' Miss Birnstingl says eventually in a more conciliatory tone.

'How do you mean?'

'The wardens at the prison. Are they all women?'

'Yes.'

'And are they cruel? I'm presuming you dealt with Daisy along with some of our other political prisoners. How are they treated?'

'We have to feed them by force, miss, as you know, but in some ways their treatment is less strict than the other prisoners. Their exercise rules, for example, and how they are allowed to talk so long as they are quiet.'

'And how do the other wardens feel about us? Are they sympathetic?'

Nancy thinks of Miss Needler and Miss Armitage, of Miss Barraclough and the Matron. She thinks of Clara, who plays her cards so close to her chest it's difficult to know what she thinks. 'Everyone's different. A lot of them agree with you, I'm sure, but some of them don't.'

'And yet they have as much to gain from the vote as any of us. Perhaps more.'

'Yes, miss. I believe so.'

'Then why on earth do you do the things you do?'

'It's our job, miss, the same with the suffragettes as with the other prisoners.' Nancy hesitates, thinking that it is not a good enough answer. 'Most of us don't have a lot of choice, miss. Not a straight choice anyway. I can't be sure of that, because I haven't worked there very long, but if I were to guess, I'd say it was true.' The maid brings in plates with sardines on toast and some sautéed potato. She takes away the remains of their eggshells.

Nancy fully expects to be asked to leave as soon as breakfast is over and she doesn't know what she might say that will change that. But if she's learned anything from the suffragettes, it's that they speak their mind, so she can't be blamed if she does the same and anyway, she's got nothing to lose.

'Could I ask you a question, Miss Birnstingl?'

'Go ahead.'

'I think you disapprove of me.'

'That isn't a question.'

'No. But do you? Do you disapprove of me?'

Miss Birnstingl hesitates. 'Perhaps.' She takes a pinch of salt from the dainty Chinese bowl in front of her. 'But then I hardly know a thing about you. You are a woman. That at least is something. And yet you are our jailor.'

'Only I would understand it if you did disapprove of me. I wouldn't think it unreasonable.'

'Whether I approve of you or not isn't the point, Miss

Cooper. I don't approve of very much about Daisy Divine and yet she is also in my house. Surely the issue with you is about trust? And I can trust Miss Divine completely. As for you . . . well . . . we shall see. I take it that you no longer consider yourself in the employment of Holloway Prison?'

Nancy bursts into tears. It happens so suddenly and with such force that there's nothing she can do about it. Perhaps it's the thought of being asked to leave. Or maybe it's the Duchess, unwilling to even acknowledge her with an open eye, though she clearly must communicate with Miss Birnstingl. Well it's both those things and more – it's the whole hopelessness of the situation.

Miss Birnstingl offers no words of comfort. She carries on eating and is halfway through her breakfast by the time Nancy manages to stem the flow of tears.

'Well, then,' she says at last. 'If you are to stay with us, I suppose I shall have to find you something to do. For the time being you can help Mary around the house. All these additional guests won't make her job any easier and I don't want to lose her.'

When breakfast is finished, the maid seeks out Nancy with a look of glee. 'You can start with the brasses,' she says, taking her into the kitchen and pointing to the pots and pans that hang from the rack on the ceiling. 'Once you're finished with them there's the brass-work on the front door.'

Nancy doesn't complain. In fact she is glad to be given something she can do well and she polishes the pots and pans till they gleam. When she goes outside to start on the door, she sees a different man standing at the lamppost. He's still in plain clothes but the suffragette was right – he watches her far too closely to be anything other than a policeman.

When she returns to the kitchen, Miss Birnstingl is spooning broth into a bowl from a saucepan on the stove. She puts the bowl on a tray and fills a glass full of water, adding lemon juice and a couple of drops of something from a small blue bottle.

'I can do that,' Nancy tells her, hoping to be allowed into Daisy's room.

'I can manage quite well myself. Thank you.'

'She should be eating better food than soup. There's some chicken in the kitchen. Why don't I bring her some of that?'

'Because her body isn't ready for it. She needs at least a week before she can move on to proper foods.'

'But a little can't do her any harm, can it? I could chop it up small.'

'It isn't the size of the mouthfuls, Miss Cooper. You haven't been listening.'

Nancy realizes she is behaving like her mother. She tries to think it through, why she is saying what she is, what the feeling is behind it and then she says, 'The prison doctor thought Daisy could die. Will she die?'

Miss Birnstingl gives her a straight look. 'I haven't lost one yet. But she will need the most careful attention.'

By the evening, Nancy still hasn't seen the Duchess and she creeps up the stairs, having made an excuse that she is tired and ready to retire to her room. The house is so quiet she half expects to find a ghost waiting for her in place of Daisy. She knocks softly on the door and enters. Daisy lies asleep, or at least Nancy thinks so. She stands at the head of her bed, waiting for her to open her eyes or to speak, the way she would when she visited her cell in the middle of the night.

She fetches a hairbrush from the dresser. 'Tell me if this is too much,' she says, 'but I'll be ever so gentle.' She sits beside the Duchess and runs her fingers through the end of Daisy's hair. It feels dry and brittle, like it might just break and crumble away, so she brushes lightly, moving from the scalp down to the shoulder. 'I used to do my sister's hair,' she tells her, 'when we were younger. I used to brush it every night till it shone like a jewel.' She picks out the hairs that have come away on the brush. 'There now,' she says, rising from the bed and replacing the hairbrush on the dresser.

'Thank you,' whispers Daisy.

21

It is the bicycle that draws Clara's attention. Propped up against a wall, its black enamel gleaming. She stops to take a closer look, runs a finger over the white rim of the rubber tyres and the soft leather nap of the saddle.

'It's not difficult to ride.' A woman appears behind her, a suffragette selling newspapers. She is dressed in a pair of deep mauve pantaloons, made specially for easy cycling.

Very daring, thinks Clara.

'It must take some getting used to,' she says.

The woman shrugs. 'A bit of practice to get your balance right but once you get there it feels very natural, like you've always known how to do it.'

'Yes. I'm sure.'

The woman gives her a wide smile and holds up the cover of her newspaper. 'Copy of *The Suffragette*?'

Clara has always drawn a line when it comes to giving

them money. The suffragettes are fine in their own way, admirable even. But it isn't for her. All that shouting and making a nuisance of yourself. And yet the newspaper makes her think of Nancy. It's been over a month and she hasn't heard another word from her sister, not even a card to say she is well. The whole thing has been playing on her mind. Not so much the thought that she might be in danger – if her sister was dead she would have heard by now – but the idea of Nancy running away to join women like these has been troubling her. She can't imagine Nancy fitting in at all. But then, as Miss Needler confided in her recently, there was something about that one, the Duchess, that Nancy took a shine to.

Clara doesn't like the thought that Nancy had been keeping things from her. That she had been changing – having ideas that Clara knew nothing about, making decisions that Clara never knew were possible. Perhaps Nancy knows something that she doesn't? Something that Clara has missed in the long hours of work or the evenings spent with Ted. She buys a copy of the newspaper then hurries away to avoid any further conversation.

When she is alone in her room, she opens the paper and flicks through the pages, surprised at what she finds. There are the type of articles she expects to see. Bold headlines such as, "I'd Rather Be a Rebel than a Slave!" or "The Militant's Path to Parliament". But it is the adverts that draw her attention. Robert Maison of Regent Street is offering henna hair colouring:

A Parisian speciality at Parisian prices. One pound, five shillings for the entire head and eighteen shillings and six-pence for roots only. All prices quoted are for ordinary shades. Pale or grey extra.

The expense is enough to make her hair drop out entirely.

There's a sale of blouses at Debenham & Freebody's, though she could buy six copies in her usual catalogue for the price of each of them. She always knew the suffragettes weren't for the likes of her. These women are after the power to go with their money. So what could they possibly see in Nancy? And what does she see in them?

'I'd rather be a rebel than a slave.' Clara has got too much self respect to be one and not enough recklessness for the other. But Nancy could be either – a slave certainly but a rebel too, if she found her courage. The two of them are closer than one thinks, joined like the top or bottom of a rolling wheel, the one leading on to the other.

She turns to the small ads on the back pages and finds a world that is closer to her own. There's a woman looking for a room to rent in Marble Arch, willing to share with women only. There's a suffrage school happening for a week in Bow, places for free, first come, first served. Nancy could be here among the ephemera as she begins a new life on her own, looking for a place to live or a job to keep her going. Clara might find a contact for her and she looks closely, trying to read between the lines for a glimpse of Nancy's face and realizing how much she misses her, like a pang of hunger that makes her heart swoon.

And then she sees the piece about a delegation. The suffragettes want volunteers for a march to petition Parliament, the week after next. Nancy could be one of them. She could be there. And if Clara goes too then she might just find her. It isn't impossible. If only she dares.

22

Nancy wakes when her door is opened. Miss Birnstingl enters with a breakfast tray. On it is a pot of tea, a plate of toast and a bowl of warm fruit compote. She sets it down on the bed and taps the newspaper that is folded and balanced on its edge. 'You should read this. You'll be selling it this morning. Felicity will come for you in an hour.'

Nancy is startled. 'Do you mean I have to leave the house?'

'Yes I do.'

'But I need to be here for Daisy!'

'You do not. Daisy will still be here when you return and I can manage her well enough myself.' She leaves the room, closing the door behind her.

Nancy stares at her breakfast tray, deciding whether she will do as Miss Birnstingl says, but she can't very well refuse and at some point she will have to trust her. She takes a bite out of the toast and unfolds the copy of *The Suffragette*. The cover has a picture of a man unleashing a fiery dragon against a woman who looks a lot like Joan of Arc. The caption reads, *The Forces of Evil Denouncing the Bearers of Light*. She opens it up, chooses an article and begins to read. After twenty minutes she remembers the time and jumps out of bed. She washes her face in the basin and brushes her hair before getting dressed and it only seems a moment before she hears a knock at the front door.

Felicity is bright and pretty, the kind of person who might wonder why anyone walks when they can run. There's something about her that reminds Nancy of Clara, how she might have been if she was a younger sister rather than the older. She tells Nancy that she is a teacher, married with a daughter but free to do some work for the cause due to the school holiday.

They take a tram to Piccadilly and stand beneath the statue of Eros where Felicity takes a handful of newspapers from the large canvas bag that she wears around her shoulders.

'Here you are.' She props them upright in the cradle of Nancy's arm. 'We sell in pairs. Don't wander off on your own.' She produces a sash in the colours of the suffragettes – white, green and mauve – and puts it over Nancy's head. 'Do you have a bag for change with you?'

'I don't have anything.'

'Here, have this.' She gives Nancy a small canvas purse that is heavy with coins.

Nancy puts the change into her handbag and clicks it shut as Felicity walks a few paces away then turns to face the crowd that are coming down from Regent Street.

'Get your copy of *The Suffragette*,' she shouts out above the noise.

The thought of doing likewise fills Nancy with terror but the passers-by are already slowing their pace to get a good look at her, so she better get on with it. She clears her throat then turns to face the opposite direction, almost bumping into a man in a bowler hat and black-rimmed spectacles. He stares at her, waiting, and she stares back, startled at what he might want, because he definitely wants something. He puts a penny in her hand, reaches out and takes the top copy from her stack of newspapers.

Well I never, she thinks, as he walks away. I sold one! And to a man! A man buying a copy of *The Suffragette*. She doesn't even know if that is allowed.

The next copy she sells is to a very posh lady who wants to talk about her own work as a Poor Law Guardian and how the system works against women who can't make ends meet. Nancy listens politely until the woman pats her on the shoulder, says, 'keep up the good work,' and leaves.

Nancy doesn't sell another paper for half an hour after that but she gets used to people staring and there are plenty of them interested, that's for sure. She even gets used to the catcalls directed at them.

'I wouldn't have you as a wife!' a driver shouts at them from his horse and cart but Felicity just laughs at him.

'I wouldn't give you the opportunity,' she shouts back.

A woman stops to ask Nancy why they have to cause so much trouble and Nancy, flustered, says that if the government did the right thing, they wouldn't have to.

She taps the cover of the paper. 'It's all in here. The answers to all your questions.'

But the woman won't buy one. She says there's ways of asking for things if you want to get your own way and any woman worth her salt knows that.

On her return to the house, Miss Birnstingl calls Nancy into the kitchen and hands her a tray. On it are a glass of apple juice and a bowl of broth. 'Daisy is awake and needs her food. I believe she would like to speak with you but please don't tax her. I will be up in fifteen minutes.'

Nancy goes up the stairs and onto the landing. She balances the tray on one hand as she knocks, then opens the door. Daisy watches her from the bed, her eyes still cloudy but focused with the same mix of curiosity and wariness that she had when they first met in her cell.

Nancy tries to smile. 'You're looking so much better today.' She puts the tray on the bedside table and picks up the glass of apple juice.

Daisy takes a mouthful and makes an effort to swallow. She places the glass back on the tray. 'I'm waiting for an explanation.' Her voice has a grate to it, as though she has to drag it up from her throat on a long heavy chain.

'I didn't know what else to do,' Nancy blurts out.

Daisy frowns.

'Why did you ask Miss Birnstingl to let me stay?'

Daisy lifts the glass to her mouth and finishes the juice. 'Curiosity.' Her hand shakes as she puts the glass down.

Nancy doesn't understand but is too afraid to ask what she means. She puts a little of the broth on the spoon, blows on it and holds it up to Daisy's mouth. 'You should eat.'

The Duchess closes her eyes before sipping at the spoon. 'Do you suppose I am kind?'

'No. I don't think so.'

'Good. I've told you before about pity.'

Nancy offers another spoonful of broth. 'I won't go back,' she tells her.

The Duchess is already exhausted from the effort of eating. 'That's up to you. But what do you want from *me*?'

Nancy can't answer very easily. She has a feeling, an ache or a twist in her gut. But she can't name it. She tries to force the feeling up and put it into words. 'I want to watch you.'

'Of course you do,' the Duchess says with satisfaction before she closes her eyes.

Nancy sells newspapers for the next three days and in the evenings she is allowed fifteen minutes to serve Daisy her supper. Miss Birnstingl watches them closely. She begins to give Nancy other tasks, like dressing Daisy's sores and managing the bedpan. When the Duchess is stronger and out of danger, Miss Birnstingl tells Nancy that she will be returning to her bookshop and leaving Daisy in her care.

'You will need to follow my instructions to the letter and that includes not letting her ladyship get the better of you. You must feed her six times a day. Do not be persuaded to stray from the menu or the quantities described. Make sure she finishes each meal. Now she has the strength to talk she can be very persuasive but be reminded that she loathes weakness and will bore of you quickly if you give in to her. I will expect a full report on my return home. Please keep notes. If you need assistance then Mary is on hand.'

'Thank you for giving me the opportunity,' Nancy tells her. 'I won't let you down.'

The following morning, Daisy looks tired. 'How is it possible I feel worse today than I did yesterday?'

Nancy delivers the glass of prune juice to her hand. 'Miss Birnstingl says you need time.'

'I was hoping to use the lavatory but my legs ache terribly.'

'Then you will have to keep using the bedpan.' She retrieves it from under the bed and places it on the counterpane. 'Do you need it now?'

'You make a better nurse than you did a warden. I never did understand how you came to work in the prison.'

'My sister found me a job. She was a warden there too.'

'It's not a job that most people would consider.' Daisy waits for more but Nancy is reluctant to talk of it. 'Was it

191

forced upon you?' Nancy nods. 'And why was that?'

Nancy shrugs her shoulders, close to tears.

'Well, perhaps that can wait. Anyway, I'm still waiting to learn what you expect from watching me?' She studies Nancy's face. 'I think you owe it to be honest with me.'

Nancy struggles with the words. 'Because . . . because I want to learn . . . how to be like you.'

'I can tell you that right now.' The Duchess doesn't seem either flattered or surprised. 'It's really very simple. You need to act on what you think and feel. We are what we do, Nancy, and if our thoughts and words are different from our actions then we either don't know ourselves or we are being dishonest.'

'Do you think so?'

'I know so.' The Duchess pauses for effect. 'Which one are you?'

'I don't know.'

'So definitely the first and possibly the second.'

'But how do you find the courage if you don't have it?'

'How can you not find the courage? To act is to be alive. Once you understand that, there's nothing else to be done.'

'But what if you lose everything?'

'Nothing can be gained without the risk of loss and most women come to realize it was never worth much in the first place.' She closes her eyes. 'Now I need some sleep.'

Nancy puts her arms around the Duchess and lifts her further down into the bed, their faces close as they hold each other's arms.

'I had a baby by my father,' Nancy tells her quietly, expecting her world to crumble but instead finding that she feels refreshed, like diving into a pool of cold clear water.

The Duchess opens her eyes.

'I gave it away. I don't even know who to.' She settles Daisy on her pillow and steps back from the bed.

'That's very sad,' the Duchess says softly. 'Perhaps it's why you remind me of my daughter. There's something about you, I can't put my finger on what it is, but I also had to give her up. It doesn't do to have a child out of wedlock in my profession.'

'Do you know where she is?'

'Yes. She was taken in by friends who agreed to bring her up as their own on the proviso that she doesn't know who I am until she is twenty-one.'

'And I remind you of her?'

'In a way I suppose you do.'

Nancy feels the warmth of a glow that begins in her belly. 'So, in a way, you want to watch me too.'

The following day, Daisy takes to walking. Nancy finds her at the window of her room, looking out over the garden.

'Do you know how long it is since I've seen a tree?' she says when she hears Nancy come into her room. 'Funny the things you take for granted, isn't it?'

Nancy's first reaction is to scold her for standing, but it doesn't work with Daisy. She puts a hand into the small of her back to support her if she faints. 'How are your legs?'

'I've always had strong legs. You don't get anywhere without good legs.' Daisy breathes in deeply, as though the window has been flung wide open. 'See that bird? Just there on the branch? See him? He's on the hunt for worms.'

'There was a bird in the prison. It was on the wing where I lived. A starling.'

'Really? How did he get in there do you wonder?'

'I don't know. He must have found a way in and couldn't get out again.'

'And they weren't able to catch him?'

'I don't think so.'

'I can see how it would be difficult. They should have shot him with an airgun.'

'What a terrible thing to say!'

'No it is not. It's the kindest thing to do for a trapped animal. Speaking of which, do we still have the policeman at our door?'

Nancy nods. She's come to recognize the faces of all three men that take their shifts at the lamppost.

'They'll be coming for me soon,' Daisy tells her. 'We shall need to be ready for them.'

In the evening, Miss Birnstingl comes to find Nancy in the parlour.

'I think it's time you and I took a walk together.' She is already wearing her coat and hat and carries a large

194

carpet bag in her hand. 'Go and fetch your coat. I will wait for you.'

Nancy does as she is told with a feeling of dread. She knows Miss Birnstingl doesn't take any pleasure from her company and is not a woman given to small talk. She returns to find her waiting with a hand on the latch and they walk out through the gate, past the policeman and on up the deserted street. Every time there is a turning towards the main road or the park, Nancy expects them to take it but Miss Birnstingl ignores them, appearing to have no direction and no purpose other than passing the time of day. With every step they take, Nancy's dread only increases until finally she stops walking altogether.

'Miss Birnstingl, I believe you have something in particular you wish to raise with me.'

Miss Birnstingl comes to a standstill. 'Indeed I do.'

'Do you wish me to leave your house? I know you disapprove of me . . .'

'Miss Cooper, I don't disapprove of you. But I do disapprove of people who do things for the wrong reasons.'

'And you think that is me?'

'Is it?'

'I don't think you are being fair. You don't know anything about me.'

'I may be old, my dear, but I know what it is to be in love.'

Nancy is caught up short. What did she mean by that? Does she think I'm in love with Daisy? The way she said it, it is obvious she does and that she disapproves. 'I'm sorry,' Nancy tells her, 'but I don't understand.'

Miss Birnstingl walks on a few steps with Nancy following at her shoulder. 'She cannot give you what you want. You do know that, don't you?'

'No. I don't know what you mean.'

'Are you familiar with the idea of a damaged healer? It describes a person of great charisma, a person who has the ability to make you feel whole one day or broken the next. Often they can give a person what they cannot give themselves. But they can only do it in bursts. They cannot sustain the responsibilities of their own actions because they themselves are broken.'

'And you think that is Daisy?'

'It is hopeless to think you can hold onto her. Sooner or later, one way or another, the two of you will be parted. So you have some choices to make.'

'And what do you think those choices are?'

'I think Daisy has it in mind to take you with her when she goes.'

Nancy catches her breath. This isn't what she expected at all. 'Has she spoken to you about it?'

'Not in any detail. No.'

They arrive at a junction in the street. There is a large red postbox on the corner and Miss Birnstingl pauses, opens her bag and looks inside. Nancy expects her to produce a letter but she takes out something that looks like the firecrackers she's seen young boys make for themselves on Guy Fawkes night, a strip of maybe eight inches held together with tape and a ten-inch fuse.

'Now listen to me carefully. I'm going to show you how to use an incendiary device.' She takes a brass lighter from her purse and flips open the lid. She feeds the device through the hole in the postbox. 'Have it ready to drop but hold on to it till the fuse is lit. Do not dangle it by the fuse or it will detach.' She strikes her lighter, puts the flame to the fuse and only lets go once it begins to fizz. 'There now. Come quickly.' She snaps her bag shut and steps away from the postbox, taking hold of Nancy's arm and pulling her the first few steps away. They quicken their pace and when Nancy glances back, the postbox looks like a smoking chimney that has fallen from a roof.

'Don't look back,' Miss Birnstingl corrects her. She chooses a road to the right and once they take it and are out of sight, they slow their walking to a normal pace. 'As I was saying, you have a choice to make and it's important you make it for the right reasons. The time is close for Daisy to move on and I presume you will want to go with her. However, I want to tell you that I am willing to let you remain in my house should you wish to.'

'That's very kind of you,' Nancy says cautiously. 'But as you say, I will be leaving with Daisy.'

'I have a friend who runs a shop. He's a nice man. He looks after his staff. He would be willing to give you a job, earning six shillings a day, if you want it. You would have the opportunity to sell newspapers in your spare time should you still wish to do so. And as I have said, you will be welcome to lodge with me until you have the means to be independent.'

'But that's not what I want.'

Miss Birnstingl becomes irritated with her. 'Daisy Divine has chosen a path that only a few can travel. You shouldn't think that she will change it because of you.'

'Why would I want to change her?'

'Because she will expect things of you that I don't think you can give or that you have given sufficient thought to.'

'Then I will have to learn,' Nancy tells her immediately, still too excited to properly understand what Miss Birnstingl has been saying.

'Very well. I can't say I'm surprised. Now you must prepare yourself. At the next junction is another letterbox. In my bag is a second incendiary device. I have shown you how to use it.'

Nancy's eyes widen.

'If you can't do this then you can't go with Daisy. There will be far greater risks and she will ask much more of you.'

Nancy sees the letterbox, a hundred yards away. A man walks up to it, posts a letter and then sets off towards them.

'There's someone there,' Nancy says and then, realizing how frightened she sounds, she adds, 'We shall have to wait until he leaves.'

'I see him. He'll be gone soon enough.' They slow their pace and smile as the man passes. Once they reach the box and there is no one else in sight, Miss Birnstingl opens her bag. She brings out the device and gives it to Nancy. 'Do it now or hand it back to me.'

'Do you have the lighter?'

Miss Birnstingl has it ready in her hand and Nancy takes it from her and lights the fuse immediately.

'Stand back,' she tells Miss Birnstingl as the postbox flares and begins to burn.

23

Miss Penny, the office secretary, knocks on Clara's door. 'It's only me.' She wafts into her office on a breeze of lavender oil. 'How are you today? Have you had any more news of your sister?'

It is over a month since Nancy ran away but Clara still resents her life becoming office gossip. 'No, Miss Penny. Nothing since her letter.'

'Oh dear,' Miss Penny says brightly. 'You must be terribly worried.'

'Is there anything I can do for you?'

'Miss Hardgrave would like to see you in her office immediately.'

'Thank you, Miss Penny.' Clara rises from her desk.

'Just to warn you, she has a gentleman visitor with her. A Member of Parliament, I believe she said.'

Clara is immediately on her guard. 'Do you know what this is about?'

'No, miss. I wouldn't like to guess.'

'No,' Clara agrees, her head already full of the possibilities.

'I'll put the kettle on so you can have a lovely cup of tea when you come out.'

Clara makes her way to the Matron's office, knocks and waits at the door.

Miss Hardgrave opens it herself. 'Miss Cooper. Good. Do come in.'

The gentleman in question is sitting in the Matron's place behind the desk. He has a sheaf of papers in front of him and a fountain pen at the ready. The Matron offers Clara the chair directly opposite him.

'This is Sir Herbert Randolph, MP. He'd like to ask you some questions regarding the incident with Constance Rigby.' The Matron retreats to the fireplace and sits in a spare chair, her sensible shoes just visible at the edge of Clara's vision.

Sir Randolph removes his reading glasses. 'Miss Cooper? Please sit down.'

Clara takes a seat.

The gentleman places his hands on the table in front of him. 'I am here on behalf of a Parliamentary committee to report on the use of a water hose during the recent protest by Constance Rigby. I understand you were the most senior member of staff present at the time?'

'Yes, sir. I was the most senior member present on the wings.'

'And this was your first day in the post of Prison Supervisor?'

'Yes, sir. I was only recently promoted.'

'Did you know of the men's visit in advance?'

'I found out perhaps an hour before the gentlemen arrived.' Clara tries to think ahead, to work out how much she should say and who she should be loyal to. From the corner of her eye, the Matron's feet move closer together. 'Miss Hardgrave asked me to meet them and assist them on their visit.'

'And when did you find out they intended to use a water hose on the prisoner in question?'

'They asked to visit the yard, sir. That's when I saw it being prepared.'

'And you didn't think to question them about how it was to be used?'

'I remember thinking it was unusual, sir. I couldn't see why it would be necessary.'

'But you didn't query them?'

'No, sir.'

'Why was that?'

'They were policemen, sir. And a man from the Home Office. I presumed they had the authority.'

'Did you think to seek advice from your superior?'

'No, sir.' Clara wonders what she might have done had they not been men.

'And yet you have a duty of care to the prisoners here.'

'And a duty to keep order, sir. For the benefit of everyone.'

Miss Hardgrave interrupts. 'Miss Cooper has shown herself to be a very thorough officer, Sir Randolph. I had every confidence in her ability to oversee the visitors who were in charge of the operation.'

'Though it appears to have been misplaced in this instance.' Sir Randolph replaces his glasses and makes a note on the paper in front of him. 'Thank you, Miss Cooper. That will be all.'

Miss Hardgrave shows Clara from her office and Miss Penny instantly appears in the corridor, ushering her into the secretary's room and placing a cup of tea in her hands for which she is very grateful.

'You look pale, Miss Cooper. Have a seat and tell me all about it. Was it to do with the suffragette girl and those men from the police?'

'It appears I am to get the blame for it,' Clara tells her. She is angry at the unfairness of it all and yet unable to shake the feeling that perhaps she was to blame, that she should have done things differently.

'I'm sure they won't think that,' Miss Penny reassures her, but they both know it's not true.

Clara drinks her tea, trying to work out what the consequences will be for her. She hears Miss Hardgrave's voice outside the door as she escorts the MP back to the main gate and when she returns, Clara is waiting outside her office.

'Miss Hardgrave? May I have a quick word?'

The Matron brings her back into her office. 'I thought

you did very well, Clara.'

'What will happen, ma'am?'

'Nothing will happen, Clara.'

'But the report? What will happen to the report?'

'Everyone will blame everyone else and it will be put down to a flaw in the system with a recommendation that it shouldn't happen again. After that, the report will be filed away and that will be the end of it.'

'I had the feeling that I was being blamed, ma'am, that what happened is being put down to me.'

Miss Hardgrave consoles her with a hand on her arm. 'One always feels that way when asked difficult questions.'

'But it would be the most convenient conclusion for everyone else, wouldn't it, ma'am?'

'I have already submitted my report on the incident and referenced your work here in the most positive manner. The incident will be put down to over enthusiasm on the part of the police and an error of judgement by yourself, Miss Cooper.'

'That doesn't seem fair.'

'As you say, it is in the interests of everyone concerned.'

'Everyone except for me.'

'The blame has been apportioned to those it will do the least harm and will be forgotten soon enough. You have no need to be worried, Miss Cooper. It is only a little black mark in an otherwise most promising career.'

'Will I be disciplined?'

'I doubt it will come to that.'

Clara has the feeling that this has all been settled, that this outcome was decided even before the men arrived at the prison and however unfair that may be, there is nothing she can do about it and there is nothing that Miss Hardgrave will do for her either.

'You must trust me, Miss Cooper. This will all blow over.' Miss Hardgrave leaves Clara standing at the door and goes to sit behind her desk.

The sudden distance between them seems exaggerated to Clara, as though the two of them are not in the same room any more but watching each other from different sides of a valley or gorge. And it looks lonely to stand where the Matron is. It will be lonely for Clara too if she should ever get there and she wonders how she ever came to envy this woman with her career.

'Do you have any further questions, Miss Cooper?'

'No, ma'am.' Clara reaches for the door. 'Thank you for helping me to understand.'

24

Miss Birnstingl has asked both Daisy and Nancy to join her in the parlour immediately. They arrive to find the maid turning up the lamps and drawing the curtains so they can't be seen from the street. 'They will be here in ten minutes,' Miss Birnstingl tells Daisy. 'Quickly. We should be ready.'

'What's happening?' asks Nancy. 'We're leaving, aren't we?'

Daisy is already unbuttoning her dress, helped by the maid who slips it from her shoulders then folds it neatly and places it in the hessian sack that is one of a pair on the large oak table. She seems to know what is going on.

'You too.' Miss Birnstingl nods for Nancy to take off her dress.

The sacks already contain a change of clothes – a hat, a pair of gloves, a warm coat, a spare pair of stockings – and

Nancy lays her dress on top of them. She lifts her hair and pins it up.

'Go to the front bedroom,' Miss Birnstingl instructs her. 'Wait there and count the policemen who arrive till we call you.'

Nancy hurries away without further questions. She climbs the stairs and goes into the darkened room. From the window she can look down on the policeman by the lamp-post. He is still on his own, his breath visible on the cold night air and Nancy stands back from the glass, aware that she is only wearing a petticoat and undergarments. She can see the street just as well from here.

She looks out along the road. Everything is still and quiet. In the road there are two parked motorcars. A cat wanders slowly in the gutter with its nose to the ground. Nancy waits for something to happen and then it does, a screech of brakes that scatters the cat as three motorcars arrive quickly, each of them pulling to a stop outside the front gate. The policeman jerks himself upright as the doors are flung open and out jump the women, twenty or more of them, all dressed identically as milkmaids holding hessian sacks that they sling over their shoulders. They wear blue gingham dresses, white aprons and yellow straw hats that sit on top of their blonde braided hair and they run from the pavement, quick as anything, pouring through the gate and slamming the knocker against the front door. The cars leave as quickly as they arrived.

The policeman doesn't know where to look or what to

do. He puts a whistle to his mouth and blows repeatedly. Within seconds, two more motorcars appear and screech to a halt but by then the women are already inside the house. Police spill out onto the pavement, looking left and right, wondering what is going on. Some of them are in uniform, some are not. Nancy counts eight of them in all.

'Nancy!' Miss Birnstingl calls upstairs from the hall. 'Come quickly!'

Nancy hurries from the bedroom and out onto the landing. The hall below is packed tight with milkmaids, each of them identical, but in the middle of them stands Miss Birnstingl, her black dress looking bleak amid all the colour and prettiness.

'Come quickly,' she calls again and waves Nancy down the stairs.

Nancy pushes through the chattering women and Miss Birnstingl loads her into the parlour where there are still more milkmaids. Nancy looks around for Daisy, doesn't find her and suddenly wonders if this is to be a trick on her too, that they might try to separate her from Daisy.

'How many police did you count?' asks Miss Birnstingl.

'Eight. There are eight of them.'

Miss Birnstingl nods. 'Then we have a good chance.'

Nancy is handed over to three women who clothe her quickly, holding out her arms for the dress. They lift the apron over her head and tie it at her waist, before they bring the bright blonde wig, arranging the braids to hang over her shoulders and pinning the straw hat in place. A woman brushes her face with white powder and then puts a big rosy red bloom on each cheek. In no time at all, Nancy looks just the same as everyone else.

'You must stay with Daisy,' Miss Birnstingl tells her calmly. 'When you pass the gate, run to the left. After a hundred yards you will reach a turning. A car will be waiting for you.' Finally, after all this time, the old lady smiles at Nancy, her cheeks flushed with excitement. 'Good luck!' she says. 'I'm going to miss you.'

One of the milkmaids suddenly takes hold of Nancy's hand. 'Don't let me go,' she says and Nancy recognizes Daisy, smiling weakly beneath her make-up. They are handed their sacks of spare clothing.

'Hurry, ladies!' Miss Birnstingl calls out to everyone in the parlour and they move out into the hall and stand three abreast, everyone tight as a tin of sardines. Nancy and Daisy are deliberately positioned two thirds down the line.

'Let me carry your sack,' Nancy offers but Daisy shakes her head.

'I'll have to manage. It'll mark me out if I'm the only one without.'

'Can you run?'

'I can do my best.'

Miss Birnstingl claps her hands. 'We shall leave on the count of three,' she announces and puts her hand on the latch of the door. 'One! Two! Three!' She flings the door open and stands aside. 'Now go!'

The women sprint from the house. Six of them make

straight for the gate where the policemen stand waiting. Four others dart to the left and right, running across the flowerbeds, making for the waist-high wall that they scramble over, scraping their palms against the flint and brickwork.

From the doorway, Nancy sees a policeman make a grab for the first of the milkmaids, catching clumps of dress as he swings her around, pinning her back against one of the large black cars. Another milkmaid is tripped and falls into the gutter, but she clutches at a raincoat, bringing the man down with her. There are whistles and shouts as the milkmaids break through and scatter in all directions being chased by bewildered policemen.

A space opens out ahead of her and Nancy dashes through the gate, her shoe kicking a dislodged helmet that spirals away into the open road. She turns left and runs along the pavement with Daisy one step behind, wheezing and already out of breath. After they have gone twenty yards, she looks behind to see if they have been followed. Daisy is already falling behind and almost at a stop, her hand clutching at her waist.

'Come on!' Nancy urges her on.

Behind them, figures are wrestling in the darkness. On the other side of the road, two milkmaids are running, laughing, skidding past a man in a bowler hat who watches the scene unfolding with interest.

The Duchess has slowed to a walking pace. She puts a hand out, beseeching Nancy to slow down and wait. She's taking deep breaths and has dropped her sack as she clutches her waist.

'Oh God,' she gasps. 'I don't think I can do it.'

Nancy runs back and picks up her sack. 'Come on,' she tells her and puts a gentle arm about her. 'We're nearly there.' But she still can't see the car or the corner of the street. Instead, she notices that the man on the other side of the road has fixed his attention on them and is watching closely. No bother, she thinks. He must be a resident, out for a quiet evening walk and wondering what the hell is going on. But then he takes his hands from his pockets, his eyes fixing on Daisy and she knows he's been looking for her all along.

'Come on,' Nancy barks. 'We've been spotted.'

Daisy straightens up and they run again, staggering, holding onto each other as though they're in a three-legged race, their knees knocking against each other's. Nancy looks back over her shoulder. The man is following them. He starts to run, his raincoat flapping out behind him.

He's shouting, 'Over here! She's over here!'

And then Nancy sees the waiting car, its engine running and the back door already opened, ready for them. It begins to edge along the pavement towards them and they rush forwards but the man is at their heels, close enough now that he's sure to catch them. Nancy hears his boots and she swings her sack on the turn, catching him full on the shoulder and knocking him off balance so that he falls heavily. He curses. Daisy reaches the car. She falls into the

211

back seat and the car shunts forward again allowing Nancy to take the last few steps and throw herself inside. She lands on top of Daisy who groans and flattens herself against the black leather seat. The open door hits a lamppost and swings itself shut as the car accelerates away and the last thing Nancy sees is the face of the policeman, getting back on his feet as he puts a whistle to his mouth.

Daisy wriggles beneath her, struggling for air and moaning. Nancy sits up quickly.

'Stay down,' orders the driver from the front seat as she steers the car out onto a main road. 'We're not out of the woods yet.'

Nancy slips down onto the floor between the seats. She's astonished to actually be inside a motorcar. And with a woman driving! Her father wouldn't know what to think. The excitement and the fear of it course through her, making her want to shout out loud.

Daisy moans again from the seat above her head.

Nancy reaches up and puts a hand on hers. 'Just breathe. Breathe deeply.' She follows her own advice, taking in big gulps of air, and when she feels calmer, she says, 'We did it. We got away.'

They drive for ten minutes, maybe more, though Nancy can't tell in what direction. From the floor she sees street lamps and shop lights. She hears the rumble of a passing tram. When the car comes to a stop they're in a quiet street, a terrace of tall Georgian houses.

'Here we are then,' the driver announces and turns in her

seat to look back at them, the peak of her cap framing her face in silhouette. 'How is she?'

Daisy forces herself to sit upright, gripping the front seat with her hand. 'I'll survive,' she says wearily.

The driver gets out, comes round to the back and opens the rear door. She offers her arm which Daisy takes, stepping uneasily from the car. Nancy lets herself out and follows on behind.

The driver takes them towards a bright red door set in the nearest house. It opens immediately when they knock. The maid says she's been expecting them and shows them into a tall hall, lit by a chandelier that hangs from the ceiling above. She takes them towards a set of double doors, knocks, then opens them up to a room full of people, all of them dressed in evening attire and holding cocktail glasses or flutes of champagne. The maid abandons them. Suddenly the conversations stop and everyone turns in their direction. Whatever is going on, Nancy hadn't expected this.

A man approaches through the crowd. 'Daisy!' He wears a black tie and dinner jacket, has his hair greased back and a finely clipped moustache. 'Daisy!' He comes to a stop in front of them, laughing, his arms held out wide as he looks back over his shoulder at his party guests. 'But which of these beautiful milkmaids is she?' He delivers his line in a mocking tone, as though he were in a village pantomime.

'Oh, Rupert, don't be foolish,' Daisy says wearily. She leans against Nancy. 'I need a chair.'

The man called Rupert hasn't stopped smiling. He

summons a maid who arrives with a chair for each of them and once they are seated he kneels in front of Daisy. 'Oh my dear, but you do look awful. Let me get you a brandy.'

'For the first time in my life, I think I'd prefer a glass of water.'

A waiter brings a tray of drinks. He pours water into tall glasses and gives them one each.

'The wonderful Daisy Divine!' Rupert announces to the assembled guests. 'Recently released from Holloway and fleeing the attentions of our best police to be here with us tonight.' There is a ripple of applause. 'And now you really must tell us everything!'

'Oh, Rupert, I'm so very tired,' says Daisy. 'You can't imagine.'

'But my dear, you have an audience.'

'She's ill,' says Nancy in her mother's tone and then blushes at her rudeness.

'And who is this?' Rupert asks, the edge of his mouth struggling to keep its smile.

'This is Nancy,' Daisy tells him. 'She's my little sister in arms.'

'Then you are welcome.' He turns to the butler who has appeared from the hall. 'Broadhurst, will you ask Mrs Higgins to make up two rooms immediately.' He turns back to the women. 'It will only take a few minutes but we can't let you go before explaining your costumes. I assume they are a disguise?'

Daisy leans forward in her chair, finding the strength

from somewhere to perform. 'There we were,' she begins, 'wondering how we would leave our safe house now that I'm recovered enough to be able to walk. It has been a month since my release and Asquith was getting ready to re-arrest me, we were all sure of it.' She takes another sip of her water. 'The house we were lodged in was surrounded by police, front and back. They knew where we were and there was no chance of escape. So we hatched a plan . . .'

You could have heard a pin drop.

And Nancy listens to the story. Though she knows how it ends, she is as transfixed as everyone else in the room. Weak as she is, Daisy Divine is still irresistible.

25

Ted arrives looking worried and serious. 'Do you still want to do this?'

'You shouldn't have taken the time off work,' Clara tells him but she's glad he's here.

Great George Street is busier than usual, a steady flow of people making their way to Parliament Square. Most of them are men. Some look like they are here to make trouble, little groups of three or four with surly faces, their fists stuffed deep into their trouser pockets. And then there are the curious, the couples walking arm in arm, come to see what all the fuss is about. Ted and Clara walk quickly, skipping out into the road to avoid a large group who are all chatter and nervous laughter. They pass newspaper sellers, a woman with copies of *The Suffragette*, and a man touting *The Socialist*. In Tothill Street, the horses are sensitive and twitch their ears. The policemen fidget on their backs.

A whisper spreads through the crowds, a sense that something is happening. 'They've set off. They'll be here soon enough.'

Ted and Clara pause, wondering where the best place is to stand and watch.

'I don't like the look of this,' Ted tells her.

Clara ignores him. She is nervous enough without him adding to it. 'You can go if you want,' she tells him, but he doesn't move. Ahead of them, people have stopped walking, anxious to go any further, wanting to be close but not too close.

'What are the chances of finding her?' Ted pleads. 'It's like a needle in a haystack.'

A man pushes a leaflet into Clara's hand and she stuffs it into her handbag without a second glance. At Westminster Abbey, a line of boys cling to the railings. Behind them, some American sailors have climbed a wall and are standing on top holding thickly cut sandwiches and bottles of beer.

'Over there,' Clara says. 'I'll get a better view from up there.' She leads Ted over to the wall. 'Help me up, will you?'

Ted frowns but he puts his hands on her waist and lifts, her shoes scrabbling at the brickwork till she's sure of her footing.

'Come and have a bite of my sandwich,' one of the sailors calls to her. 'Come and have a taste. It's a good one.'

She dismisses him with a turn of her head and tries to concentrate. She can see the square quite well from here. The green is packed tight with people, mostly rough-looking men in cloth caps and grey woollen jackets. Behind the square stand the Houses of Parliament, the entrance three deep with police.

'You all right up there?' Ted calls up to her.

'Don't worry, chum,' one of the sailors calls out to him. 'We'll look after her.'

'Here they come!' A shout goes up from further down the street.

Clara looks for the women but all she can see is the top of a banner between the hats and parasols. Is that her? Will it be Nancy? It has been less than two months since she saw her but somehow Clara expects her sister to look different, to be changed in some way.

The crowd goes quiet as the women process toward the Abbey, the road opening up before them as people push their way to the pavement then turn back to look, curious to see what sort of women might think of doing such a thing as this. Will they be harridans spitting venom? Or beautiful and brave? Like the witches from *Macbeth* or Joan of Arc?

Clara can see them now, six women walking in a line across the street. All of them wear long black dresses and as they pass, Clara can read the word DELEGATE stitched onto the white stars of cloth on their chests. They each carry pages from the petition, rolled up into a scroll. But none of them are Nancy. Clara's heart sinks.

Ahead of the women, the road is blocked. A wall of men stand waiting, flat caps pulled down as far as their eyes. There are twenty yards of space between them and the delegation. Then there are ten. The men refuse to budge. The crowd holds its breath. The women will never get through. They haven't got a chance if the men won't move.

'Please make way!' the woman holding the banner shouts ahead. 'We are here to petition the Prime Minister.'

'Get back to your kitchens!' comes a call from the crowd.

There's some laughter and the crowd creeps closer, more confident now that the tension has been broken. And then a foot sneaks out, from some boy or man, a laced black boot that catches the trailing toe of the closest suffragette so that she trips and falls. A photographer bursts forward into the space ahead of her, his camera flashing tungsten as her scroll rolls away under the feet of a man in a leather apron and bowler hat who must have closed his shop to come and watch. The crowd swells forward again. The people at the back push to get a better view and Clara loses sight of the woman but she can still see the other suffragettes who walk up against the line of men. The men push them backwards but the women come again. This time the men catch hold of them by their waists, turn them around and throw them to the ground. Someone snatches their banner and passes it back into the crowd who bat it between them so it darts like a gadfly above a pond before it disappears for good.

The women get to their feet. They're going to try again.

'Let them through,' someone pleads from the crowd. 'Let them have their say! It's only fair.'

The suffragettes step up again, close enough that they could kick the men or kiss them. This time the men pin their arms to their sides, lift them off the ground and spin them round, throwing them back behind them so the women are swallowed into the crowd and have no chance of escape. The men close in. Clara can see the suffragettes being pushed and shoved. She sees a woman's head, sees another's arm held up high, the women appearing then disappearing as they are passed through the crowd like packages, or bits of wood adrift in the sea.

Three policemen arrive at a run and put their shoulders to the mass of men, hoping to rescue the women and bring them back into the safety of the street. A bag of flour flies through the air and hits the helmet of the one in the middle, turning the shoulder of his uniform from black to white.

Then Clara sees another banner coming through the crowd. More women. Another delegation. There are shouts from across the square where a third party must be approaching from a different route. Is that Nancy? Clara thinks she sees her. She can't be sure but it could be. A hundred yards ahead of her the woman is lifted up above the crowd for a moment and then disappears from view.

'Help me down,' Clara shouts to Ted and he holds his arms out wide to catch her as she jumps.

He tries to hold her back. 'You'll never find her,' he yells above the noise. 'Not in all this.' He has a hold of her arm but Clara frees herself and makes a run for the square, pushing her way between the shoulders of the crowd. 'Clara!' he shouts after her as the crowd closes in. 'Clara!'

The crowd shifts as people push closer trying either to see

or break out and make for safety. And now Clara is among them, pushing up against the backs of taller men who block her view so that all she can see is the very top of Big Ben. She puts her head down and pushes hard with her legs, digging her heels in, then slipping round the shoulders of the man in front, her fingers brushing the arm of his twill jacket.

'Excuse me,' she shouts out as she comes through. 'Excuse me.'

Every time they turn, she has a chance to push her way past. The ground under her feet changes from cobblestones to grass. Ahead of her, something is happening. There is laughter and a loud cheer.

Someone calls out, 'Give her one for me!'

A sudden surge drives everyone to the left. The man in front of her trips and falls to the ground taking three or four men with him. Clara is pushed from behind. She steps on a hand, stumbles, then falls against a man who is just getting to his feet and they both fall together, Clara landing on her side with her face in the mud. As she tries to get up, another man lands on top of her and she goes down again. A walking stick fixes itself in the grass, just inches from her eye before a hand takes hold of hers and pulls her to her feet. She half expects it to be Ted but it isn't, it's someone else, a man in a linen suit who nods at her and then is gone.

To the left of her, a line of mounted police moves through the square spreading panic. The crowd compresses squeezing Clara so tight that if she were to lift her feet from the ground she could still stand upright. The lack of control, of not being able to move where she wants, makes her panic.

'Clara!'

She thinks she can hear Ted's voice calling to her but she can't see him, can't even turn her head in the right direction. Someone has a hand on her back. Someone has a hand on her thigh, on her buttock, on her breast, pinching at her. The crowd twists itself like a flock of birds as the horses come through, their teeth bared against the bit. One of them comes so close Clara sees herself reflected in its eye. And now she desperately wants to leave. This is too frightening. Too dangerous. And Ted was right. The chance of finding Nancy in all this is nigh on impossible.

She struggles to break free, pushing hard to her left instead of straight ahead and then she suddenly breaks loose, falling forward into a circle of space, a clearing where one of the delegates is crouched on the ground taking deep breaths. The woman looks up at her, perhaps expecting a friend. Clara looks away. She had thought she was brave but she is not. Now all she wants to do is leave.

'Let me through,' she says to the men in front of her. 'I'm not with them. Please let me pass.'

And the men do.

Behind the circle of men the crowd is thinner and she darts between the gaps, heading back toward the Abbey and the safety of Great George Street. A hand grabs hers. Ted is beside her but he has lost his hat and has an ugly bruise above one eye. She puts a hand to his face and he flinches from her.

'Don't.'

She touches his cheek. He brushes her hand away.

'You're angry with me.' She can see his humiliation. Ted only came to protect her but he couldn't even protect himself. And now he blames her.

'I can't go back to work looking like this. I'll get the sack.'

'You'll have to think of something then because that bruise won't go by the morning. Tell them you got set upon in Soho then they'll feel sorry for you and won't read the riot act.'

Ted bristles and Clara wishes she hadn't said it. 'Don't be angry with me.'

He glares at her, sullen and silent.

'Ted?'

'I'll see you. I've got to go.'

She takes hold of his arm. 'Not before you tell me why you're angry.'

'I don't know.'

'Yes you do. Better to tell me now than later. I can't do anything about it if I don't know what's bothering you.'

'It's stupid, that's all.'

'What is?'

'All of this independence malarkey.' He stares at her defiantly. 'If people were just decent to each other none of it would be necessary.'

'And is that how you feel about me? That I'm being stupid.'

'I always try to do the right thing by you, Clara.'

'I know you do.'

'But it doesn't make you happy any more. Half the time I feel like I'm walking on eggshells.'

'And I make you feel like that?'

Ted looks ashamed to have said it and Clara realizes that this is not just today. Ted has been going cold on her for a while now and she wonders how she missed it.

He steps away from her. 'Clara, I really do have to go.'

'Will I see you Wednesday?'

Ted shrugs. 'I suppose so.' He leans across and kisses her lightly on the cheek and she watches as he walks away, thinking now she might lose him.

26

Nancy is given a large double bedroom next to Daisy. It is on the second floor and looks onto the back of the house where there is a long thin garden terraced with flagstones and planted with overhanging trellises of ivy and wisteria. The room has a four-poster bed with crisp white sheets. Directly opposite the bed is a marble fireplace with armchairs either side of it. Nancy walks around the bedroom, still in her nightgown, touching the figurines of naked cherubim. She is gaping at a large brooding seascape on the far wall when the maid knocks and enters with a basket of kindling and coal.

'Good morning, miss.'

'Good morning,' says Nancy, embarrassed, and she gets back into bed, pulling the sheets up around her as the maid rattles the grate and busies herself with the fire. 'Would madam prefer breakfast in her room this morning?'

'Is Miss Divine awake yet?'

'I have just been in, miss. I'll bring her breakfast up directly.'

'Then I'll have mine brought up to me as well. Actually, could you bring Miss Divine's breakfast to me? I will take it into her.'

'As you wish, miss.'

Nancy wishes she wouldn't address her like that. If the maid only knew where Nancy came from. But of course she knows! It must be obvious as soon as she opens her mouth that the two of them have more in common than separates them. Nancy gets dressed quickly, putting on the same dress she left home in, so if the maid can't tell by the way she speaks, she'll know as soon as she sets eyes on her. Well, what of it? She is here as a guest of Miss Daisy Divine and she doesn't have to answer to anyone else.

It takes two maids to bring up breakfast. It consists of steamed finnan haddie, omelettes, mushrooms and a dish of small peas. There are buttered muffins and coffee in a silver pot. The butler arrives with a serving tray on wheels and transfers the dishes from the trays which have been used to carry them up.

'Will this be sufficient, miss?'

'Yes. Thank you.' Nancy is overwhelmed at the quantity of food. 'That'll do very nicely.'

She wheels the trolley out into the hall, knocks on Daisy's door, then enters. Daisy is sitting up in bed, her hair still down around her shoulders, and Rupert sits on the bedside next to her. He wears a white flannel suit with a red cravat. Something about him disgusts Nancy and she tries not to look at him.

'I brought your breakfast, Daisy.'

Rupert stands and crosses to the window. 'I have servants that can do that, Miss Cooper.'

'I'd prefer to do it myself,' she says, though she hasn't the nerve to lift her head. She pushes the tray past him to the bedside then sits on the crumpled sheet he has just vacated.

'Put it over by the window,' Daisy tells her. 'I shall have it there.'

Nancy pushes the tray over to the window and sets it on the small table.

Rupert is obviously irritated by her presence. 'The maids will think you're after their jobs.' He runs a hand through his hair. 'I'm serious. If you want to keep the staff onside, you should let them do their work.' He turns to Daisy as she leaves her bed and finds a gown. 'Darling, you're looking so much better this morning. You frightened the life out of me last night, turning up in that state.' He retrieves his hat from the foot of the bed. 'I have some business to attend to, so I'll be gone for a day or two. The staff have been told to give you everything you need, so don't be afraid to ask.'

Daisy takes a chair at the window.

Rupert leans down and kisses her on the lips then straightens up to find Nancy staring. 'Good day, Miss Cooper.'

'It's obvious you don't like him,' Daisy says once he has left.

227

'Who is he?'

'Rupert? He's a very rich man who adores me.'

'Do you trust him?'

Daisy arches an eyebrow. 'We understand each other. He won't go to the police, if that's what you mean.'

Nancy pours herself a cup of coffee. 'How long are we going to be here?'

'I think another few weeks of this and I'll be strong enough to get back to work.'

'Do you mean the theatre?'

'No, my dear. I mean firebombing. I've missed it terribly.'

Nancy behaves as though she didn't hear. 'I should contact Felicity. I can be out selling newspapers while you are getting your strength back.'

Daisy shakes her head. 'It's too conspicuous for you. I'm afraid those days are over.'

'Then what am I to do with myself?'

'You don't have to do anything. Relax! Have the staff run hot baths for you all day. That's what I'm going to do.'

Nancy pouts. 'I don't feel comfortable here.'

'You're being silly and I won't allow it. Anyway, this isn't his home. It's just a place he uses to entertain the friends his wife disapproves of.'

'You should eat your breakfast before it gets cold.'

Daisy picks up her knife and fork and begins on the omelette. 'Every time you are angry with me you get me to eat. Do you know that?'

'It's for your own good.'

'Hmm . . . He's a dish though, isn't he? Nancy? Don't say you haven't noticed?'

Nancy lifts the little plates and scoops something of everything out for Daisy. 'He looks like a rat.'

'I suppose he does a bit. Not your type then. What about the Scandinavian look? Blond hair and blue eyes? I knew one once. He was a count or some such. Very considerate in bed.'

'You shouldn't talk the way you do. You only do it to shock me.'

'Rubbish! Anyway, more people should talk the way I do. People can be so pretentious, don't you think?'

Nancy stands and puts her plate back onto the tray.

'Now you're not talking to me. And you're still behaving like a servant. Leave that plate alone and sit back down.' She pats the seat next to her. 'Come on. Are you jealous? You are! I can see it in your shoulders.'

'That's ridiculous.'

'Of course it's not. You can tell a lot about a person just by looking at them. Even something as simple as the way someone walks in a street.' She looks towards the window as though the proof of it might be passing the house right there and then.

Nancy joins her at the window. 'How do I walk?'

'Like an apology.'

Nancy's face crumples.

'I'm being honest.' Daisy pats the seat again and Nancy sits. 'Our bodies betray us, Nancy. They communicate all

229

the things we don't wish people to see. Acting can be as much about letting go as it is about control. When people look at me they should see a part of me and not. So when I'm on stage I need to be both a master of myself and not. And when I look at you, I think . . . well actually, if I'm being honest, I don't think you want a body at all. That's why I was so surprised when you hit that policeman. I half expected you to go back and apologize.'

'I didn't know what I was doing,' Nancy tells her but she is pleased that Daisy saw it.

'Exactly. See what happens when your body takes over? Look at you now. You are sitting up straight and your shoulders have moved back. That's pride, that is, seeping into your backbone. Can't you feel it? The emotion and flesh becoming one. You should remember what it feels like.'

Nancy takes hold of her hand and squeezes.

The Duchess allows it for a moment before shaking her away. 'And remember this too,' she says seriously. 'I like men. I find them exciting. And I like Rupert. At least for now.'

27

Later that week, Daisy knocks on Nancy's door. She gives her messages, two white envelopes, to be delivered by hand. She gives her money for fares and food.

'Both envelopes must be delivered only to the person to whom they're intended and you will need to wait for their response.'

The first address is in the East End. Nancy takes a tram and then a bus, asking the conductor to tell her when she gets there. He comes to find her when the bus reaches Spital-fields, pointing to a large church across the street from where the bus has pulled to a stop.

'That's where you want to start. Haberdasher Street is round the back of it somewhere. You can always ask.'

She finds the house in a row of terraced cottages, not unlike her father's house. A group of girls are chalking hop-scotch on the pavement while the boys kick a ball against the end wall. She finds the house without needing to ask again. The door has been left wide open and Nancy can look through to a small parlour and a set of dark stairs. She checks the name on the front of the letter Daisy has given her, then knocks and waits. A little girl walks into the parlour and stands sucking at her thumb and staring. She looks about three years old, dressed in a pinafore that has a stain down the front.

The sight of her makes Nancy feel uneasy. 'Is your mother at home? I'm looking for Rosie.'

The child eyes her curiously.

'Go on in.' A boy appears at her back, one of the children from the street. 'She'll be out the back.'

Nancy steps into the parlour, sees a door through to the back of the house and walks past the little girl. There is a table with three wooden chairs and a stove that is lit. A young woman can be seen through the open sash window, hanging clothes out on a line of rope that runs across the yard.

'Miss Church?'

The woman turns and frowns at her. She comes inside. The little girl wanders in and stands with her back to the wall, still watching Nancy.

'Miss Church?'

'I told them you'd have it by Monday.'

'Sorry?'

'I told her not to send someone round. I can see you all right by Friday. I'll come to the offices in the afternoon, the way I normally do. I don't want you coming round here.'

Nancy retrieves the white envelope from her bag and holds it out. 'You *are* Rosie Church?' Nancy recognizes her as one of the women who came to Miss Birnstingl's and disguised her as a milkmaid. 'It's a letter from Daisy. She asked me to deliver it in person.'

The woman suddenly realizes who she is. 'Well, why didn't you say? Coming round here calling me "Miss Church". I knew I recognized you from somewhere but I couldn't put a place to you. Frightened the life out of me.' She takes pity on the little girl. 'Come and sit at the table, Hilda. I'll get you something to eat.'

She takes the letter from Nancy's hand then crosses to a cupboard where she brings out a loaf of bread, cuts a slice and spreads some jam from a pot that she keeps on the window sill. 'Here you go, darling.' She hands it to the little girl.

Nancy is assuming she'll have to read the letter for the woman but Rosie opens it and reads herself.

'Tell her we'll be there,' she says after a moment. 'It'll take a few of us, mind, but I'll be done at the Palladium by seven.' She folds the letter and slips it into the pocket of her apron. 'Would you like a cup of tea?'

'No, thank you,' says Nancy, then thinking she might have been rude tells her, 'I have to deliver another message.'

'You might as well. You need to wait a minute while I make it up for her.'

'What's that?'

'She's asked me to give you a little something for her.' Rosie reaches up and fetches a tin from a shelf above the door. 'Hilda, go on outside will you. Go and find that little Jamie, he'll play with you.' When the girl doesn't move, Rosie picks her up, carries her across the room and puts her down by the door. 'Get off with you. You can come back in half an hour.'

Nancy waits for her to leave. 'You've got a lovely daughter.'

'She's not mine. Heaven forbid!' Rosie takes the lid from her box. 'The kids round here are in and out of all the houses but Hilda takes a special shine to mine.' She brings out a clump of marine sponge, all soft and yellow, cuts a lump the size of a small fist and shapes it into a ball by rolling it between her palms. She sprinkles it with a white powder, then pours something from a little glass bottle which it soaks up.

Nancy comes forward to the table for a closer look. 'What's it for?' she asks, thinking of a soothing bath for Daisy's poor legs.

Rosie wraps a string net around the sponge and pulls the drawstring tight. 'Stops the babies,' she says very matter-of-factly. 'Do you need one yourself?'

'No,' says Nancy. 'No, thank you. I won't be needing that.'

'Here you go then.' Rosie fits the device into a little round tin and pops the lid on. 'Tell Daisy she can settle up with me another time.'

'I'll tell her.'

'See you Friday,' Rosie says as she sees her to the front door.

The address on the second letter is a strange one, a Miss Edith Garrud at St Cuthbert's Hall in Euston. Nancy takes the bus back into town, gets off at Trafalgar Square then walks up towards Gower Street. The hall is easy enough to find and she pushes open the double doors. Once inside, there is a vestibule with another pair of double doors, partly glazed, so she can look into the hall. And what she sees is the most extraordinary sight. Scattered about the room are pairs of women, each attacking the other. Most of them have weapons of some sort, either umbrellas or small wooden clubs, and they set about each other with gusto, letting out loud yelps and grunts as they launch their assaults.

Nancy slips inside and stands with her back to the door, feeling overdressed in her hat and coat. The instructor acknowledges her from the far side of the room, signalling for her to wait where she is, then works her way through the class, shouting instructions at the grappling women.

'Use your brolly to disarm her! That's better.'

When one woman throws her attacker over her shoulder, she claps her hands in encouragement.

'That's excellent. Just as I showed you.'

Eventually, she reaches Nancy. 'Can I help you?'

'What on earth are they doing?' Nancy can't help herself asking.

'And who are you?'

'I beg your pardon, Miss Garrud. I have a letter for you from Daisy Divine.'

Miss Garrud takes the letter, opens it and reads the two pages of closely written handwriting. She has an honest face, plain but straightforward, with a no-nonsense nose. 'Please let her know I will make the arrangements.'

'Yes, thank you, I will.' Nancy's eyes stray back to the women in the hall.

Miss Garrud fans her face with the letter. 'Daisy suggested you might like to join us. We provide protection for the Pankhursts against re-arrest by the authorities. That and other assignments such as yours.' She fetches a club from the belt around her waist, takes Nancy's hand and places it in her palm. It's shaped like a skittle but has the weight and size of a truncheon and Nancy can feel the violence of it, how it is weighted to be swung from above the head and sits in her hand so comfortably. It only has one purpose. And she's scared of it. She can feel the fear in her fingers. Miss Garrud glances back at the fighting women. 'Why don't you try it with me now?' She takes a step back, suddenly poised and alert.

'No,' Nancy says emphatically. 'No. Thank you very much, but no.'

When she arrives back at the house, there are lights in the upstairs rooms. Daisy is wearing an evening gown and sits next to a roaring fire.

'How did it go?' she asks. 'Did you meet the fearsome Miss Garrud?'

236

'You told her I might like to join them!'

Daisy laughs. 'Do you hate me? I thought you might find it fun to put all that anger to good use.'

'She said I could attack her with a wooden club!'

'And did you?'

'No!'

'That's a shame. You would have felt much better for it, although you'd have come off the worse. She's a black belt in ju-jitsu, whatever that is. Did you bring one of those clubs home with you? Apparently, if you hit a horse on the back of the knees with one, it'll sit down and unseat the rider.'

'Is that useful?'

'Absolutely.' Daisy gives her a mischievous smile. She takes a sip from a glass of gin and tonic. 'And did you see Rosie? Is she able to come next Friday?'

'She said she would.'

'Good. And did she give you something for me?'

Nancy fetches the round tin from her bag, looking like the little girl, Hilda, all sullen and watchful.

'I assume you don't approve but Rupert will be here tonight and I've already had one daughter.'

'But how can you? How can you complain about the way men treat us and then . . . well you know . . .'

Daisy watches her closely, her lips pursed. 'Listen to me, Nancy. I know what men are. I know how they work. Occasionally I even enjoy their company. But don't ever make the mistake of thinking I don't believe in the cause.'

'Yes, but . . .'

'It's known as having your cake and eating it. So let that be the end of it.'

Nancy makes a point of locking her door and going without supper. When she hears him arrive, issuing instructions to the butler in the hallway, she pulls a pillow over her head and tries not to imagine what Daisy is doing in the room next door. She sleeps fitfully and wakes in her clothes. Outside the bedroom window, the light is bright enough for mid morning. She listens to the shout of a rag and bone man, the heavy hooves upon the cobblestones and the slow scrape of cart wheels. When she visits the bathroom, she catches sight of Rupert's back as he disappears through Daisy's bedroom door, his shirt tails hanging over bare legs. He makes a point of rattling the key in the lock of Daisy's door.

Nancy takes a walk in the park and stays there past lunch time. In the afternoon, Daisy comes into her room, walks straight to her and hugs her and Nancy allows herself to be held, putting her chin on the top of Daisy's shoulder and detecting a fragrance on her neck that she hasn't smelt before. Probably a gift from Rupert.

'Are we to leave this week?' Nancy whispers. 'Please tell me it's soon. I don't think I can bear very much of this.'

Daisy takes hold of her hand, squeezing her fingers gently. 'We shall be gone by Friday.'

28

When she sees the man, Clara is walking on the brick path that circles the park near the prison. He is ahead of her, going in the same direction as herself, so she only sees the back of him, but there is something about the man that reminds her of Ted. She doesn't know why. He doesn't look like Ted. His hair is blond where it shows beneath his cloth cap and he walks differently. Ted is usually so optimistic, he has a spring in his stride, but this man seems the opposite, walking with his shoulders hunched as if against an ill wind. But then, at the suffragette delegation in Westminster, Ted had walked away from her in just the same way. That must be what reminds her of him.

She quickens her pace, fearful she might lose him. She wonders what on earth she is doing following a stranger in the park. And then she thinks that Ted might be about to leave her, that however much she has ignored the feeling, it has been with her since they last met.

She blames herself, goes over their time together searching for tiny little clues, like combing for lice in a lovely head of hair. What might she have done to drive him away? There was that time she wouldn't let him take her to the music hall in Hoxton because she thought it was too vulgar. Or when she insisted they shared a plate of fish because it was a dish served for two and she wanted it more than the beef. Ted had said he didn't mind but he had eaten slowly and never said how much he liked it. She'd thought she had the right to express an opinion, especially as she was the one paying for it. But that was a problem too. Ted never looked easy when she insisted on paying her way. He found it excruciating, though he never said so. He just went quiet. All the humour gone out of him. It had been a long while since he pulled her leg about something.

She is closer to the man now. Almost within touching distance. The man turns and looks at her. He must have heard her coming and he makes space for her to pass him on the path but Clara looks away, sees a park bench at the side of the path and makes a show of sitting down. The man continues walking and Clara, feeling embarrassed and stupid, tells herself that he looks nothing like Ted and she ought to think of something else.

Miss Penny, the office secretary, is to leave the prison and be married. She announced her news only the other day with a diamond engagement ring that she wore to work, a sure way to invite questions, although it was the last thing Clara wanted to talk about. Miss Penny wouldn't let her get away so easily. She told her that Ernest was an older man but all the better for it. 'You need a man who's mature enough to know his way around.' In Miss Penny's experience, younger men were never serious in their intentions whereas the older man had enough experience of life to know what he wanted.

But that isn't the problem with Ted. It is she that can't decide what she wants.

She manages to convince herself that she has been selfish. That she's not meeting his needs. That she isn't what he looks for in a woman. Ted likes her to be different. He told her so. But no man wants to be under the thumb, do they? She searches for the man again, looks out across the park, and now he is some distance away. She watches him pass behind a line of trees.

She begins to despair. The two of them are still caught in the same impossible game as when they started seeing each other. The more space she takes for herself, the less there is for Ted. So it's not only about her independence. It's about him too. Ted's got to change too. But then he wouldn't see the need. He said as much to her, and who can blame him? He must like things the way they are. He must like himself just the way he is.

She reaches for her handbag, opens it up and brings out a handkerchief. She blows her nose.

She had asked Miss Penny how long she and Ernest had been seeing each other, and when she replied that it was two years, Clara had said, 'Goodness. But how do you keep him interested?' Miss Penny had forgiven her rudeness once she guessed that Clara must be talking about her own experience.

'That's younger men for you.' She had leant in close and lowered her voice to a whisper. 'My advice would be to hold a little back. Make him work for it.'

Clara had blushed, realizing that Miss Penny was referring to sex. But Ted has been as good as gold since she pushed him away in the park. He hasn't put a finger on her. And that must be difficult for him. Clara stops herself. She drums her fingers repeatedly on the ornate iron armrest of the bench, wondering why she is finding excuses for him. Why does she always come back to blaming herself? Is the lack of sex difficult for her too? She doesn't know. All of that is so confused. Having a body that tempts her and a head that shames her. If Ted only understood about her father then it might help them move forward. She thinks about telling him. But she can't do that for the fear that he'll think less of her, that she will revolt him, the same way she revolts herself when she remembers what her father did. When she can't sort out the loving and the loathing. That's the worst of it. The pity of it. That her body isn't her own to do with as she pleases and that sex is not simply an urge or a feeling but a negotiation, a trade off, like shaking hands on a deal when a piece of her is still owned by her father. That's not fair for either her or Ted.

She looks out across the neatly cropped turf. There is that man again. Now he is coming towards her. He has circled the park and the path is bringing him back to her. He'll be by her side any moment. He'll walk right past the bench where she sits.

Clara stands up, puts her bag back on her shoulder and hurries away before he gets too close.

29

Rosie Church arrives the next afternoon with two other women from the Actresses' Franchise League.

'All right, Daisy?' she asks as she comes into her room. She nods at Nancy. 'Miss Cooper.' She takes paints and powders from her bag and lays them out on the edge of the dresser.

'What shall we be this time?' asks Daisy, sitting at the dressing table and checking her face in the mirror.

'What's the last thing you'd expect?' Rosie asks, looking at Nancy.

'Umm . . . I don't know . . . a fisherwoman?'

Rosie shakes her head. 'That'll never do.'

'A man!' says Daisy, clapping her hands in delight when Rosie nods. 'Oh, I do so love dressing up!'

The women take suits from a case and hold them high so they fall out flat. 'You need to look respectable but not rich.'

Rosie puts a hairbrush to her lips as she thinks it through. 'What about a bank clerk with his apprentice? Do you think you can pull it off?'

'Of course I can pull it off,' Daisy tells her. 'But it's out of the question. I would never stoop so low.' She picks up the bowler, one of a selection of hats laid out on a chair beside her. 'I shall be a theatre director. An impresario. I think I can manage that very well indeed. Do you have a long silk scarf?' She puts the hat on her head and admires herself in the mirror. 'You can be my boy,' she tells Nancy.

'Chief technician,' Rosie corrects her. 'A theatre director wouldn't be travelling with a boy.' She bunches Nancy's hair up at the back. 'This is going to be a problem. We can't have you wearing a top hat. Ideally, you'd wear a cap or a trilby. Something like that.'

'You can cut it,' Nancy tells her. 'Cut it as short as you like.'

'Are you sure? Once I start on it, there's no going back.'

'I won't mind.'

Rosie raises her eyebrows. 'See, Daisy? Dedication to her craft. Where did you find her?'

'I didn't. She found me.'

Rosie holds a pair of scissors over Nancy's head. 'Shoulder length or shorter?'

'I want it all gone,' says Nancy, suddenly serious and determined.

She watches in the mirror as Rosie gets to work quickly, cutting off long lengths of hair and dropping them into a paper bag at her feet. With every snip of the scissors Nancy feels unburdened. She is becoming less herself. Less of the little girl she grew up with, less of the woman she finds so uncomfortable to be with. She is being transformed into someone new, someone she has only glimpsed until recently but is now reflected back to her in the flesh. And this can't be taken back. Like a kick or a punch, it won't be undone.

Once her hair is cut short, Rosie goes more carefully, taking her time to shape the sides and parting it to the side. Nancy watches every movement and each time Rosie pauses, Nancy turns her head, noticing how her chin seems less soft and how her ears stick out. She has never liked her ears but she likes them now.

'Can you shave the back of my neck so it stops in a straight line?'

Rosie slips the razor from its sheath and scrapes the back of her neck carefully. When it is done, Nancy runs the tips of her fingers across the bristles, tickled pink at the daring of it, her nerves fizzing like a fuse.

'Where are we going?' She asks Daisy.

'Manchester.'

'And what shall we do there?'

'Plant a bomb.' Daisy turns to see if the colour is draining from Nancy's cheeks. 'The house will be empty. No one will be hurt.'

'Yes,' says Nancy.

The women find a corset to trim her figure. She slips an old woollen suit over her collarless shirt, then chooses a flat cap to complete the disguise. She looks at herself again in the mirror. Is it really this easy to become a boy? She struggles with the buttoned fly of her trousers then stands back, admiring herself. She catches Daisy eyeing her suspiciously.

'What do you think?'

'You're not my type,' Daisy tells her, 'but I suppose you'll do.' She stands up from her dresser. 'I hope you intend for me to have a paunch,' she tells Rosie. 'Any theatre director who's any good has a paunch. It's only the ones who don't make any money that are stick thin.' She holds her arms out wide so the women can put padding in her overcoat.

When they are ready, they pack their own clothes into the suitcases that they will take with them to Manchester. Rupert appears at the bedroom door to wish them farewell. He walks Daisy along the hallway with his arm around her waist.

'Write to me,' he says at the front door.

'I won't.'

He kisses her cheek. 'Then don't leave it so long before you visit again.'

'Thank you, Rupert. You've been a brick.' Daisy takes hold of a silver-topped cane from a rack by the door. 'Is that our cab?' She blows him a kiss on her way out. 'Give my love to your wife.'

They travel to Euston station, pay the driver and walk through into the ticket office. Daisy does all the talking and she manages to find just the right tone in her voice, though it's Nancy who looks the most convincing, sauntering along

247

the concourse, fiddling with the coins in her pockets, and wondering how easily she's taken to wearing trousers. She touches Daisy's arm then points to the platform where their train is being prepared for boarding.

'We've got a few minutes yet.' She looks around the crowded concourse.

A man stares fixedly at the large white clock that hangs above the entrance, cigar in one hand and a newspaper tucked under his arm. A couple of porters manhandle a large trunk onto a trolley while beside them a florist fills the buckets on his barrow with lilies and roses and bright yellow daffodils.

Nancy gives a little tug on the sleeve of Daisy's coat. 'Have you noticed?'

'What?'

'No one looks at you when you're a man. I mean, they see you, but no one tries to hold your gaze. They just register you in passing.'

'Horrible, isn't it?'

Nancy re-adjusts the cap on her head. 'No. It's terrific. It means I'm not on show. I don't have to be pretty all the time. Look here! Have you seen the way I walk?' She takes ten paces away, turns and then walks back. 'See what my legs do when they don't have to be ladylike?'

'Your deportment leaves a lot to be desired,' Daisy scoffs. 'In my opinion you're over acting.' She puts a finger to her false moustache. 'If it wasn't for the thrill of deception I would be utterly miserable, I can assure you.'

'I'm going to buy a pack of cigarettes and smoke them on the platform.'

'I bet you don't.' After a moment she adds, 'Actually, it would be quite useful for one of us to have a light on us. We'll need it for later.'

Nancy's heart skips a beat. She's been so taken with acting as a man that she'd quite forgotten why they are making the trip in the first place.

'Well go on then!' Daisy tells her. 'There's a tobacconist just over there, but be quick about it. We have a train to catch.'

Nancy walks across to the booth, thinking through how a man might behave with a tobacconist. He would know his brand, for a start. She picks one out while she waits for another customer to be served. She won't bother trying to change her voice. Better to be comfortable than try too hard.

'A pack of Navy Cut and a box of matches,' she says when the man looks at her expectantly. She stops herself from saying please. Do men say please to each other when a woman's not in earshot? Perhaps not. The tobacconist doesn't seem to mind and he passes the cigarettes over the counter without a second glance. Nancy stuffs the packet in her trouser pocket, feeling like it's the best thing in the world not to need a purse or a handbag.

'Come on then,' she tells Daisy, returning with a lit cigarette hanging from the corner of her mouth. 'We've got a train to catch.'

Their carriage is already half full and they wrestle their

249

cases down the aisle till they reach their seats. Daisy looks up in despair at the luggage racks.

'Here, I'll do that.' Nancy takes the case and swings it up, glad that no one stands for them with an offer of help. She stores her own case beside it and the two of them settle into their seats as the train pulls away from the platform through a pall of smoke.

Daisy picks up a newspaper from the free seat opposite, unfolds it and slaps the spine with the back of her hand to make it behave. She obviously has no intention of talking so Nancy takes a look around the carriage, curious at the other men, noticing how they slouch rather than sit upright. She makes a note of their open knees then does the same. A little while later she walks down the aisle of the train, not worrying if she catches the eye of a lady or two because they always look away. She buys a bottle of beer from a man with a trolley and stands drinking at the open window in between the carriages.

When she returns, Daisy is in conversation with a couple in the next row, telling them about the production of a play about Joan of Arc that they are bringing to Manchester.

'We have dressed her to look like Emmeline Pankhurst,' she informs them blithely. 'To catch something of the mood sweeping the country.'

Nancy thinks that's taking things a bit close to the wire but the couple don't appear to have noticed anything untoward.

'She used to live in Manchester, before she moved to London,' they tell her proudly.

'Of course she did,' Daisy replies graciously. 'But now she belongs to all of us.'

Once they arrive, Nancy is told they have to walk.

'It should only take fifteen minutes and we ought not take a cab.' Daisy looks at the street names to get her bearings. 'No point in leading them straight to our front door, is there?'

She strides away down a side street with Nancy struggling beside her, a suitcase held in each hand.

'How long will we stay here?'

'We won't. We'll meet our contact, pick up the bomb and lie low till the small hours.'

'The bomb?'

'Yes, my dear. The bomb. Well it's more of a large incendiary. What did you think we were going to use?'

Nancy shrugs, trying not to look anxious.

'The target is a short walk from the house. It belongs to an MP but he hardly ever uses it.'

'And where do we go once we've done it?'

'We shall leave immediately. We don't want to be anywhere near Manchester once the news gets out. There's a small station where we can catch the early train. We'll travel a few stops, change, then pick up the mainline.'

'Right.' Nancy breathes deeply, the way you do if you are stuck on a boat in rough water.

They turn down a street of small cottages. Beyond the end of the road they can see open countryside. The house they want is at the far end of the street, the last one before it turns into a muddy lane that disappears between the hedge-rows. Daisy knocks softly. The door is opened by a woman in an apron. She looks confused.

'Yes? Can I help you?'

Daisy lifts her top hat, showing her hair pinned up high, and the woman laughs. 'You better come in.'

'We had you fooled, didn't we, Mary?'

'I didn't know what to think.' She shows Daisy through the hall towards the light in the kitchen, taking Nancy by the arm and ushering her forward so she can close the front door. 'Welcome.'

From the kitchen comes a man's voice, deep with a thick Manchester accent. 'Miss Divine?'

Nancy freezes at the sound of a man. She glimpses him as he stands from the table, the legs of his chair scraping on the tiled floor – a bearded man in shirt and braces, his cap still on his head.

'My husband,' Mary explains, leading Nancy on into the kitchen.

'It's an honour to meet you,' he says.

Daisy smiles graciously, as though she already knows. They shake hands.

'Mr O'Callaghan.'

The man turns to Nancy with a broad grin. 'I haven't got a clue whether you're a bloke or not, but you're very welcome too.'

'This is Nancy,' Daisy introduces her.

'Welcome, Nancy. Come in and have a seat.' He pulls two

chairs away from the table. 'Thank God you didn't decide to come as policemen or we'd have been out the back door. Wouldn't we, Mary?'

'We might be yet.' The woman puts a kettle onto the top of the range then brings out cups, a small pot of milk and a plate of oatmeal biscuits.

The four of them sit close around the table, drinking their tea and swapping pleasantries till Mr O'Callaghan says, 'Right, then. Down to business.' He produces a piece of paper from his pocket and flattens it out on the corner of the table so they both can see the hand-drawn map.

Mary comes round to stand behind Daisy's chair, then traces the route with her finger.

'You take the lane outside. You can't go wrong. Keep walking till you come to a crossroads. You'll see a wall right opposite. That's the house you want. If you keep on to the left there's a gap where the wall has crumbled and you can climb in there. At the gatehouse there's a cottage where the housekeeper lives with her husband but that's at the front of the house and this'll take you in through the back. Once you're done, come back to the lane where you went in and carry on up, away from the town. The railway station is a fifteen minute walk – first train out is at 5.35. That should give you plenty of time if you blow the house at half past four.'

Nancy gets distracted by the mention of the bomb. It must already be here in the house. She hadn't thought about it till now, what with everything being so warm and cosy, but it must be. She looks furtively around the room. There's nothing out of the ordinary but it must be here, hidden away, perhaps under the staircase, or locked into a cupboard. A bomb in this house. She wonders who made it. Was it him or her? They both seem so ordinary. She watches Mary put the kettle back on to boil. Mr O'Callaghan is telling Daisy about the couple that live in the gatehouse, turning a matchstick between his fingers, looking for all the world like a gossip at a pub table. But there'll be a story to these people, a path that leads right up to this house where they live with their secrets.

Now that the plan has been discussed, the conversation dries up. Daisy has become unusually quiet and that makes Nancy anxious. She becomes aware of the clock ticking on the mantelpiece.

'It's going to be a long night,' Mary says.

She brings a fresh pot of tea and Mr O'Callaghan says, 'That won't do,' and fetches a half bottle of whiskey from a tin on the shelf above the range. 'Will you join me?' he asks Daisy.

'Better not.'

'I'll stick to the tea,' Nancy tells him, so he pours a dram into the bottom of his cup and drinks by himself.

'I'll be off to bed, then, if you don't mind,' he says, once he's had the last of it. 'Mary'll sit up with you but I have to be at the yard for six.'

The clock on the mantelpiece says ten-thirty. He shakes their hands again and wishes them luck before taking himself upstairs and the women sit in silence, listening to the ceiling creak and moan about the weight of him.

Mary produces a deck of playing cards and they play gin rummy, with Nancy and Daisy taking turns to try to beat her, though she wins every time. They switch to the backgammon board but Mary still proves unbeatable and Daisy gives up, folding her arms crossly and staring into nowhere. She drums her fingers on the table top.

'How many rooms does the mansion have again?'

'Seven bedrooms upstairs. Three bathrooms,' Mary tells her patiently. 'Do you need to look at the drawing again?'

'No. I was just thinking . . . '

Mary asks them questions – about the Pankhursts, about living in London, about the theatre – and Daisy becomes something of her old self, giving her news about the cause or telling her stories from her time in Holloway. They try not to look at the clock until finally, it tells them the time is three-thirty.

Mary spreads her hands on the table. 'It's time for you to leave.'

She brings them into the hall where a holdall now sits on the doormat, waiting for them patiently. Mary picks it up as though it is nothing more than a bag of shopping. She hands it to Daisy and Nancy can see it's heavy, so she says, 'Shall I take it?'

'Oh, no!' Daisy keeps both hands on the handles. 'This one is especially for me.'

Mary O'Callaghan kisses her cheek. 'Best of luck to you.' She squeezes Nancy's fingers. 'The first part of the track'll be muddy till you reach the lane, so be careful to keep to the edge.'

The two of them walk briskly, the moon giving them just enough light to judge the edge of the ditch to the side of them, and when they reach the lane, their shoes are surprisingly quiet on the cobblestones. Soon they come to the crossroads with the stone wall. It's about eight feet high and shields the house from view but they follow it till they reach the gap, then scramble in through high nettles and the loose ends of brambles which Nancy kicks out of the way, glad the two of them are still wearing trousers. At the edge of the trees they look out across a meadow of short grass. The mansion lies in front of them, perhaps two hundred yards away, its windows dark and gloomy.

Daisy kicks at a rock by her foot. 'Bring that with you, will you, Nancy? You're going to need it.'

Nancy kneels and picks up the rock. It's heavy but not too large for her fingers to get a good grip of it. Daisy is already starting out across the grass and Nancy runs to catch her up. At the back of the house there's a set of steps, guarded by two stone lions who sit and watch them pass. At the top of the steps is a wide brick terrace. They pause to assess the back of the house. A row of tall glass doors open out from a reception room and Daisy chooses the last of them then presses her face to the glass and listens.

'We'll get in here,' she whispers. 'Once we're inside you can use the torch. You need to take the staircase then look in every room on the top two floors so we can be sure it is empty.

I'll check downstairs and choose the right spot to leave our little friend.' She closes her fingers around the rock in Nancy's hand. 'Are you scared?' When Nancy nods she says, 'Good. You ought to be.' She steps back from the door, bringing Nancy with her. 'Go on then. Give it a good strong throw.'

Nancy lifts the rock above her head and launches her stone at the middle of the glass and there's that terrible moment when the silence shatters but then returns immediately. The rock has left a hole that will allow them to walk straight through if they can bend low enough to avoid the sharp edges that still cling to the frame, but they wait where they are, listening out for any sign of movement. There's nothing. No shouts or footsteps. No rooms being suddenly lit. They step gently across the shards of glass. Like walking on ice. A small lump of it sticks to the sole of Nancy's shoe and she scrapes at the parquet flooring till she scuffs it out. The two of them are now standing in a long tall room. Daisy hands her a small torch and the beam picks out a grand piano, its legs still showing beneath the dust sheet. They find a door that must lead into the hall.

'Go on. Be quick,' Daisy prompts her and Nancy leaves to find her way upstairs.

In the hallway, her torch picks out the gilt-framed paintings of horses and dour-looking men in uniform. She discovers the staircase and follows the carpet that runs up its middle till she stands on the first floor landing. Straight ahead of her is the first door but she hesitates to open it. Should she shout out something before she turns the handle?

No. Better not to alert anyone who might be there. But she's being silly. There's no one home. She already knows. And if there is then that is why she's checking the rooms. To alert them. Though what she would say if someone were to suddenly appear, doesn't bear thinking about.

She knocks on the door, feeling like a fool as she waits for an answer that she hopes won't come. She turns the handle, letting the door swing open, half expecting someone to jump out from behind it. She steps inside and swings the beam around a bedroom, all laid out in dust sheets, the wardrobe standing up like a ghost in the torchlight.

'Hello?' she calls out. 'Anybody home?' She realizes how ridiculous it is to sound so friendly, like some unexpected guest dropping in for tea and a chat. Nobody here. She closes the door.

In the next room along, she finds the same thing, a room full of covered furniture.

'Good evening!' she announces loudly. 'The ball will begin in ten minutes. Food to be served as a picnic on the terrace.' She feels better already. She tries the next room and then the one after that, touching the edges of the furniture with her fingertips, wondering how it might be to have a house so big and not even live in it.

In one room she rips the sheet from a piece of furniture and finds a desk with an embossed red leather top. She opens one of the drawers and finds writing paper, a box of blotter and a fountain pen which she has a sudden urge to steal. She picks it up, turning it in her hand to reveal the name

Reginald Hillingsworth engraved along the barrel. It can't do any harm, can it? Soon the whole place will be nothing but ashes and she likes the idea of a memento, to keep these memories alive in the long nights ahead, when she hardly believes it ever happened at all. A real man wouldn't think twice about it.

She puts it straight back down.

Better hurry up. She runs from the room, continuing along the corridor, flinging open every door and shouting, 'Votes for women!' as she puts her head inside. She never knew it was possible to feel this free. At the end of the corridor, a second staircase takes her up into the servants' quarters where she bangs on the doors. Nobody here either. She takes the stairs down, remembering the layout to the house and where she began. 'Daisy?' she calls out loud from the foot of the staircase. 'Daisy? Where are you?'

A flashlight at the end of the corridor startles her but it's Daisy's voice that calls to her.

'Come on. Time to go.'

Nancy runs to meet her but Daisy is already gone, disappearing into a room where Nancy finds her crouching against a wood-panelled wall. She holds a length of fuse in her hand that she trails out along the floor.

'As soon as I light this, we go straight through that door over there. We can go out the way we came in.'

Nancy nods, a lump in her throat the size of a fist. 'How long do we have before . . . ?'

'A minute. Perhaps less.' She takes a box of matches from

her pocket. 'Go and stand by the door. These fuses can be fickle.' She strikes a match as soon as Nancy retreats. 'Ready?'

'Ready.'

Daisy puts the flame to the fuse and as soon as it starts to fizz she is up and running. 'Go on then!'

Nancy turns for the window, her flashlight picking out the edges of the glass as she ducks back out into the night air. Halfway across the terrace, she turns to check on Daisy who is right behind her. They reach the stone steps and are just passing the lions when there is a loud explosion, a kind of *whoomph* as a fireball expands from the hallway, lighting the broken window with a faint yellow glow.

'Run!' Daisy shouts, and Nancy turns and sprints out across the grass, making for the line of dark trees. Nancy gets there first. She turns to find Daisy who is breathing heavily as she stops under the shadow of a large oak.

'Are you all right?'

'Not really. I'm completely shattered. But I'll make it to the station on time, don't you worry. Just give me a moment.'

They look back at the house. The windows of the ground floor are now a bright fierce orange and Nancy expects to see the silhouettes of men come running with buckets. When no one arrives she almost feels sorry for the building, meeting such a lonely end.

'It's really very beautiful,' Daisy says of the fire. 'But I suppose we shouldn't stay and watch.'

They retreat to the wall, find the gap and slip through, out into the lane.

'What time is it?' Nancy asks after she has checked up and down.

Daisy slips a finger into the pocket of her waistcoat, scooping out the watch on a chain and tilting the face till it catches enough of the moonlight. 'Four forty-five. It's only a short distance to the station, so we have plenty of time.'

They spill into the middle of the lane and begin to walk. Either side of them are tall hedgerows and Nancy wonders how they'll escape if a bobby on a bike comes whistling down after them, but soon enough the hedgerow gives way to fencing and the fields open out, all silver and blue in the faintest of dawn light. From somewhere or other, a horse whinnies in the darkness. The sky behind them has a faint orange glow, like a sun about to rise, and Nancy can't be sure if it's real or from the fire. They pass a single house, still unlit and sleeping. A few hundred yards more and the lane widens out into a proper road where they can see the station, the signal standing out against the moon like a scarecrow.

Daisy checks her watch again. 'We have fifteen minutes yet. Better lie low till we see it arrive.'

To their left, a gate leads into a field and they click it open and step behind the waist-high hedge, crouching together like foxes hiding from the hunt. After a few minutes they hear the strain of a bicycle chain and Daisy takes a look above the hedge.

'Station master,' she tells Nancy as she ducks back down.

He parks his bike and undoes the padlock on the chain across the door. After another five minutes, the two of them decide it's time to go and they creep back out onto the road just as a train shunts down the line toward them.

Daisy straightens her top hat. 'Do I look respectable?'

Nancy reaches out and picks a burr from her tie. 'You'll do.'

They arrive at the station just as the train pulls to a stop and Daisy produces the tickets that Mary gave her before they left the cottage.

'Lovely morning, isn't it?' she says to the station master.

'Beautiful,' he replies, clearly surprised to have customers at such an early hour.

They board the train immediately and find only one other person in the long carriage, a farm hand who alights at the next stop along. Nancy begins to relax as she watches the fields rushing past. Two stops on and they switch trains. This station is bigger than the last and already has a good many people on the platform. Daisy finds a bench and sits in the very middle with her suitcase at her feet.

'We got away with it.'

The two women smile at each.

We got away with it. Nancy turns the phrase in her head as though it is a piece of oak on a lathe, ready to be fashioned into whatever she chooses. Who'd have thought she could do all this and get away with it? She takes another cigarette from the packet she bought yesterday, leans against the wall at her back and begins to smoke, waiting for the train which arrives on time to take them away from Manchester.

30

Usually Clara returned home in the evenings when they would both be there, but this time she arrives on a Thursday afternoon when her mother will be alone with her washing. She uses her key to let herself in and there is a moment, after she has stepped across the threshold, when she has the parlour to herself. The room has long been her father's domain, an arena for the grudges that are played out in the family, but before that there had been a time when it belonged to her and Nancy, a place where they would sit and do their homework or press their noses to the window to see which children were out playing in the street. The room is warm this afternoon. Welcoming.

In the kitchen, her mother has her back turned, bent over the large tin bath, wringing the life out of a shirt.

Clara leans against the frame of the door. 'Hello,' she says.

Her mother startles, glancing quickly behind before straightening up. 'How long have you been there? You frightened the life out of me sneaking up like that. Is something wrong?'

'Nothing's wrong. I wanted to see you. That's all.'

Her mother looks uncertain. 'Your father's not here.'

'Yes, I know. It was you I came to see. I thought we might talk.' She knows her mother will give her short shrift if she has the chance, so she says quickly, 'It's been a long time since we had some time to ourselves.' She steps into the kitchen. 'How about a cup of tea? I can make it. You sit yourself down.'

'I haven't the time to sit down. These clothes won't wash themselves.' Her mother leans back across the tub, takes a nightdress from the water and begins to rub it vigorously.

Clara fetches the kettle. She fills it with water and puts it on to boil. She uses the smaller of the two green teapots, takes some cups from the dresser and two teaspoons from the drawer.

'Something's happened, hasn't it?' her mother says without looking up. 'You wouldn't be here if something hadn't happened.'

Clara thinks she should admit that Nancy is missing but then they will have to talk about her and her sister will fill the room, taking in all the air that Clara wants for herself.

She brings the cups of tea to the table, slides the chairs out from underneath. 'Come and have a minute, Mother.' She reaches out and takes her mother's hand, all wet and wrinkled from the water and colder than she wants it to be. She can still remember, as a little child, how it felt to hold her mother's hand, to have her close and careful, to be in no doubt she was loved.

Her mother shakes herself free but she comes and sits down, wiping her fingers on her apron. 'I don't know what all this fuss is about.'

Clara doesn't know how to begin. For so many years they have trodden paths that only lead away from each other and now she is bewildered. She doesn't know what she wants to say. She takes her purse from her handbag, finds the sovereign and puts it on the table between them. 'I wanted to give you this. It's for yourself. Not for him.' She covers it with a pot of sugar to make it look less indecent.

'I don't want it. I wouldn't know what to do with it.'

'You could do anything. You should treat yourself. Buy a new hat.'

'I don't need a hat.'

'Well a new dress then. There's a new store opened up in the high street . . .'

'And what would I tell your father when he sees me wearing it?'

'Well then. Don't buy anything at all. But put it somewhere safe. You never know when you might need it.'

Her mother drinks her tea then puts the cup back on the saucer. She glances at the washtub.

'I've been seeing a man, Mother. His name's Ted.'

'Have you now?' Her mother is grateful to be on more

certain ground. She takes the pot and pours her cup half full. 'So now we've got to the bottom of it. Has he asked you to marry him?'

'I think he wants to.'

'Do you have to?'

'No, Mother!' Clara resents being asked, resents the way her mother cheapens being told. 'But I don't know what's the right thing.'

'It can't be so hard. You must like him?'

'Did you like Father? I mean, you must have done or we wouldn't be sitting here now.' She thinks of herself and Ted. How it is with the two of them. Perhaps there was a time when her mother was just like her and her father just like Ted? 'How did you know he was the one? Was he good-looking?'

'I don't remember.'

'I don't think you've ever told me how the two of you met.'

'I don't remember that either.'

'But you must do!'

'He was just there, Clara,' her mother says defensively. 'He grew up a couple of streets from me so he was always about.'

'And what made you want to marry him? Did *you* have to?'

'It's what people do, Clara. They've always done it and they always will. For better or for worse.'

'But there should be some joy in it? Shouldn't there?'

The offence stiffens her mother's chin. 'Has he got a good job, this man of yours?'

'I've got a good job, Mother! Actually that's part of the problem. I've got a job that I'm good at. Or at least I thought I was.'

But her mother has never approved of Clara working. She reaches out for the sugar pot and moves it aside then slides the sovereign back to Clara. 'I don't want it. You keep it for yourself. Or give it to your sister. There's bound to be something she wants with it.'

Clara thinks of her bicycle, of how giving this meant longer to wait for that beautiful machine.

Her mother returns to the washtub, taking up again with the nightgown that she lifts and soaks, lifts and soaks, using her knuckles to rub at the hem of it. 'I'll tell your father you dropped by. He's always interested in the both of you.'

Clara puts the sovereign back into her purse, busying herself with the clasp on her bag.

'When will we be meeting Ted, then?' her mother asks. 'You'll need to let me know so I can get some cake in. I don't want him thinking we go without.'

'I'm not sure.' Clara realizes that this is currency, that she has used the secret of Ted to buy her mother's favour and now her mother is cashing it in. 'Soon enough, Mother.'

'You can bring Nancy back round too. It's about time she paid us a visit. She's always been ungrateful, that girl.'

'Nancy's gone, Mother. I don't know where. She left the prison and I don't know where she is.'

267

Her mother's hands stop long enough to take the news in. 'What do you mean, you don't know where she is?'

'She's safe. I know that because she wrote and told me but I don't have an address for her. She's taken up with the suffragettes, at least that's what I think. So she could be anywhere and we're not likely to find out anytime soon either.'

If there's one thing her mother disapproves of more than women who work, it's women who protest about their lot in life. Or perhaps she's thinking how her husband will react once she tells him.

She puts her hands back into the bath tub. 'Well then, just yourselves then.'

'Yes, Mother,' she says, 'just the two of us.'

31

Nancy puts her face into the wind that comes in off the sea. It is stronger on the path that climbs up from the beach and she closes her eyes, turning her head from left to right, feeling the salt scrub away at her skin. She lifts her chin, exposing the softness in her neck. She undoes the top button of her shirt. They have been in Tenby a week since they arrived from Manchester. A few months of this would have her looking like a sailor but there won't be time for that. Daisy is already champing at the bit. She says they'll be gone before another week is out, whether or not she gets a letter of instruction.

A motorcar approaches on the road behind, its engine laboured on the upward climb, and she waits for it to pass, then turns for home, tapping the borrowed walking stick in rhythm with her feet. She pulls the cap closer to her eyes as she passes under the monkey puzzle tree which frames the view down to the pretty little harbour. Mrs Evans – who refers to herself as 'only recently widowed', though it's been five years since Arthur passed away in a motorcycle accident – will be starting on the kippers and scrambled eggs. She watches a skiff slip out across the water. Another five minutes and she'll drop down into the town, passing by the doors of the pink and blue terrace that looks out at the sea. She takes her cap off as she closes the front door to the guesthouse.

'How was that, dear?' Mrs Evans comes through into the hallway carrying a silver teapot.

'Lovely,' she says. She has only seen the sea once before, on a holiday to Whitstable, where her father had put her on a donkey and bought her a stick of rock both the evenings she was there. She joins Daisy at the table in the big bay window as Mrs Evans settles the teapot down between them, then turns the milk jug so the handle points to her instead of Daisy.

'You should have gone with her, Miss Divine. Get some colour in your cheeks.'

Daisy has not set foot outside the guest house since they arrived.

'I can't run the risk of being seen,' she says, repeating what she said yesterday.

'Oh, my dear, I doubt anyone in Tenby would recognize you. We don't bother much with the theatre. Or the news, for that matter. That's London business to most of the people here, though of course, some of us like to keep abreast.'

'I'm sure that's true, Mrs Evans, but it would only take

one. A single soul with an enlightened mind and I could be returned to jail.' Daisy reaches round for the milk. 'A woman passed this very window in a fashionable hat only half an hour ago. So you see, anything is possible.'

Mrs Evans flushes red and takes herself back to the kitchen.

'That was mean,' Nancy tells her.

'What was mean?'

'Well, rude then.'

In the hallway, there are only photographs of Arthur, a sprig of rosemary on top of each, but there are portraits of Mrs Pankhurst on the bedside tables in both their bedrooms and Nancy thinks that shows a woman who knows her own mind as well as a little bit about the world. She pours herself a cup of tea.

'If we have kippers again, I think I'll scream.' Daisy scrapes her knife across the toast. She looks particularly fine when she frowns, like a storm still out at sea, all the beauty of her mixed in with the possibility of danger. This morning, framed by the light from the window, she looks like a portrait, a proper picture in a gallery. Nancy could sit and look at her all day.

Daisy notices her staring. 'Are you *ever* going to wear a dress again?'

'I can't decide. It's difficult with my hair so short.'

'It's not difficult. You wear a wig. I will send for one from London . . .'

'Please don't. I wouldn't wear it.'

'Wouldn't you? How very independent. I've noticed quite a change in you since we arrived.'

'I like it here.'

'You can stay if you like. Mrs Muggins has taken a shine to you, I can tell.'

Mrs Evans returns with the kippers and eggs. 'There we are now.' She sets the plates down proudly as the letterbox rattles and she hurries out, scoops the letters from the mat with a complaint about the state of her back, then returns with a fistful of envelopes. 'There's something here for you, Miss Divine. Probably the one you've been so anxious about.' She hovers behind the chair but Daisy lays the envelope down on the table in front of her.

She picks up her knife and fork. 'Thank you, Mrs Evans. These kippers look especially good this morning. Oh and look, is that a ray of sunshine? Perhaps I will take a walk this morning after all.'

Mrs Evans forces a smile. 'I'll be in the kitchen if you need anything else.' She closes the door behind her.

'Well?' Nancy asks as soon as they're alone. 'Aren't you going to open it?'

'I most certainly will.' Daisy pushes the kipper round her plate. 'Where do you suggest I walk if I don't want to parade myself round town?'

'There's a path that winds up above the harbour. You won't meet anyone.'

'You'll have to take me.'

'I've only just got back.'

Daisy reaches for the clutch bag on the chair beside her. 'That reminds me, I have something here for you.' She produces an envelope and hands it across the table. 'You must keep this safe.'

Nancy thinks immediately of Clara, that she might have somehow found a way to write. She opens the letter and reads. It is from a Miss Connolly. The address is in London. It starts, 'To my darling Nancy, I hope this finds you well,' and then continues to tell her about some people she's never heard of. Peter is having an awful time of it at work. The children are loving their new school mistress and of course, Bertie will be home again at Easter, so that will be a god-send. She sends her love and hopes to see Nancy soon.

'What is this?' She hands the letter to Daisy. 'It must be a mistake.'

Daisy gives it back without a second glance. 'It's the address of your contact. Keep it safe. You should write to her in a similar style whenever you need to. Don't include anything incriminating and always give an address at which you can be reached. That is all she is interested in.'

Nancy reads the name and address again. 'But why do I need this?'

'So they can keep tabs on you, of course.'

'No, I mean, why should I need my own contact? I've always presumed that was you.'

'You belong to the cause, Nancy. Not to me. This shows we have accepted you as one of our own. It's a mark of trust.'

'But surely it's unnecessary if I'll always be with you.'

'You should take nothing for granted. I could be arrested at any moment and besides, you are not my lapdog any more.' She wipes her mouth with the napkin, perhaps thinking she has been unkind. 'This assures your independence. Now, if we are going on this walk I need to fetch my hat and coat.' She stands up from the table. 'Well come on then! We need to go while there's a break in the unrelenting misery. As soon as the sun realizes it has arrived in Wales it is bound to leave.' She takes her own letter from the table, puts it into her clutch and goes out into the hallway.

Nancy pushes the last forkful of scrambled egg around the rim of her plate, wondering what all this is about. It should feel good to get a letter like this. Like being promoted in your job. She should be pleased, she knows she should. And yet she feels she is being abandoned. That's the feeling she can't get rid of. That the person she loves is about to hurt her.

Daisy puts her head around the door. 'Well come on then. I'm not going to find this blessed walk on my own, am I?'

32

The oystermen come in off their smacks, hauling rowboats up onto the shingle. They shoulder heavy sacks to the edge of the beach while Clara and Ted watch from the roadside. She is fascinated by the sea, always has been, though she has never been able to hold the memory of it exactly. Not like it is. Not like this. The fish stalls on the Camden Road don't smell fresh enough and there is nothing in London like the sound of a wave breaking on a shore, the soft crumple of applause as the pebbles suck the water down.

She had met Ted at seven o'clock that morning, found him waiting under the station clock at Victoria. 'Where are we going then?'

Ted had waved the train tickets under her nose. 'It's a surprise.'

But Clara knew full well.

She had mentioned the seaside only the week before,

told him of the family holiday in Whitstable, where she and Nancy rode on the backs of donkeys and ate ice cream every day. She hadn't seen the sea since then and she told Ted how she missed it, knowing full well what he is like, though she had still let him cover her eyes so she wouldn't see the destination on the board at the front of the platform.

She had bought a new bag for the occasion, larger than her handbag but not so indecent in size to suggest that she has planned to stay overnight. It held a change of undergarments, a second pair of stockings and a douche, wrapped in a woollen shawl together with the small bottle of vinegar and a packet of baking soda.

Ted puts his arm through the strap of the new bag as he reaches for her waist. 'Come on now.' He draws her away from the sea. 'We ought to look for a place to eat or we'll run out of time.'

'There's a place not far from here,' she tells him. 'We passed it only a few minutes back, the hotel with the dining room that looks out to sea. I'm sure it was where we stayed before.'

'We can try that then.'

'That'd be nice. But not yet, Ted. Let's keep walking to the edge of the bay. I want to see what's around the corner. Come on. It won't take long.'

They are only a short distance from the Tankerton Slopes, where her father had sent her mother with Nancy, telling them to fetch him the last pebble from the very end of the beach. Clara had wanted to go there too, not back to her father's room at the hotel. She wants to go there now, not for a pebble but as a kind of reclamation. A rewriting of history with her own hand.

The two of them walk out to the edge of town. Once they round the bay, she can see the beach stretch away into the fading light and she wonders how far her mother went and why she stayed away so long. She sits on a bench, patting the wooden slats beside her, and when Ted sits, she kisses him, her hand stroking the back of his neck, like tickling a trout before you catch him.

She wonders what he would say if he knew what she had in her bag, if he knew that all he has to do is ask and she'll give herself to him. She kisses him harder and he responds but then pulls away as though he doesn't trust himself.

He makes a joke of it. 'Blimey, you must be starving,' and wipes his mouth with the back of his hand then stands up from the bench. 'We ought to think about getting back.'

'It'd be nice not to have to, wouldn't it? I mean to stay till tomorrow. If we could. I don't have to be at work till the evening.'

Ted looks uncertain. 'I told my father I'd be back tonight. He'll be worried if I don't turn up. Either that or he'll think I've been up to no good.'

'It wouldn't do any harm, would it?'

'I don't like to worry him.'

'But we could, couldn't we? If we wanted to.' She wants to tell him that the hotel has a sign in the window for vacancies but she can't do that, can't make it sound like it is

277

her idea. It should come from him. If it doesn't come from him then she'll sound like a loose woman and anyway, she needs Ted to feel in control. That's the whole point of it. To give him what he wants.

Ted stands awkwardly. He puts his hands in the pockets of his trousers. 'I couldn't afford it. Not together with a proper meal.'

Clara has money in her purse for the both of them but today is Ted's treat. He made a point of telling her. So she needs to do it properly.

'I'd be happy with a bag of chips,' she tells him. Now she sounds cheap. She reaches out and takes his hand. 'I'd rather spend more time with you than have a posh meal out. I seem to remember the food there isn't very good anyway.'

'Then let's do it properly. I mean if we want to stay over then we ought to plan it out. Make sure we don't upset anyone. That way we won't draw attention to ourselves.' He pulls her up from the bench and brings her face close to his. 'I can wait. In fact I'd rather wait. If we're going to do it, we should do it right and get engaged.'

But that's just what Clara wanted to avoid.

They walk back into town. The hotel looks less inviting than it did when they passed earlier, the front of it unlit in the darkness and a couple of old blokes standing at the bar.

'Let's not bother, Ted,' she tells him, feeling defeated.

'Are you sure?'

'I'm certain.' All she wants now is to get back to London.

'You're right. We'd be better to save the money for the next time. We can come again, can't we?'

'Of course we can.'

'Well then, let's do that. We can find something quick to eat at the station.' She buttons up her coat and readjusts the bag on her shoulder so that it swings behind her hip. She tries one last time to please him. 'What are you doing Wednesday? I saw my mother the other day and she's invited us back for tea. I've got the afternoon off and you could come after work, couldn't you? Only I need to let her know. She'll want to lay on something special.'

She hasn't seen Ted look so happy in a long while. So there then. She's managed to give him what he wants. By doing things properly.

'I'll make sure I've got a good suit on.'

'The grey one?'

'That's the only other one I've got.'

She reaches out and straightens his tie. 'You can wear your homburg.'

'I think I will,' Ted says. 'Yes. I think it'll make just the right impression.'

33

'Mrs Evans, you have been too kind!' Daisy makes a full turn in front of the mirror and assesses the alterations to her mourning gown. She puts her hands on her hips. 'I have to say, you've managed the waistline beautifully.'

'Against my better judgement, as you know, but if you don't mind being scandalous . . .'

'I love a bit of scandal, Mrs Evans. You don't know how long it's been.'

'Daisy!' Nancy scolds her.

'Never you mind, Nancy. I've had time enough to get accustomed to her ways and she means no harm in it.' Mrs Evans takes the hat from its box – a modest toque with a band of black leaves and a veil of lace. 'I suppose this will do well enough.'

Daisy stoops to allow her to pin the hat in place then unfastens the veil and lifts it down over her face. 'It's really very dignified. I shall make sure everything is returned to you as soon as we arrive.'

Mrs Evans shakes her head. 'There's no need for that.' Her eyes fall on a picture of Arthur standing on a beach, holding a sea bass by its tail. 'I won't have need of it again, Miss Divine.'

Nancy fastens a pin into the black crepe armband on the sleeve of her suit. 'I'll make certain she behaves appropriately while she's wearing your dress, Mrs Evans.'

'I know you will, dear.' Mrs Evans pats the back of Nancy's hand before she leads them out into the hall where their bags are already packed and waiting. 'Please give my regards to Mrs Pankhurst when you see her.'

'I didn't realize you knew her?'

'No, Miss Divine. Not in person. But I did have the honour of once attending a rally and to hear her speak is to have a friend for life.'

'Exactly.' Daisy shakes her hand.

Nancy kisses her cheek.

'I shall certainly miss all this excitement,' Mrs Evans tells them and she wipes away a tear with her little lace handkerchief as she closes her front door.

The two of them make a strange pair on the slow train to Swansea, the young man looking taciturn and the grieving widow, altogether far too full of life. They change trains, securing a carriage for themselves on the journey to Reading.

'I shall make a terrible show of weeping if anyone looks like they might come in.' Daisy settles herself into a seat by the window as Nancy heaves their cases into the rack above. 'Thank God we've left the back of beyond. That's all I can say.' She lifts her veil and looks for Nancy's approval. 'I'm going to tell them. From now on I will only lodge in cities and if they ever send me to the country, I shall simply refuse. We have to draw the line somewhere. Don't you agree? Nancy? Are you listening to me?'

Nancy has taken her seat and is looking out of the window. She nods her head, trying to give the impression she is listening when in fact she's doing nothing of the sort.

'I don't know what's got into you.' Daisy pretends to admire the view, taking an interest in a herd of cows. 'You must be tired from all that fresh air.'

Nancy fixes on a tree standing alone in the middle of a field. It is replaced by a river that meanders. A solitary man fishing. She has a feeling something's wrong, but she can't put her finger on why that should be. She's felt it since the letters arrived last week, a sense that something between them has changed. One moment Daisy is distant, caught up in her own thoughts and yet unwilling to talk about them. And if she is not aloof then she's like she is now, trying to jolly things along. But that's just the way she is. It could have nothing to do with Nancy. It could be some other matter entirely, like news of her daughter or a new young man she has made plans to meet. So perhaps Nancy is imagining it.

Perhaps it is nothing at all. Yet the feeling persists that Daisy is slipping away from her.

'Did I ever tell you that policemen have to pay for their helmets if they lose them?'

'Pardon?'

'Policemen.' Daisy fixes her with a determined stare. 'If a policeman tries to arrest you, knock his helmet off. Chances are he'll scurry after it thereby giving you an opportunity to escape. It's a useful thing to know.'

'I'll try to remember.'

Daisy nods. She reaches for her bag, finds her purse and opens it. She puts a banknote into Nancy's hand. 'This is for your expenses. Make it last as long as you can. No need for receipts. Mention money to Miss Connolly when you need some more and she'll understand.'

Nancy has never had a banknote in her purse before. All her life has been coppers and small change. Paper money isn't for the likes of her. She could do anything she wants with it and most people would be pleased, but it makes Nancy scared. She tries to hand it back. 'It's too much.'

'It can't be too much since you don't yet know what you need it for.' Daisy snaps her purse shut and turns to face the window.

The last time Daisy put a piece of paper into her hand it felt like they were sealing a bond. This feels like breaking it. Nancy folds the note and puts it in her purse beside the tickets for the train.

They alight at Reading and the porter directs them to a

modest-looking guesthouse that has vacancies. Daisy asks for two singles and of course, it wouldn't be right for them to share, but their rooms are on different floors, an unfortunate occurrence that only seems to exaggerate the distance between them. Before they part, Daisy hands Nancy a letter with the name of their contact in Leatherhead, telling her to memorize the meeting place and the address of a house in the East End where she will escape to once it is done. The intention is to set fire to the clubhouse of a golf course in the constituency of an MP noted for his objections to their cause. Nancy was pleased when Daisy told her the plans yesterday. It felt intimate. But now it feels the opposite.

She closes the door to her room and sits on the edge of her single bed. She is tired. So very tired and yet all she has done is sit on a train. When she closes her eyes, she aches all over. In her joints and bones. An anxiety that nags at her. She lies back on her bed, spreading her arms out up above her head and suddenly thinks of her mother, an image of her standing at their kitchen table, before she turns and leaves the room. What a strange thing to remember! It's nothing at all, no memory to speak of, and yet here it is, coming into her head. And there have been others too, all of her family, arriving like spectres to knock on her door then standing there mute. Waiting for her.

The thought makes her feel weak and Miss Birnstingl told her that Daisy abhors weakness.

She finds the letter with the details for tomorrow and reads them carefully, testing herself till she knows them off by heart. This is important. It is a chance for her to be useful. To make Daisy need her just as much as she needs Daisy.

She takes herself to bed, deciding the rest will do her good. Tomorrow she will be stronger.

Daisy misses breakfast. A waitress delivers a note to Nancy's table saying they will meet for a late lunch. Nancy calls the woman back to the table. 'Has she checked out?'

'Oh no, miss. She asked to be allowed to lie in this morning.'

Nancy chooses to believe the waitress then doubts herself. After breakfast, she goes out of her way to walk past Daisy's room and then she does it again after another hour, hoping that they might meet by chance or else she might find a maid who can tell her if Daisy is still sleeping. She resists the urge to knock on Daisy's door but arrives early for lunch and takes a table that allows her a view of the front desk. By the time Daisy arrives, she could almost kiss her.

'You look better for a good sleep.'

'Thank you. I was very comfortable. You seem to have cheered up too.'

'I think I have.'

'Good.'

'I memorized the details from the letter.'

'Did you? I didn't think you would. I thought you rather resented being asked.'

'Not at all.'

'Tell me the name of the golf course.'

'Hillybrooks Golf Course. On Sandyman Lane.'

'And our contact?'

'Miss Miles.'

'Good. I have planned for you to be in charge on this. I think it's time you were given the responsibility. Miss Miles will accompany you and be your look out. She will take her orders from you, unlike our bomb maker who takes orders from no one and will only deliver to me in person. That means I will have to accompany you to Leatherhead. There will be others too, a delegation from the local branch who intend to paint a slogan across the eighteenth green.'

'But you will be there with me?'

'I will return to London as soon as the bomb is collected.'

'To the address in the East End?'

Daisy looks embarrassed. 'I'm needed elsewhere. Nancy . . . the house in the East End . . . they're good people. They will look after you.'

Nancy can't stop the tear from falling. Daisy frowns. She finds a tissue from her bag, then holds it to Nancy's cheek as though she doesn't know what to do with it. Nancy takes it, wiping her face before she blows her nose. 'You've been planning this, haven't you? I knew you were. When were you going to tell me?'

'I have just told you.'

'When will I see you again?'

'Nancy . . .'

'What?'

'Oh, don't be so melodramatic! I'm sure I didn't teach you that!' Daisy checks her watch.

'But you are going to leave me? That's the point of this, isn't it?'

'I leave everybody, Nancy. You know that.'

Nancy raises her voice. 'Then why did you ever let me stay in the first place?'

Daisy takes hold of Nancy's hand. 'You said you wanted to be like me,' she says quietly. 'Well, this is me. It's who I am.'

'Selfish?'

'Yes. Sometimes. But always myself.' She takes her hand away. 'Besides, I thought you wanted to be independent?'

'I don't want to be alone.'

'Often the two go hand in hand.'

'Is it because I bore you?'

'No, Nancy. You don't bore me. You just don't need me any more.'

'But I do. I do need you.' She tastes a sudden bitterness on her tongue. 'How soon before you tell your daughter who you are?'

'Nancy, that isn't important and I'd rather not talk about it.'

'She won't want to know you. You know that, don't you? I wouldn't want to know you. Not if it was me.'

'That was spiteful.'

Nancy crumples. 'I can't do this without you.'

'Anyone can set fire to things, Nancy, and an understudy always suffers from nerves. It will be all right on the night. You wait and see. You will be magnificent. Quite the leading lady.'

But Nancy thinks that isn't what she meant at all.

*

They take the train to Leatherhead and arrive after dark. Daisy has become like Clara, an older sister who points out useful things like the road that leads to the golf club or the direction the police are likely to come from once they are alerted. They wait at one end of a bridge that spans the River Mole and they have nothing to say to one another.

Daisy checks her watch. 'Maude won't be late. You can always rely on her.'

'You should leave.'

'I can't leave.' Daisy looks out across the bridge. 'She won't give you the bomb. She says it has to be me.'

A few minutes more of silence and Nancy says, 'Well, she's not coming.'

'She'll be here,' Daisy tells her. 'She probably thinks you're a man and has taken fright. Look. Her she comes now.'

Nancy turns and sees a woman trudging toward the other side of the bridge, a bag of groceries in each hand. She gives Daisy the one with a couple of leeks sprouting from the top.

'Hello, Maude.' Daisy nods at the leeks. 'It was turnips the last time, wasn't it? I hope you don't want them back.'

'They're from the garden. You should hang on to them and make yourself a soup. Be a shame to blow the buggers up.'

'It's good of you to throw a supper in. This is Nancy, by the way. She's in charge tonight, so remember her face. You might be working for her again.'

Maude glances at Nancy disapprovingly. 'Does she always dress as a man?'

'If I choose to,' Nancy tells her pointedly.

'Then I'll know what to look out for.' Maude looks Nancy firmly in the eye, sizing her up and committing her to memory. 'Well, it doesn't do to stand about talking.' She turns around and trudges back across the bridge.

The two of them head back the way they came, each step like a metronome, pacing them till the end of the piece. Nancy knows that now there is nothing to stop Daisy leaving. No reason for her not to take the first train out of town.

They find the road that leads up to the golf course. A young woman waits at the junction. Beside her, two bicycles are leaning against the lamp post.

'Miss Miles?' asks Daisy.

'Nancy?'

'I am surprised you don't recognize me. Actually, this is Nancy.'

Miss Miles laughs nervously. 'Oh, I do beg your pardon. How silly of me not to realize!'

Daisy hands Nancy the grocery bag then kisses her on the cheek. 'You'll be good, darling. You can do it.'

'Anyone can set fire to things.'

'But most people don't.' She puts her hand on Nancy's shoulder. 'You're one of the special ones.' She pulls away quickly. 'We shall see each other again. I'm sure we will. It'd be a shame if we didn't.' She offers her a handshake. 'Goodbye, Nancy.'

'Goodbye, Daisy.'

And then she walks away.

Miss Miles swings the handlebars of a bike toward Nancy. 'We ought to hurry up. The others have already been there half an hour.'

'I can't ride a bike,' Nancy tells her. 'I've never learnt how.'

'Really! Gosh. I hadn't thought of that. I suppose I better give you a backy and hope nobody sees us.' She wrestles the bike around and stands forward, offering Nancy the saddle. 'You can put the bag in the basket on the front.'

Nancy thinks she shouldn't let go of the bag, the way Daisy wouldn't let her take it in Manchester, but she'll have trouble staying on a bike as it is, so she puts it in the basket and holds tightly to Miss Miles's waist as she scoots along the darkened lane. At the clubhouse there are four bicycles discarded on the ground and they find the women already kneeling on the eighteenth green, painting large white letters on the lawn.

'Right, we better get to it.' Miss Miles takes her to the back of the building, a single storey timber house with a veranda that overlooks the course. 'I thought you might be able to break in here. What do you think?'

Nancy says she may as well. She feels numb, as though she's not really part of what's happening.

'I'll keep watch out at the front,' Miss Miles says and then takes herself off.

Nancy looks about for a rock but there's nothing like

that on the veranda. She sees a row of clay flowerpots, picks one up and throws it. The inside of the clubhouse is a large single room with clusters of tables and chairs. She puts the bag behind the bar and lights the fuse. She walks back outside and stands at the back of the green feeling none of the excitement she did at the manor house in Manchester.

The fire has already spread to the roof where there is a weather vane with a cockerel that twists away from the heat. From here she can see the light from the town spread out before her and beyond that there is darkness. She suddenly feels very small. She puts her hand in her pocket, finds the pack of cigarettes and stands smoking as the fire becomes brighter. She becomes slightly nauseous. Perhaps it is the cigarette. She hears the whistle of a train heading out across the countryside. Even with a fire, the world can be a cold place.

The women on the green have finished their graffiti.

'Leave the pots and brushes where they are,' calls Miss Miles, 'we need to leave now.'

Nancy stays where she is. 'Don't worry about me,' she tells them. 'I like to watch it burn. I'll find my own way home.' She lights another cigarette then listens to the scrape and rattle of bicycles being lifted, the scrunch of tyres setting off on the road and then the silence, blistered by the crackle and pop of burning wood.

She is alone on stage. It is the final scene and she is standing in the spotlight but she has forgotten her lines and there is no one here to prompt her and she can't improvise, she can't act. How did she ever come to believe she was an actor?

Soon there is a faraway bell. Not loud but insistent. Another bicycle, a squeal of its brakes and a crash as the rider lets it fall to the ground. A whistle is blown. The constable who arrives at the back of the clubhouse is on his own. He discovers Nancy standing alone on the grass with a leek in each hand.

'Did you see them, sir?'

'Who?'

'The women that did this.'

'How do you know it was women?'

'Because . . .' He points at the large white letters, glowing golden from the firelight.

Votes for Women.

'So you're a detective?'

The policeman looks at her queerly. 'Can you be of any help, sir?'

'I did it, Officer,' she tells him. He doesn't believe her. She can see it in his face. She takes off her cap and flutters her eyelashes at him. 'I did it all by myself.'

34

Ted has bought flowers, a bunch of daffodils with the stalks wrapped in bright green paper. 'They're for your mother. I want to get some cigarettes for your father too. Only I want to get the right brand. No point in giving him the wrong ones.'

'They'll be the right ones if they're free.' Clara thinks he looks nervous. 'We're only going for a cup of tea.' She straightens the collar of his shirt. 'You look nice though. Didn't you wear that suit the first time we went out?'

'I keep it for special occasions.'

'You'll probably get married in it.'

'I probably will.'

'Well whoever it is, she'll be lucky.'

Ted looks confused but she's only pulling his leg, giving with one hand then taking it back with the other.

He sees a kiosk at the side of the street and hurries over. 'Here. What does he smoke then?'

She points to the Navy Silk Cut. 'Either those or the Redford's, the ones with the Union Jack on the front.'

Ted buys a packet of each and puts them in his inside pocket. 'What does he like to talk about?'

Clara snorts. 'I haven't got the foggiest idea. Only don't mention Nancy. If he knows already then he won't like it one little bit and if he doesn't know then you don't want to be the one to tell him.'

'Right. Yes of course. I'll just play along then.'

'Here. This is the street. Our house is halfway along on the right there.'

Ted looks down the row of terraced cottages. 'It's pretty much the same as ours. Two up, two down? Has it got a kitchen out the back?'

'That's right.'

'Well they're very nice. Very nice indeed.'

Clara has the impression he'd be happy living here his whole life and she gets a sudden urge to start running, to flee as fast as she can and not stop till she's somewhere different, somewhere she doesn't recognize at all.

Ted fiddles with the cuffs of his jacket as they wait for the door. Her mother answers in her Sunday best, a navy-blue jacket and a skirt that she's had ever since Clara can remember. She brings them into the empty parlour where Ted shakes her hand firmly.

'These are for you, Mrs Cooper.'

'Flowers? Well aren't they pretty? We don't often have flowers but I've got just the right vase for them.' Her mother takes Clara by the wrist. 'Would you mind giving me a hand in the kitchen? I think it's up on one of the high shelves and I'm not so steady on the chair as I used to be. We won't be a moment, Ted.'

She walks Clara into the kitchen, closing the door behind her to reveal her father, waiting for her, still in his shirt sleeves and collarless.

He takes hold of Clara's upper arm and hauls her closer to his mouth. 'I've told your mother not to mention your sister,' he mutters in her ear. 'Better that he doesn't know or he'll run a mile.'

Her mother's face has already turned sour, as though it's Clara and not Nancy who has brought bad luck on the family.

Clara pulls her arm free and takes a chair to the shelf where they keep the vase.

Her father follows her, still speaking in an urgent whisper. 'What does he do then, this man of yours?'

'He works in a bank.'

'Does he?'

'Nothing too fancy. He's behind the counter, but he thinks he might have prospects. Why don't you go and ask him yourself? He doesn't bite.'

Her father snarls at the suggestion he might be afraid. 'I don't mind if he does. Nothing to be scared of in my own home.' He takes himself away into the parlour.

Her mother holds the back of the chair as Clara steps up and reaches for the vase. 'We've got tea and sandwiches.

Pickle and cheese. And a Victoria sponge. But I want you gone within the hour. Your father doesn't want to be disturbed any longer than he has to and I've got a mountain of housework still to do.'

'Isn't he pleased then?'

'He's got better things to think about.'

'That'll be fine, Mother. We've both got things we want to do as well.'

She hands the vase down to her mother who dusts it off with a cloth. Clara replaces the chair at the table then goes into the parlour, fearful of leaving Ted for too long with her father in one of his moods. She finds the two of them by the fire, her father in his armchair and Ted in her mother's seat. The packets of cigarettes are on the mantlepiece, the first of them already opened.

'So you think there'll be a war then, Mr Cooper.'

'Bound to be if they keep up the insults.' Her father leans back in his chair. 'It was the same with the Boers. You can't be all talk. You've got to back it up or they'll think you're going soft.'

Clara goes back to the kitchen where her mother is warming the teapot with a swill of hot water. She lays the tray with cups and saucers, collects the jug of milk from the window sill and goes to the drawer where they keep the silver teaspoons.

'What are they talking about?' her mother asks anx-iously.

'The war.'

'What war? You go back through, will you? I can manage the tray.'

Clara takes a chair back into the parlour so she has something to sit on.

Her father breathes out a cloud of smoke that hangs in the air above the fireplace. 'You'll be signing up then?'

'I suppose I will if it comes to it.' Ted leans forward, flicking ash into the fire the way Mr Cooper had a moment before.

Clara remains standing. She didn't know he smoked. At least he never has with her.

'You'll need to be married within the year then. I wouldn't want my daughter left on the shelf without a pension.'

'Father!' Clara glares at him.

'It's better to be frank about these things.'

'I agree,' says Ted. 'There's a lot of things to consider.'

'And you shouldn't go thinking we've got a pot of money for you either. It's hard enough to get by as things stand.'

Clara feels like she's being packaged up and parcelled off, like a ledger of goods to be signed away and taken on by someone else. 'I'm on a decent salary myself, thank you, Father.'

'That won't last though, will it?'

Her mother enters with the tray of tea. 'Fetch in the sandwiches, would you, Clara?'

Clara stays put behind the chair. 'I've got enough saved up to marry when I choose but I won't be deciding on anything until I've bought myself a bicycle.'

Her father throws his eyes at her like a dagger.

'I want a new one too. They've got them for six pounds three shillings in a shop in town.'

'Waste of bloody money,' he spits. 'I won't have it in the house.'

'You won't have to now that I'm gone.'

Her mother comes between them with a plate of sandwiches that she fetched from the kitchen herself. 'I doubt that Ted will put up with that kind of nonsense,' she says and offers him the plate.

Her father takes two. 'What do you think of women riding bicycles then, Ted?'

'It's not something I've given a lot of thought to.'

'Father thinks they accentuate the female form,' Clara tells him. 'And women shouldn't be seen to have legs, should they, Father?'

'Whatever next?' says her mother.

'Only hussies ride bicycles.'

'And suffragettes, Father. I see them on their bicycles all the time.'

Her father stands up suddenly. He'd have hit her for that if they weren't in company. She can see the violence itching at his fingers. He reaches above the mantlepiece for his cigarettes.

'I expect we could save for a car,' Ted says quickly. 'I hear they're only going to get cheaper and my father thinks in twenty years' time we'll all be using them one way or the other.' He smiles at Clara weakly. 'You'll look lovely sitting in the passenger seat.'

'The sooner we have a war the better.' Her father sits back down. 'It'll put a stop to all this nonsense. What did you say your father does, Ted?'

'He's a foreman.'

'Is he?'

'Yes. A metalwork factory. Not a large place but with a good reputation.'

'Still. He might have a bit put by.'

'There's Victoria sponge still to come.' Mother collects the plates then stands over Ted as he finishes his sandwich. 'Clara, will you take these through and bring the cake from the table?'

Clara does as she is told. In the kitchen, she wipes away the crumbs then rinses and dries the plates. What was she thinking of, bringing Ted back here? She can't remember why on earth she wanted to do it.

She brings back the cake and serves it herself. 'We better be going once we've finished this.'

'Yes,' says her mother and her father stays silent.

'It's been very nice,' Ted tells them. 'And this is the best Victoria sponge I've had in a long while.'

'Yes,' says her mother.

'Right then,' says her father.

When they shut the front door, Clara walks so fast that Ted has a struggle to keep up.

'Clara?' he calls her back. 'Clara?' He takes her arm to slow her pace. 'C'mon now.'

'Don't you dare tell me how nice they are!'

'Right. I won't then. Well you did warn me.'

'Right.'

He puts a hand around her waist. 'I don't mind you bringing a bicycle into the house.'

'Then you should have said so.'

'I was trying to keep the peace.'

'Keeping your head down more like it. Anyway, what house? We're not about to get married. We're not even engaged.'

'I'd have asked by now if I thought you'd say yes.'

'Ted, don't.' She walks away towards the main road.

Ted catches up with her. 'I won't ask then. At least not until you've bought that bicycle and need somewhere to keep it.'

'Ted? Do you wish sometimes that things could be different? That we could be different?'

'How do you mean?'

'Don't you get scared at the thought of becoming like your parents?'

'I wouldn't mind. They're decent enough people. You'll have to meet them then you can see for yourself. I'd like you to. If you want to.'

'Perhaps,' she says. 'In a little while, when I'm ready, but not straight away.'

'No,' says Ted. 'Not straight away.'

35

Nancy knows she should say something at her trial. Daisy wouldn't think twice about it. The last time she was in court she told the judge exactly what she thought of him. But Nancy lacks the projection needed for such a stage and anyway, she doesn't trust her mouth. It makes her vulnerable, like a secret tunnel into a walled city, and she has hardly said a word since she confessed to that policeman. She thinks instead of tiny creatures with hard shells. Of beetles and crabs. A tortoise. Anything that retreats inward and resists. The judge passes sentence without an interruption.

The policeman who brings her from the dock is kind to her. 'Mind the step there.' He holds her arm gently as he leads her down a set of stairs. She thinks he's after a little piece of her heart to make him feel better about himself.

A second policeman waits at a heavy door. His keys are already in the lock. 'We've got a coach ready to go.'

'That's a relief,' her policeman tells her. 'Better to get it over and done with.'

If he knew how the familiarity of the locks and doors is a comfort to her, he might stop trying to wheedle her out with reassurances. The Black Maria is parked in the yard with its rear door open.

'It's unpleasant,' he says, 'but not as frightening as it looks unless you hate small spaces.'

'I prefer them.'

'Well then, you should be fine. The journey will take about an hour all told, depending on whether the driver has to pick up along the way.' He smiles at her in a fatherly manner. If she knocks his helmet off he'd have to grovel at her feet. He takes her arm again and guides her up into the van. 'First open door you come to, go inside and sit yourself down. I'll follow you in to lock up.'

The van has a passage the width of a man. She passes three locked doors, arrives at one which hangs open and goes inside. She sits down. Her shoulders touch both walls.

The policeman appears at her door. 'Good luck,' he says before closing it. He turns the key in the lock. She hears him step down from the van. 'All ready to go, Bob.'

She folds her hands into her lap, tucks her feet under the bench and sits in the darkness, as still as a whelk in the crevice of a rock. When her toes begin to tingle, she resents them and keeps her feet where they are, refusing to give in to their complaining. When they become numb she thinks, there, that'll show you, and enjoys the small sense of victory.

The van comes to a stop. Voices. A woman singing an old song that she's heard before from gypsies selling rosemary. Another key in a lock. Then on again. Stop. A rattle of keys. This time they could be at Holloway. The thought brings her back into her body. The worry of who might be waiting for her extends like a worm along her spine. Miss Jackson. Mrs Armitage. It could be any of them. Perhaps it will be Clara, but she hopes not so soon, not the first face she sees.

The door opens suddenly. 'Come along now.' It's a different policeman. This one is perfunctory. 'Follow me.'

When she stands, the blood rushes back into her feet with the vengeance of a thousand needles and she can only hobble from the van. She takes the steps slowly, holding onto the edge of the door and cursing under her breath for having made herself limp. She joins the line of other prisoners then waits, trying to shake some life into her legs, aware that it makes her look nervous or agitated or a bit strange. A skirt would hide it better than the trousers. She sneaks a glance at the warden in charge and sees Miss Barraclough reading from the clipboard, apparently unaware of who Nancy is. But she must have seen her name? Nancy runs a hand across her cropped hair. Does she really look so different?

The women are led up the steps and into the large reception room. Opposite the door are a line of dark-blue dresses that she quickly puts faces to – Miss Needler, Miss Barraclough – all of them seem at pains not to look at her with the exception of Mrs Armitage who glares in her direction. They are taken through to the holding cells and Nancy is put in with a prostitute who looks at her with undisguised contempt and prefers to stand rather than sit on the bench next to her. Mrs Armitage arrives. It would be her. She has forms to fill in.

'Name?'

'Nancy Cooper'.

'Occupation?'

'None.'

'Address?'

'No fixed abode.'

Mrs Armitage tuts. 'Religion?'

'Church of England.'

She shakes her head. 'The shame of it.'

They are taken to the bathroom and told to undress. Mrs Armitage stands and watches, pursing her mouth to stop herself from saying more. But Nancy feels nothing. No anger or resentment. Not the usual sense of shame she feels unclothed. It's as if her body doesn't belong to her, the same way it didn't when she gave birth, as though it has a purpose of its own, and she thinks of it as just another garment, to be put on or taken off, changing her from a man back to a woman.

She is suspicious of the pleasure of hot water and sits up straight in her bath, scrubbing herself roughly with a loofah. In the dressing room, she takes the first green dress from the top of the pile. Red and black stockings. She is proud to put them on. Miss Barraclough pins a badge to the front of her dress with the number of her cell and she does it carefully, making sure the needle doesn't dig into her skin. This little act of kindness puts a hand around her heart. Her cell number is 417 and Nancy wears the badge like a medal.

She is taken to the wing that houses the suffragettes and she listens out for them as she passes their doors, feeling stronger for belonging but glad she doesn't have to meet them. All she wants is to be alone.

Her cell is everything she hoped for, though now it seems cluttered where before she found little comfort. She rolls up her mattress and stacks it against the wall. She takes her plate and spoon and the books on her shelf, stowing them in the same place. She considers the wooden chair a luxury and she picks it up, testing the strength of the legs and back. She doubts she can break it with her bare hands but if she can find a place to lever it, a corner of the room perhaps or the boards of her bed? She sees the bars on her window, pushes a leg between them and yanks until the joint comes apart. She tries a second leg and then the back, breaking the chair piece by piece until its parts lie in the corner of the room with everything else.

In the olden days, there used to be monks, holy men, who would retreat to a place outside the town, a cave where they would be visited by people who brought food and water in exchange for prayer. Now that she is behind her cell door, it's as if the world isn't there. Or rather that it has been reduced to a spy hole, the width of an eye, which watches her refusal to act and insists instead that they act upon her.

She removes her clothes, then sits naked on the bare

boards of her bed, watching the bull's eye, wondering which of the wardens might come to look at her. Perhaps Clara is there now, spying on her, the way Nancy used to with Daisy, trying to discover what makes the two of them different. She sits straighter, tries to imagine her spine as the handle of a broom reaching from the neck to the coccyx, all her vertebrae in a line. She meets the gaze of the little glass ball and tries not to blink.

The door opens like a cut in the wall. A woman walks across the gash of light and for a moment it could be anyone. Then she sees it is Clara.

36

Clara stands before the locked cell door. The number 417 is painted in white letters above the spy hole, and she repeats it to herself, trying to fix the number against the name she knows so well. If she is to do as she instructed the other wardens and treat her sister like any other prisoner, then she must remember to use it instead of Nancy's name when the two of them are not alone. She takes a step forward and puts her eye to the glass. The sudden nakedness shocks her and she steps back from the door. The loss of control makes her feel faint. She gives herself a talking to. She's of no help to either of them like that. This is happening. This is actually happening and nothing she can do will change it now, so she better get used to it, the same as Nancy has to. She takes a deep breath to clear her head then steps back to the door.

Her sister is hardly recognizable. Her hair is the most

obvious thing, cropped short like a man's. But it's not that. It's the way she sits bolt upright, her breasts unapologetic, her hands laid calmly on each of her thighs. Nancy was never like this. Never brazen and bold. She wouldn't say boo to a goose. And Clara feels diminished by her, as though it is her and not her sister who is the younger child. She'd never dare take a baby from her now.

She lifts the keys from her belt and unlocks the door. She goes inside, closing it firmly behind her.

The two sisters eye each other warily.

'Why are you naked?' Clara fetches the nightgown from the corner of the room where it is draped over the remains of a broken chair. She holds it out and shakes it, then gathers it up into her hands till it is bunched at the neckline. 'Put this on.' She walks across to Nancy, expecting her to raise her arms, like a child being dressed.

Nancy folds them in front of her chest. 'I'll only take it off again.'

Clara thinks of forcing the nightgown over her head, of making her respectable the way she would with the other prisoners, but she can't pretend that this is not her sister or that this is just another day at work. She walks back to the corner of the room and puts the nightgown back where she found it. 'I've been dreading this,' she says to the wall. 'I was hoping that when you got arrested, it wouldn't be in London. That I would see your name on a list from Manchester or Liverpool.' She turns to see Nancy watching her. 'Are you all right?'

Nancy shrugs, her shoulders assuming the same expression as her face.

'I tried to find you. I went to Parliament Square for the delegations and I saw you, but I couldn't reach where you were because of all the fighting and the crowds. But I saw you. I couldn't believe you had the nerve to do it. That must take a lot of courage, to walk up to those men, knowing what will happen to you.'

'It can't have been me,' Nancy tells her flatly. 'I wasn't there.'

'Oh. But I thought it was. I was sure.'

'It can't have been. I've been busy elsewhere. I've been doing other things.'

'Yes. The report said you've been convicted of arson. Oh Nancy, what have you done?'

Her sister stares at the door, as though too much of this might break her.

Clara tries to reassure her. 'I've told the wardens they should treat you with the same respect as any other prisoner but I can't do you any favours, Nancy.'

'I don't want you to.'

'Will you go on hunger strike?'

Nancy nods.

'Well then, I shall excuse myself from restraining you. I won't force you to eat against your will.'

'Why not? If you want me to live it's only natural.'

'Well then. I'll try to do what I think is for the best.'

Nancy suddenly laughs. 'Christ Almighty, can you imagine Father's face if he were here now?'

The sudden change brings them closer, the way they used to be back at home, behind the closed door of their bedroom.

Clara giggles. 'He'd be blowing a gasket.'

'He'd lock the door on both of us and throw away the key.'

She sits on the bed beside Nancy. 'Do you want me to tell him? He knows about you running away and joining the cause but should I let him know about this?'

'I don't care.'

'You're only saying that because you're scared. You'll have to face him sometime.'

'Will I? I can't imagine when.'

'We'll have to manage this the best we can.'

'Yes.'

'But are you all right? Really?'

'I don't know. I think so. And you? How are you?'

'I don't know. I suppose I'm much the same as usual.' Clara puts her arms around her sister. Hugs her. Holds her shoulders and her waist, the way she did when Nancy was in labour. 'I'm sorry about the baby. I was wrong. I know that now. I should have found a way of doing things differently only . . .'

'You did what you thought was best.'

'I tried to.' Clara stands and brushes down the front of her dress. 'Well then. I better get back to work. If there's anything I can do for you then I will.'

'You can visit me. Come in the middle of the night. Stand by my bed and watch me sleep. You can brush my hair.'

Clara gets up to leave. 'We'll have to wait and see.'

As she is locking the cell door, she sees Miss Hardgrave advancing along the gantry.

'So your sister is back with us,' she says as she arrives. 'These are unfortunate circumstances but I told you she would turn up sooner or later.'

'Yes, ma'am, though it wasn't an affair of the heart as you suggested.'

'Do you think not? If there's one thing I can't fault the suffragettes for it is their passion.'

Clara puts her keys back into the lock. 'Would you like to speak with her?'

'No, Miss Cooper. There is no need for that. Actually, I need to speak with you. Would you accompany me back to the office? I'd prefer to talk with you alone.'

Clara follows the Matron down the metal staircase and through the locked gates that separate the wings from the administration block. She will tell the Matron, once they are there, that she is unwilling to partake in the restraint and force-feeding of her sister, nor will she be party to any other forms of discipline that might be considered necessary during her stay at the prison.

But Miss Hardgrave has no interest in that at all. She offers Clara the chair opposite her own.

'I have the form here for your sister's detention.' She slides a typewritten sheet across the table to Clara. 'Please note that the details are correct. In particular, it states her age as nineteen.'

'Yes, miss.'

'A full five years too young to apply for the post of prison warden, a post that you yourself recommended her for.'

'Yes, miss.' Clara hadn't expected this. The shock of it ties her tongue.

'I also took the liberty of sending away for your own particulars. You are twenty-three, are you not?'

'But, ma'am . . .'

'Still too young to be a prison warden, let alone a Supervisor.' She reaches out and pulls the paper back to her side of the desk. 'There is no possibility of me overlooking this.'

'But, ma'am . . .' Clara stammers. 'I can do the job, ma'am. You know I'm very good at it.'

'Which is why it is with the greatest regret that I have to inform you of your dismissal, to take place with immediate effect.'

'But . . .' Clara needs to grip the arm of her chair from a sudden fear of falling.

'Miss Cooper, I can't ignore it. I turned a blind eye to the story of your father's illness. You told me he'd made a good recovery while your sister seemed to think he had died. In the circumstances, I decided against curiosity. But this is in black and white and it is more than my job is worth.'

Clara regains some composure. She recognizes the Matron's tone well enough to know there is no chance of a change of heart. 'I understand, miss,' she says quietly.

The Matron opens her drawer, the one where she keeps the mints, and retrieves a piece of notepaper. 'Your sister's details included an address that she has listed as permanent. A Miss Birnstingl of Kensington. I have copied it down for you, as you may need it in the future. Below it you will see the name of a lady who I understand has responsibility for recruiting women to a new police force. Obviously I can't provide you with a reference but perhaps, one way or another, you might find a way . . .'

'That's very kind, miss.'

'As a word of advice, you will always find that honesty is the best choice. In the end, it is our virtues that mark us out for who we are and our lies that will find us out.'

'With the greatest respect, miss, I don't believe we had a choice at all. Neither myself nor my sister.'

'Then I hope the benefit of hindsight instructs you otherwise. May I have your keys, please?'

Clara unfastens the leather belt around her waist and puts it on the desk top. She feels bewildered, unsure whether she is setting herself free or losing the key to everything. In all the time she's spent here, she never could decide.

37

The morning bell wakes Nancy at 6 a.m, an hour later than she used to have to get up as a warden. She hears their shoes on the gantry before her door opens and Miss Needler tells her she needs to slop out. 'And you can't go out like that. Do we need to dress you?'

'I won't wear the prison uniform.'

Miss Needler takes a deep breath. 'You should choose your battles, Nancy. You'll be a long time on your own in the coming weeks. No need to make it harder.' She leaves the door ajar.

Nancy puts her feet on the cold floor. The shift of balance makes her lightheaded. She waits a second, stands, then goes to the bucket and crouches over it. Once she's done, she swills the contents around, looking for a sign that her body is already changing and disappointed that there's nothing out of the ordinary to be seen.

She puts on her prison uniform then walks out onto the gantry, busy with wardens coming in and out of cells, their eyes flitting towards her then away again. In the sluice room a woman is already at the sinks, an older suffragette who she used to supervise, and Nancy is thankful for the rule of silence as she rinses. She fills a second bucket with clean water, finds a scrubbing brush and carries both buckets back to her cell.

She sets to work on the floor, scrubbing with a vigour she never had at home, cleaning right up into the corners and under the door. On her hands and knees, the hunger shifts like a bubble in a spirit level, becoming lighter and less insistent, then falling like a stone to the bottom of her stomach when she stands.

The kitchen staff clatter their way along the landing, bringing loaves of bread and little dishes of butter. A woman leaves her allocation on the edge of her bed, pouring milky tea into a mug before she leaves. Nancy moves the loaf and butter to the floor. The rule is that it cannot be removed until the following day when it will be replaced with the same. Or perhaps it will be something different? A tasty plate of something from the kitchen would be their first concession to her. She drinks her tea in gulps, thinking it will flush her out.

In forty-eight hours, if she eats nothing, they will begin to force-feed her and she won't leave this cell until they believe she is in danger of dying. Before then, her routine will be the same as any other prisoner. She goes to chapel.

She does some needlework – darning prison stockings and sewing arrows onto dresses. She finds her fingers are familiar with the work, that they take to it with a sense of relief. She's always had her father's hands, thick and workmanlike, and it's satisfying to make them obedient, to make them do women's work. In a few weeks' time, they will look different, thinning to the bone and ridding themselves of her father's likeness.

She exercises, walking with the other suffragettes like birds in formation. Like geese or swans migrating. There's a lightness that comes with hunger, a feeling she can fly.

Two women adopt her and they set a fast pace, talking as they walk. 'How is it we've never met before?'

'I'm new,' she tells them. 'My name's Nancy Cooper.' She mentions Daisy and Miss Birnstingl, to get their respect.

'Welcome,' they say and begin on a second round of the yard. 'Will you go on hunger strike?'

'Yes.'

'You're braver than we are. Good luck.'

She feels she doesn't need it.

Returning to her cell, she becomes giddy on the stairs and has to pause, holding the railing with her head bowed. The other prisoners wait with her until Miss Needler moves them on, annoyed at the delay and taking Nancy by the arm to hurry her along to her cell where she lies on her bed, limp with exhaustion but glad of it, satisfied that her body is complaining. She treats the bread and butter on the floor as a mark of her defiance rather than a temptation.

During the night she wakes suddenly, a smell of rank sea-weed in the top of her nose. She must have been dreaming of Tenby. She gets up, walks to the door and back, then sets herself a target of twenty lengths and goes back and forth, pacing the floor as she counts out her total. She sleeps again.

In the morning, when she comes to slop out, her urine is a deep yellow brown. Like autumn. She scrubs the floor till she faints. A moment later, as she comes back to herself, the kitchen girl arrives, looks at her, then steps over her leg and replaces the loaf and butter with new ones. She drinks her tea, sitting on the floor with her back to the wall, reminding herself she's already halfway there.

She goes to chapel. They sing 'Abide with Me' and instead of mumbling through the words, Nancy has an urge to sing, to make her hollowness vibrate, and she fills her lungs with air and then forces it out, thinking that this must be the most glorious feeling in the world and wondering how she never knew she had a voice. She imagines herself as a flugel-horn or better still, a clarinet, darting its way across the scoresheet with a huge orchestra behind her.

She faints again, this time on her way to needlework. She is excused the exercise yard. Her hunger now is not insistent, more of a regret that her body has come to cope with. But the complaining has moved into her arms and legs, her muscles clinging to her bones and moaning like distant relatives at a funeral. She's taken a dislike to them. She might disinherit them. They're not hers anyway. Her arms belong to the wardens and police who use them to move her from one place to another, like handles on a heavy bag.

In the night she dreams of buildings burning as she runs from them, the heat on her back making her heart feel cosy as a buttered bun.

When she wakes, Miss Needler is in the centre of her cell, standing hand on hip and glaring at the loaf and butter as though she blames them. 'No more leaving the cell for you, please.' She takes the food away, returning later with a girl from the third division who takes out the bucket and scrubs at the floor with a lack of application. Miss Needler allows her to leave with the job half done, as though she means to demonstrate that this cell no longer belongs to Nancy, that she needs to retreat further from the world.

Nancy remembers Daisy, how she told her girl exactly what she wanted. But she doesn't want to think of Daisy. She forces herself to think of something else. Clara comes to mind. She wonders what she's doing now that she has lost her job, whether her stomach is lined with butterflies, just the same as hers. She thinks of birthdays, a present waiting on the table in the parlour and Clara shaking her awake saying, 'You lucky thing!' Today feels like one of those days. A special day. Like her first day at school, holding hands as her sister walks her solemnly to the door. Today has the same inevitability, a sense of herself being marked out, of being noticed; a day when the world takes her in hand. The doctor will come for her this morning.

Above her bed is a small cobweb, stretched between the

angles of the wall and ceiling. It's a safer place to watch what they do with her and she scuttles up when she hears the young doctor's voice. He brings five of the wardens with him. From here on the ceiling she can see he is already beginning to bald. They take hold of the girl's arms and drag her from the bed to the chair. They kneel at her feet, holding her ankles against the thin wooden legs. They twist her arms behind the back of a chair as the doctor holds a stethoscope to her heart and then holds her chin in the palm of his hands saying, 'You must open your mouth.'

The girl clenches her teeth. Nancy can see the muscles bulge on the side of her cheek as he tightens his grip and reaches for the metal clamp, but it does no good. This girl has always had good teeth and she can pull herself tight as a razor clam buried deep in sand.

The doctor asks for a narrower tube and his tone when he talks to Mrs Armitage is matter-of-fact. None of the charm or special attention he used with Nancy. Miss Needler undoes the clip on the funnel, uncoils a second tube and attaches it. The doctor approaches from the front. The girl struggles. Nancy watches her shifting in her seat and she thinks, go on, girl, don't give him an inch.

He takes hold of her nostril between his thumb and forefinger, turning it upward and out, and then he inserts the pipe, pinching the end of it to make it fit, then pushing it slowly up inside her head.

The pain makes her fall from the ceiling, makes her tumble back into this girl so that suddenly she is right there,

319

38

Her mother knocks on the bedroom door. 'Clara?' She pushes it enough to put her head around. 'Can I come in?'

Clara sits at the dresser in a pink and white silk dress that she found in a sale. It is bare at the shoulders, pretty enough for the occasion but not so out of the ordinary that it can't be worn again.

'You look nice,' her mother says. 'I had a cotton dress when I got married. It had a lovely bit of lace across the middle of it. Second-hand mind, and I had to sell it again the week after the wedding but I thought it was beautiful. Made me feel like a queen for the day.'

'I thought you couldn't remember.'

'Some things you never forget.' She brings a chair over to the dresser and sits beside her, putting her handbag down onto the floor. She touches Clara's hand, holds her fingers for a moment. 'I brought some bay leaves for your hair.'

'I've already put it up,' she says uncertainly.

'Yes.'

Clara takes the clasp from her hair then shakes her head so that her hair falls down below her shoulders. 'Go on then.'

'Aren't you done yet?' her father shouts up from the bottom of the stairs.

Her mother stands quickly and goes to the door. 'You be quiet now!' she shouts back down at him. 'We'll be ready when we're ready.'

She closes the door and comes to stand behind Clara. She puts her fingers through her hair. 'There's a way of doing it that's more subtle than a wreath.' She takes the cutting of bay from her handbag. 'I've made it softer, see? But it was only cut this morning so it's still got a bit of spring in it.' She begins to weave the bay carefully into Clara's hair, sometimes over and sometimes under so that it seems to have grown there of its own accord, and Clara sits like a cat being stroked, thinking how soft her mother's hands are. When the last pin is in place her mother steps back to look at her work.

'What do you think then? Will it do or do you want it back the way it was before?'

Clara admires herself in the mirror. 'You've turned me into a goddess.' She catches an expression on her mother's face that she hasn't seen since she can remember, a kind of sparkle in the eyes.

'Stop your fussing or we'll miss the bus!' her father shouts out.

The two of them ignore him.

'I got you this.' Her mother reaches back into her bag and hands Clara a little square box, already open to show the delicate silver bracelet inside. 'It belonged to my mother and she gave it to me on my wedding day. It's not expensive but it's pretty, I think.'

'Something old,' says Clara. She makes to kiss her mother on the cheek but her mother flinches.

'Better get going.'

When they come downstairs her father is pacing the room. 'Are you done with all your preening? Five minutes it took me to have a shave and put my suit on. None of this bloody nonsense.'

Her mother goes to the hooks by the door and fetches her coat. 'It's a bride's prerogative to be late on her wedding day.'

'She'll be lucky if he's there at all, never mind making him wait for it.'

'Now you watch your mouth, Tom Cooper. If she's anything like me, it'll be the one day she gets to keep for herself and I won't have you spoil it.'

'I'll have a say in my own house.'

'And it'll be an empty house if you're not careful.' Her mother turns on him with her finger lifted. 'I mean it. If you ruin her day I'll leave you for good and you can think on it while you're skivvying for yourself.'

Clara has never heard her mother speak that way before and she fears the worst of it but her father doesn't dare. He walks to the door and fetches his hat.

'You've got a new hat, Father.'

'Your mother bought it.'

'Well it looks very handsome.'

He opens the door, letting in the sunlight and the smell of hops from the brewery. 'Come on then.'

As they walk down the street, the children stop their playing and the wives come to their doors and stand in their aprons, clapping their hands and calling out good luck to her.

A group of men are smoking at the corner. 'Morning, Tom. Are you giving her away then?'

'Tried to sell her but we couldn't get anything for her.'

'Get away with you,' her mother tells them as they go on past.

On the omnibus, there's an old lady that coos and pats Clara's hand. The conductor won't take any money for their fare but lets them ride for free and all of this fuss makes her feel special, makes her feel better for deciding to go through with it.

They get off at Highbury Corner and walk the short distance to the church, her father leading the way with her mother by his side. Clara drops back a step or two and watches them, the way they come together and apart, her father setting the pace and her mother coaxing from a step away, suggesting he slow down or speed up, getting him to look this way or that.

So this is how it is then. Everyone does it.

She begins to feel nervous. In an hour or so it'll all be

done. She falls further behind, suddenly doubting again that she's made the right decision. Ted's a good man, she tells herself. And he loves me.

At the steps to the church her parents wait for her to catch them up.

'We'll go inside and say our hellos,' her mother tells her. 'Your father will come back when they're ready for you.' She leads him up the stone steps, leaving Clara on her own in the spring sunshine. If she were to walk away now, everything would be different. That must be how Nancy had felt when she took off from the jail. Everything wagered on the impulse of a moment.

Ted has hired a photographer and the man comes outside and sets his tripod up on the pavement.

'I can do a quick one now if you like,' he tells her. 'A portrait with the church in the background.' He takes his camera from its wooden box, sets it on the top and starts to screw it into place.

'Hello, Clara.' Nancy's voice.

She turns to find her arriving at the wrought iron gates. She still has those dark marks beneath her eyes but there's some colour in her cheeks since the last time Clara saw her and she has let her hair grow longer.

'Nancy!' Clara runs the couple of steps to meet her. 'You said you weren't coming!'

Nancy kisses her quickly. 'I wanted to wish you luck.' She hands Clara three stems of lilies, tied up with blue ribbon. 'These are for you. Something blue.'

'You'll come inside, won't you? Now you're here you might as well.'

'It'll only set him off. You know what he's like and I don't want to spoil your big day.'

'It'll be worth it.'

'I'm not ready to see him, Clara. Maybe one day, but not today.'

The photographer interrupts them. 'Are you ready?'

'Can you take the both of us?' Clara drags her sister in front of the camera and they stand in each other's arms as the flashlight pops.

'I better go,' Nancy says and gives her another quick kiss. 'Come and visit me in the bookshop.' She runs a few steps then calls back. 'And bring Ted with you. I want to meet him.' She skips from the pavement and crosses to the other side of the road.

'Everyone's inside,' their father calls out from the church doors. He takes the few steps down to her. 'Let's get this over and done with then.' He offers her his arm.

'Hang on a minute,' she says. 'I'm not ready yet,' and she steps away but then stops, unable to move one way or the other.

'I told you he'd be waiting. Over half an hour he says he's been stood there.'

'He's been waiting a lot longer than that,' she answers, annoyed to have his voice in her head. 'It won't do him any harm.'

She looks back along the road, hoping for a sight of

Nancy and is in time to see her sister turn the corner of the street.

Nancy is riding fast on a bicycle, the ribbons of her boater stretching out from her head, her bright blue Liberty dress flying free in the breeze behind her.

Acknowledgements

Thank you to everyone at DFB, in particular my editors, Bella Pearson, Anthony Hinton and Hannah Featherstone.

Thanks as always to Sallyanne Sweeney for your patience and careful observations.

And to Tanya Smart, always generous and wise.